The Jewels of Allarion - Book Two

The Queen of All Light

By

Theodora Fair

Copyright © 2002 by Theodora Fair

All rights reserved. No part of this book shall be reproduced or transmitted in any form or by any means, electronic, mechanical, magnetic, photographic including photocopying, recording or by any information storage and retrieval system, without prior written permission of the publisher. No patent liability is assumed with respect to the use of the information contained herein. Although every precaution has been taken in the preparation of this book, the publisher and author assume no responsibility for errors or omissions. Neither is any liability assumed for damages resulting from the use of the information contained herein.

This is a work of fiction. Names, characters, places, and incidents either are the product of the author's imagination or are used fictitiously. Any resemblance to actual events or locales or persons, living or dead, is entirely coincidental.

ISBN 0-7414-1260-8

Published by:

INFINITY
PUBLISHING.COM

519 West Lancaster Avenue
Haverford, PA 19041-1413
Info@buybooksontheweb.com
www.buybooksontheweb.com
Toll-free (877) BUY BOOK
Local Phone (610) 520-2500
Fax (610) 519-0261

Printed in the United States of America

Printed on Recycled Paper

Published October, 2002

Dedication

To Patrick,
whose love and gallantry
rescued the real Elanille from untimely oblivion.

taf

The Chant of Life

Light and Death are one.
Love and Dark are one.
Truth and Time but move
Eclipsing each other in tune.

We live and are of Earth.
We die and are of Fire.
In the Air we fly free
In the Circle of Time
To our birth in the Sea.

None can change what we are.
None can change what we must be.

Prologue

    Her arms were numb. The weight of Kyrdthin's body slowed her breath. Janille sat through the cold, dark night gently rocking him. The sharp gravel of the driveway beneath them cut deep, but she did not care. Emptiness ached in her chest, but she could not weep. Over and over she chanted the last words of the home spell, "...Home to Love. Home to Love..."
    They had won. The Dark Lord had been thwarted. The Twin Kingdoms of Arindon and Frevaria were united and a new age had begun in the light. Her children, April and Willy, now ruled jointly as Queen Avrille and King Willarinth. They had won, but at what price? Janille looked down at the burden in her arms. Kyrdthin, her dearest love lay lifeless. She drew a star sign on his cold forehead. An early morning breeze began to stir. Somewhere a bird sang.
    "I have to find the way home," she said aloud. "I can't leave him here in this alien place. I have to give him the honor due the great man, the great magician that he is."
    Another bird began to sing, another and another. A faint line of pink crept between the easternmost oaks. The cottage set inside the circle of those five old trees was full of memories and dreams. Thirteen years she had lived there guarding the children from the Dark. It was here she had hoped to return with Kyrdthin when the battle was done. The east brightened. There was not much time. With a sigh of resignation Janille began the most powerful ritual she knew.
    She eased Kyrdthin's head reverently to the ground then stood up. The sun was almost up. Her body ached from her long, cold vigil as she hurried back to the cottage. She pulled the quilt from the bed, pocketed a box of matches from the kitchen, then headed to the garage to look for a can of gasoline. Outside again, without as much as a glance at the coming dawn, she soaked the trunk of each guardian oak with fuel, then dribbled a thin line around the circle joining them. Kyrdthin's six-foot body was heavy and awkward but she managed to wrap him in the quilt and drag him to the porch. She struck a match, setting the first oak ablaze. She

struck the second and the third, racing from tree to tree ahead of the sun. Four, five and she was done just as dawn broke free from the eastern hills.

She held Kyrdthin's face to catch the first ray. From the center of her makeshift star sign she sang the song of the home spell that had always brought him back to her. This time she sang for both of them, willing the magic to take them home. "Five for One. One for Five. Hie thee home..." she chanted as the towering flames engulfed them.

Chapter 1

"I don't trust him."

"Gil, I respect your concern," said King Will. "But Frebar has more than supported us. He has done nothing in these two years of our reign to warrant such suspicion."

"That is precisely why I don't trust him."

"Now Gil," Queen Avrille cautioned their aging advisor. "Don't let old hatreds affect what we must do today."

"You are giving him an heir," Gil insisted.

"We are sending him his grandson to foster, nothing else," Avrille argued.

"What do you expect my father-in-law to do, Gil, abdicate when the boy reaches majority?" said Will

"Now that would be worthy of the old fox," said Gil. "Yes, set Kylie up as a puppet king and all Arindon would be afraid to challenge him because their darling wears the crown…"

"Gentlemen!" exclaimed the queen. "We are here to discuss Kylie's fostering not a succession. Arindon and Frevaria are one kingdom, our kingdom. Does anyone doubt that our own children…"

"Who are only one-year-old and daughters not sons…"

"Gil please," begged the queen. "Let's stop and take a moment to brew a pot of tea before we continue."

Gil leaned back into his chair and folded his arms across his chest. His thin face was still flushed. His mouth was drawn into a straight line. King Will refused to sit. He paced angrily. His boots steps rang the length of the royal study and back again.

Queen Avrille hung the teakettle over the fire. She hated political discussions. As she waited for the water to boil she thought about the events that had brought them here. She was no longer a schoolgirl living in another world with her mother and foster brother. That world was gone. Her mother was gone. And now she was not only expected to be an adult, she was a queen. Willy was her husband, her king and father of her twins. Why? Why…?"

"Only magicians can brew tea by just staring into the fire, April," Will teased.

"I wish Uncle Hawke were still here," said Avrille grabbing a pot holder. "He would know what to do."

"Kyrdthin's wisdom and magic are missed by all of us," said Gil.

"It's more than that, Gil," Avrille said with a catch in her throat.

"Yes, I know," said Gil taking the teapot from Avrille's trembling hand. "Kyrdthin's greatest magic was his love for us."

"Let's remember him as we drink our tea and settle this business today," said Will.

Gil nodded his agreement.

It was not an easy decision. Will knew that Frebar had sworn homage to them and reclaimed Avrille as his daughter, yet his temper still rose at the thought of Frebar disowning his infant daughter and banishing his queen simply because of the child's Allarian appearance. Will looked at his wife as she poured them another round of tea. Queen Avrille's luxurious hair was bound back in a coil with a strand of pearls. How he had loved to pull her thick braids when they were children! His fingers longed to touch it now, to feel the dark cascade as it had felt, tumbling heavy and wet when they used to frolic in the pools of Allarion. She had been cooperative and very desirable then. He took a long sweet sip of tea, stretched his arms over his head and waited to catch her eye.

"What are you thinking Will?" said Gil following the young king's gaze with a smile.

"Nothing," said Will returning his attention to the problem at hand. He knew he had to be cautious. He had to make the right decision. Frebar had never recalled his border patrols when the kingdoms united and the Delven threat vanished two years ago. Kylie was also Frebar's eldest daughter's son and a strong claimant to the throne. He tried to push his fears and uncertainties aside and concentrate on the present. Kylie was seven. Fostering was the custom. All he had to do was…? Will drained his cup and set it down with finality.

Gil looked up. Seeing the determination in Will's face he pulled up his chair again and their discussion resumed. Avrille let her tea get cold. Her thoughts were a jumble. Her heart reached out to Kylie. Couldn't these men consider the little boy who would be sent away from the only world he knew? Frebar favored the boy with gifts and holidays and the child responded with affection....She turned her attention back to her husband and their advisor.

"Maybe the whole idea of fostering is obsolete," Gil was saying. "Why should a child spend seven years away from home during such an impressionable age?"

"My sister wants Kylie to go," said Avrille.

"Why would a widow willingly want to give up her only son?" said Will. "You'd think she would beg to keep him near her."

"We all know the boy's obsession with violence and revenge since his father's death," said Gil.

"But it's been four years!"

"And those four years have taken a heavy toll on my sister," said Avrille. "I know what she is suffering. I took care of Kylie too don't forget."

"There haven't been Delven in the kingdoms since our coronation. What has he got to revenge against?" Will started to pace again.

"Sit down, Willy," said Avrille. "Who cares if he has a real reason? Kylie takes it out on his mother and anyone who tries to take care of him. And the constant warring between him and his sister…"

"Lizelle is another matter entirely," said Gil.

Avrille absently refilled their teacups. "We are getting off the subject gentlemen," she reminded them.

"Yes, it seems we have two separate issues here," said Gil. "That of trusting a young Arindian nobleman for fostering in Frevaria and Princess Elanille's problems in rearing her granted very difficult children."

"There is another very important issue," said the queen in a controlled but commanding tone. "What about Kylie the child? Where can our nephew best learn love and trust and courtly manners? How can my sister's pain be lessened? She is only twenty three and already she has endured several lifetimes of grief. Just once consider someone's feelings rather than the good of the kingdoms."

"That's two issues, not…"

"Shut up Willy."

"What about my feelings, April? What about the feelings of all the people of the kingdoms?"

"Just shut up Willy!"

Gil waited. Counseling the headstrong royal pair tried his patience. He poured himself another cup of tea. "Another cup either of you?"

"No thank you," Avrille snapped.

"Will?"

"How can you think of tea when everything is going wrong, Gil?"

"If I may advise Your Majesty?"

"Lay off the formal stuff, Gil..."

"Then more straight forward, Will. When everything is wrong, the only thing left to do is to drink tea. Let's all have another cup shall we?"

Avrille hung the tea kettle over the fire again. Will poked at the logs, carefully avoiding her gaze. The Twin Kingdoms were blossoming under their rule but Gil could see the storm clouds brewing between them and wondered how it would all end.

Eventually it was decided that Kylie should go to his grandfather in time for the Solstice celebration under the condition that Frebar would consent for an honor guard to accompany him. Gil drafted the document and dispatched it promptly.

Gil returned to the rooms he shared with Marielle. He entered quietly, trying not to disturb her sleep. Her pale, thin body was curled beneath the heavy satin comforter. He pulled the covers up over her shoulders and brushed her forehead with a kiss. Her silver hair rustled on the rose petal strewn pillow as she roused briefly.

"Sleep a little longer, my love. All is well," he whispered. Marielle sighed and dozed off again. He tiptoed across the lush green carpet. He swung open the window and looked out over the morning bustle in the town below. Over his head a prism-jeweled wind chime tinkled in the breeze. The plaza in front of the new guild hall was a riot of color, smells and sounds as market vendors hawked their wares. Arindon was happy and thriving. Harvests had been plentiful. Industry and education flourished. Everyone, without exception, loved their new king and queen.

Marielle sighed in her sleep. Gil's heart hurt to look at her. The glory that was once the Queen of Allarion now lay wasting among the withered treasures of that fair lost land. The scented candles and dried flowers that adorned the room and the blue-tinted windows could only mimic the fresh but heavy scents of Allarian breezes and sapphire skies. The shell-lined fountain that fed the bath trickled a sad soliloquy. There were no butterflies, no birdsong.

Their decision to remain as advisors to Will and Avrille was good. Gil did not regret it, but now he was called on to help less and less.

"Are you here my love?" Marielle called.

"As always, my queen," he said hurrying to her side.

"What were you doing?"

"Looking out. It's a beautiful day."

"I wish I could see it too," she said weakly.

He arranged the plush, cloud-soft pillows on the window seat then carried her almost weightless form to the sunlight. He lovingly covered her lap with a shawl and smoothed her dull silver hair. "There goes another cart to the mill," he said pointing down the road. They watched the wagonload of grain sacks make its way past the last thatch-roofed cottage and into the trees beyond the town.

"That Mabry fellow is certainly clever. With his building skills to put Will's ideas to work, is there anything the two of them can't do?" said Marielle.

Gil did not answer. He admired Mabry. Since he and Will had diverted part of the river with a big boulder and shunted the water off into a wooden race to the big mill wheel, the town had reliable power to grind flour, saw lumber and promises of many other conveniences. Yet he still did not like the man. More and more it was Mabry's advice Will sought not his. Gil felt old and tired. He looked down at Marielle. She had dropped off to sleep again in the warm sunlight.

Avrille slammed the heavy door, took a deep, hissing breath and set off down the corridor at an angry pace. Rogarth lay down his papers as she stormed past the alcove where he was working. "My Lady," he called after her. "May I be of service to you?"

"Oh Rogarth," she said as she turned to wait for him to catch up with her. "You are the very person I need. Calm, logical…"

"What's wrong dearest lady?"

"Politics! I hate, hate politics!" she fumed. "That's all Will and Gil ever talk about. It's such an infuriating bore. Everything is such a bore…this castle…all these ignorant people." Rogarth's giant steps made one to her two but the pace suited the impatient young queen. "I want to do something interesting, something fun," she declared as they crossed the great hall. Her heels beat a sharp staccato across the fire-scarred mosaic in the center of the floor. Her whole world had changed since the chandelier blazed with magic fire and fell on the day she married her foster brother and was crowned his queen.

Rogarth followed her in dutiful silence. Avrille burst through the double glass doors that led to the garden. "I want to be free! Free of everything!" She twirled with abandon in the late morning sunlight, then stopped. The hem of her long heavy gown continued a half turn before it dropped again to her ankles. Her face sobered. "Walk with me Rogarth," she said resuming her regal tone.

Rogarth offered her his arm. Together they strolled among the arbors and fountains. When they came to the vine-covered wall Avrille stopped abruptly. "This is as far as I can go," she said bitterly. "These walls surround my life. Rogarth you can't imagine how trapped I feel."

"Perhaps I do, my lady," said Rogarth surveying the same walls. His fingers flexed idly on his sword hilt.

"You're a man. You're a soldier. You don't have to be watched and protected all the time. You don't have to behave all the time. I never have any privacy. I never get a chance to be me. Being queen isn't at all like it is in fairy tales."

Rogarth patted the hand that dramatically clutched his arm and smiled.

"I'm only nineteen," she continued. "And I'm married with not one but two squalling babies. In the world were I grew up I would have just finished school and be looking for a job and dating boys and having fun. Rogarth, you just can't know what it's like," she sobbed.

"Dearest lady," he said taking her hands. "Perhaps I do know. I feel trapped and restless here too. I am a soldier, a man of action. Though I am honored that King Will chose me to advise him, the paperwork of politics and the charade of courtly life is a heavy burden for me."

"But you have the tournament."

"Yes that was a wise decision on King Will's part," he said guiding her along the cobbled path. "Without the tournament to divert our unoccupied soldiers there would be trouble indeed. Though I think King Frebar had the best idea to just maintain military life as it was."

"Gil disagrees with that," she said stopping to admire a rose.

"Allow me," said Rogarth as he snapped the bloom and presented it to her with a sweeping bow. "My heart is at your feet Lady Queen."

"Don't tease me, Rogarth. I'm not the little girl you escorted to Allarion what seems like ages ago."

"Are you someone else?" he said with a twinkle in his eyes.

"Oh Rogarth," she laughed taking his arm again. "Yes, I am still little Avrille inside but only you can know it. You are ever my dearest friend." She stopped and looked imploringly up at him. "There is one very important thing I want you to do for me." She took a step and stopped again.

"You are my queen. You need only to ask," he said.

"No this I ask you to do as my friend." She reached up her arms and locked them around his neck. "As long as I am queen I need you to be my lifeline. I need you to keep the 'Little Avrille' inside of me alive and well. Promise me, Rogarth."

"On my honor, as a friend," he replied solemnly.

They strolled on through the garden reminiscing happily, helping each other put the cares and confinements of the present at bay for a few moments before their busy lives resumed.

Chapter 2

"But Aunt Mari…" Jasenth begged.

"No and that is final," said Maralinne with measured patience. "Four-year old boys do not go out in the woods at night. All the little animals are home in their dens with their mothers just like you are."

Jasenth stared at the floor. His lower lip quivered. His eyes welled with tears of disappointment. He squeezed them shut, determined not to cry.

Maralinne held out her arms. "Come here brave little hunter."

Jasenth looked up but stood firm.

"Jayjay, you know I love you, but there are just so many things out there that could hurt a little boy."

"Uncle Jareth goes out every night."

"And every night my heart feels alone and scared until he returns."

"Even with me here?" he said looking up into her face with wide innocent eyes.

"Having you here helps me more than you will ever know," she said giving him a hug.

Jasenth crawled up into his aunt's lap. Big boy though he tried to be, he still loved to be cuddled. Maralinne held him willingly though her legs soon ached with his weight. It was almost two years since her sister's tragic death. After Will and Avrille's coronation she and Jareth left for his cottage with Analinne's orphan. The new king and queen had granted them permission to marry and adopt the child, but the three of them simply slipped away without ceremony.

She stroked Jasenth's bright red curls and let her thoughts wander. Here she was content. Their life was idyllic and simple. Jareth hunted and fished and she tended the house and garden. Arindon castle and her life as a princess seemed far away. Her gowns and jewels were gladly replaced with peasant garb. Jareth and Jasenth were all she needed, but Jareth was gone so often, like tonight, either hunting or scouting or whatever business he did for King Will. Maralinne sighed a deep lonely sigh.

"What's matter, Aunt Mari?" said Jasenth snuggling a little closer.

"Just thinking, Jayjay," she said tying to shift his weight a little to relieve her numb legs. "Tell you what, let's wrap up and sit out on the porch and name the stars until Jareth comes back."

The night air was cool. Together they looked up at the piece of sky cupped in the circle of giant trees that surrounded the cottage. "There are the Twins," said Maralinne pointing to two bright lines of stars.

"Twins like you and my mommy," said Jasenth.

"And like the king and queen's babies," Maralinne added.

"And my daddy and Uncle King Frebar,"

"Yes, for them too."

"Then who's is it?" He cocked his head and gave her a quizzical look.

"Any one you choose, Jayjay. You say which one."

"I say it's you and Mommy."

Maralinne gave him a squeeze. "Let's look for the king and queen," she said turning him around and pointing to the north. "See the up and down 'W' shape there? That's Queen Avrille. And see that pointed box below it? That's King Will."

"Do I have a star Aunt Mari?"

"I'm sure you do but people don't usually find out which one is theirs until they are grown up."

Jasenth squinted up at the heavens. "I think I will be the big bear," he mused.

Maralinne laughed. "First, my little cub you will have to be the little bear and I will be the mama bear and..." Jasenth squealed as Maralinne growled and grabbed him in a bear-sized hug.

A meteor shot across the heavens, straight north from the mouth of the dragon stars to fall sizzling into the cup of the big bear's outstretched paws.

"Look at that, Jayjay!"

"He catched it!" Jasenth cried.

"He sure did," said Maralinne.

"Maybe it's the Big Bear's job to catch stars before they fall and get hurt."

"If you say so, little bear."

"Ho there!" Jareth's voice boomed across the clearing.

"Uncle!" Jasenth exclaimed. He broke free of Maralinne's embrace and ran out to meet him.

Jareth swooped him up.

"Anything exciting tonight?" said Maralinne as Jareth hoisted the boy to his shoulders and headed toward the house.

"No. I spent most of my time just sitting and thinking."

"You could have done that here," she replied as she held the door open then pulled it tight behind them and drew the bolt.

"Maralinne, I was thinking of you. That's why I came back so soon. That's why I came home empty handed. All I need is here, my princess," he said drawing her close. He cupped her chin and kissed her until the hard line of her mouth softened and responded.

Jasenth wiggled from his perch on Jareth's shoulder.

"Love you too, Jaybird," said Maralinne lifting him down. "Now that Jareth is home it is time for bed."

"No. No. Not yet," Jasenth wailed.

"Be a good boy, Jayjay," said Jareth. "Get ready for bed and then we will have some man talk before you go to sleep."

"A story? Please, a story."

Jareth gave him a friendly swat in the direction of the washtub. When the four-year-old was scrubbed and rubbed rosy clean Maralinne dressed him in his nightshirt and said, "I will leave you two men alone while I tidy up the kitchen."

Jareth drew the rocker close to the fire and patted his knee. Jasenth crawled into his lap and laid his head against Jareth's shoulder. The boy's red-gold curls were a bright contrast to his uncle's dark beard. "Just between us," Jareth began.

"Can't she hear us?"

"She knows when not to listen," Jareth assured him. He lowered his voice a bit. "I visited a special place tonight."

"Where? Where?"

"A special place with a story all its own."

"Tell me please. Please Uncle Jareth."

"Once there was a big bear that lived in a magic cave in Arindon wood..."

"Aunt Mari and I saw the Big Bear in the sky catch a star tonight."

"Oh you did? Well that's much like my story," said Jareth as he stroked Jasenth's bright hair and pressed the child's head back to his shoulder. "One day the bear wandered a bit farther than usual into the lands of men. He smelled smoke and heard screaming coming from a cottage. Some bad soldiers were being mean and taking things from the poor woman and little boy who lived there. The bear growled and stood up to the soldiers. But before he could stop them the soldiers killed the mother. The bear attacked the soldiers and sent them running home."

"What about the little boy?"

"He ran away into the woods. The bear tracked him and soon found him huddled in a hollow tree, frightened and exhausted. The bear lay down beside him until the boy stopped crying. Then he nudged him gently, stepped away and looked back. He did this several times until the boy understood to follow him. They traveled deep into the woods, all the while keeping watch for more soldiers. When the boy grew hungry the bear caught him a rabbit and showed him where to pick berries. At first the boy didn't want to eat the rabbit raw but soon he was so hungry he tried it and it tasted good."

"You ever eat it raw, Uncle Jareth?" said Jasenth wrinkling up his nose.

"I've done a lot of things when I had to, Jayjay, but nothing beats how your aunt makes rabbit stew, right?"

"Right," Jasenth agreed heartily.

"Well, back to the bear," Jareth continued. "On the second day they came to a river. The bear let the boy climb on his back and they swam across. A faint trail led up the steep gorge on the other side toward a beautiful waterfall. High in the rocks behind the falls was a cave. There they camped for the night. The next two days were quite an adventure. In fact they are a whole bedtime story in themselves so..."

"Tell me. Tell me," Jasenth begged.

"Well, just a preview for tomorrow night," said Jareth. "They go deeper into the cave until they come to the icy realm of the Dark Lord himself..."

"Wow! And then what?"

"They battle a spider monster and of course Dark Delven soldiers."

"Then what? Then what? Do they ever get home again?"

"Well, yes," said Jareth, allowing himself to be coaxed. "Eventually they arrive at the other side of the mountains and enter the magic land of Allarion. There the king and queen adopt the little boy and give him a happy home. Now it's time for bed."

"What about the bear?" asked Jasenth not the least bit sleepy.

"I don't know," said Jareth with a note of sadness in his voice. "The last time the boy saw him he was heading back toward the cave. Now to bed, Jayjay. I mean it this time."

When Jareth returned to the kitchen after tucking his nephew into bed, it was Maralinne who had questions to ask. "I saw the boy and the bear when we were in the cave. You said it was a time turn. What did you mean? What really happened? It's a true story isn't it? Your story? Right, Jareth?"

"You heard what I told him?"

Maralinne nodded.

"Then you know all there is to know."

King Will and Mabry the miller sat in Armon Beck's tavern with a pitcher of ale between them. "In the place where I was fostered there was a man much like you," Will was saying.

"Oh there was? A man named Mabry?"

"No, he was named Leonardo, but that's not the point. It is your way with things, your vision of how things could be that makes you two alike. It was hundreds of years before the people of his world could make the things Leonardo dreamed."

Mabry poured another pair of mugs. "But the dreams are yours, sire. I only carry them out."

"We are a pair," said Will. "I have the knowledge but I am young and lack experience. You are the master craftsman but no longer have a dream. Together, together we can rebuild the universe!"

The innkeeper replaced their empty pitcher and discreetly stepped back to give his distinguished guests their privacy. After a fresh swig from his mug, Will spread out the sheaf of papers he had brought to show his friend. For the rest of the afternoon they were oblivious to the comings and goings in the tavern. Patrons stared but kept a respectful distance as their king and his master builder conferred. The textile mill Will proposed seemed almost possible with its giant looms harnessed to the power of the river. That same power already turned grain into flour and powered the sawyer's blades. Mabry studied Will's plan. He pursed his lips, turned the plans from one vantage angle to another. He knit his brow and tapped a point. Then he traced his finger across the page and back. Finally he nodded his head and hoisted his mug. "To the future!" he said.

"To my kingdom and your genius!" said Will.

Their mugs rang with the challenge.

"Lizzie, what are you doing?"

"Drawing, Mommy," Lizelle replied with wide, innocent eyes.

"All over the floor?"

"Yes, Mommy," she said with her sweetest smile.

"Lizzie, you are a naughty girl. First for making this mess and second for talking sassy," Elanille exclaimed.

"But Grandma said, 'Draw pretty stars on the floor'. Grandma said to, Mommy."

"Grandma said, Grandma said. Your grandmother is not here and she did not tell you to draw all over the floor."

"She did too," Lizelle insisted.

"Lizzie, enough! I know you and Grandma used to have fun playing magic games. I know you still love her. I do too but she is not here now and..."

"Grandma tells me now. For real. Now..."

"Enough I said! Go ask nurse Linelle for a rag and scrub this mess off the floor all by yourself. Now!"

Elanille left the room. What else could she do? Lizzie was impossible. She was a very beautiful and very intelligent child, but she was also very naughty. Elanille made her way downstairs. As she passed the morning room, Queen Avrille called out to her. Elanille decided to join her sister and her companions.

"Good morning, ladies," she said with a sigh. She looked around the sewing circle. Their hands stopped momentarily then resumed their work

"You look exhausted, dear," said Lady Liella. "And the day is hardly begun."

"It's Lizzie," said Elanille sinking into a chair. She looked at her sewing basket but did not open it.

"More mischief?" asked Lady Cellina leaning forward with anticipation. "What has the darling terror done this time?"

"She crayoned all over the nursery floor," Elanille said then hurried to add, "But I set her to scrubbing this time."

"Did she say Grandma told her to do it again?"

Elanille nodded.

"You poor dear!" Lady Liella laid her embroidery down in her lap and reached out her hand. "Hard as it may seem, it is normal for a four-year-old to adopt an imaginary playmate."

"Liella, I remember how you used to chatter in the garden until the rest of us almost believed in your flower fairies and talking trees," said her sister.

Lady Liella grabbed her embroidery needle and began to punch her work with vigor. "Celli, I did not believe in talking trees. That was one of your tricks, hiding in the arbor and scaring me to death."

"Liella, I assure you I did no such thing. I distinctly remember..."

"Ladies," said the queen. "We are not helping Elanille by bickering over childhood pranks of forty years ago." Turning to her sister she said, "Elani, I am sure you have not breakfasted yet. Let me send for some bread and fruit. Liella, Cellina will you have a bite more also?"

"I wouldn't say no to more of those strawberries," plump Cellina announced. "Elanille, they are so luscious!"

"I'm not hungry."

"You have to keep up your strength," Lady Liella encouraged. "Perhaps just a cup tea?"

"Avrille, while you are ordering, make it shortcake rather than plain bread this time," said Lady Cellina.

"Celli!"

"Now Liella. I know what's best for melancholy."

Elanille jumped to her feet. "Stop it! Just everybody stop it!" she shouted then collapsed back into her chair.

"I'm so sorry dear," said Liella offering her a handkerchief.

"So am I," said Elanille. She twisted the handkerchief around her fingers. Her tears fell unchecked. "I apologize for my ill temper, ladies. Everything has been just too much for me with Kylie leaving and Lizzie misbehaving and no one to share it with...." Her voice trailed off as she dabbed at her eyes.

"Then share your burdens with us," said Lady Cellina. "We are no substitute for the children's dear departed father, or any man's arms for that matter, but we women open our arms to..."

Elanille burst into tears.

"Lady Cellina!" Queen Avrille's tone was sharp. "I am reluctant to reprimand my elders even though I am the queen, but your artless remarks have hurt my sister. You will be quiet and leave her consolation to those with more compassion."

The sewing circle became silent after that. Everyone made a pretense of continuing their work. When breakfast arrived Elanille looked so pale that Avrille suggested they take a tray to her room.

The two sisters spent the remainder of the morning in the quiet of queen's apartments. After breakfast Elanille dozed and Avrille stared out the window. Trebil, her little bird friend, sang a plaintive song from his cage. Avrille let the melody carry her thoughts. She and her sister were so different. She envied Elanille's golden hair and cameo complexion. Their father had wanted her. He reared her as a princess with all the comforts and attentions the wealth of Frevaria could provide. Avrille envied her sister's romantic whirlwind courtship with Sir Keilen. Though she pitied her sister for her tragic widowhood, she pitied herself more for never knowing romance at all.

She looked at her own dark hair in the mirror. She wore it up now in a style befitting a queen. She ran her fingers over the heavy braid. Today she had woven a green ribbon through it. Except for state occasion she never wore a crown, preferring the glory of her own hair instead of jewels.

"Chirp," said Trebil.

"Shh, shh, birdy love," she whispered. "Elani is sleeping."

"Story?" he chirped softly.

"Yes, Trebil, tell me a story. Make it something that will help me forget I am married to my little brother. Tell me what it would be like without these troublesome babies and this boring, boring castle."

She unlatched the door of the little golden cage. Trebil hopped out onto her shoulder. She carried him to the window and looked out into the cloudless blue of the Arindian sky. Her thoughts floated away into Trebil's dream.

A knock at the door interrupted Avrille's reverie. "Who is it?" she demanded.

The latched rattled.

"Come in," she said with a glance at her sister stretched out on the bed. Elanille roused with a yawn.

"I can't get the dumb door open," said a small voice on the other side.

"Lizzie!" Avrille exclaimed. "What are you doing here? Your mommy is tired. Can't you let her rest a while?" Reluctantly she opened the heavy door.

"Linelle sent me to say 'Mommy I sorry I drawed ona floor'," said Lizelle with a dramatically penitent face.

"Oh Lizzie," said Elanille reaching out to her daughter. "Come kiss mommy and be my good girl again"

Lizelle climbed up onto the bed and into her mother's embrace smothering her with kisses. When Elanille could finally disengage herself she set the child down. "Now run along back to Linelle, Lizzie sweet. Mommy needs to rest a bit more."

Lizelle skipped from tile to tile across the room and out the door. "Don't step ona crack or you'll break yer mother's back," echoed down the hall.

"Children! What a plague!" Avrille exclaimed as she sat down on the bed beside her sister.

"It's not easy," Elanille agreed.

"You were at least happily married and wanted children."

Elanille looked at Avrille. Lines of tension marred the once fresh beauty of her sister's face. Voicing what she suspected was the cause Elanille said, "What is wrong between you and Will if I may ask?"

"Nothing is wrong, Elani. Just not enough is right."

"Then you are happy?"

Avrille turned her face away. "Sure we are happy. It's just that after the glamour of Allarion faded and the twins were born there was nothing else. We were never in love. Will's my little brother, no prince charming to be sure. And when I failed to give him a son we lost even the charade of married life."

"You sound as if you don't care," said Elanille reaching out then withdrawing her hand.

"Why should I? Will and I can rule and parent more effectively as friends than as lovers. We have always shared something good. I just wish my life weren't so horribly boring. I could use some romance, some intrigue. I want excitement, adventure!"

"You're looking to love someone else?"

"The queen cannot love someone else." Avrille stood up and planted her feet firmly on the floor.

"Chirp, chirp," said Trebil from this perch on the windowsill. "Trebil see fast running, coming here. Run, run! Must tell queen!"

Soon there was pounding at the door. Avrille opened to a breathless serving woman.

"Lady Queen," she said sinking into a deep curtsy. "Darilla's babe is coming early and the midwife is out at the farms. With Your Majesty's gift of healing...Oh please come quick."

"I will come. Return to your mistress. Try to keep her calm. I will be there shortly."

Avrille reached for a basket and began assembling the items she would need to assist with the birth. "Why don't you come with me Elani?"

"I can't leave Lizzie that long."

"She's with Linelle."

"But I may be hours. Linelle can only do so much without relief, and I said she should take the evening off. I suspect she has a young man, though she has never said so directly."

"Then bring Lizzie along," said Avrille throwing a shawl over her shoulders. "It would do her good to get out and play with other children. Darilla has a whole house filled with younger brothers and sisters, six or seven I think."

"Who is this Darilla, anyway," asked Elanille taking the extra shawl Avrille held out for her.

"Mabry's eldest."

"Oh, the miller? The builder?"

"Yes, that's Mabry. Will was apprenticed to him when we first came here if you remember? They are a second family to him and Mabry is Will's right hand in all those wild plans of his."

"Who did Darilla marry?" asked Elanille as they closed the door behind them.

"She didn't…"

Avrille, Elanille and Lizelle left the castle by the east gate. They walked along the cobbled street to the edge of town to the modest cottage where Mabry housed his family behind the mill. The door opened before they had a chance to knock. The serving woman led them through a room full of anxious faces. Avrille and Elanille entered the small bedroom at the rear of the house. Lizelle was left to the scrutiny of six pairs of eyes. She quietly sat down on a bench near the bedroom door.

"It's gonna be breech, Lady Queen," wailed the serving woman. "And I don't have the knack for turnin' it."

Darilla lay in the bed flushed and exhausted. Her cry was weak and frightened as a contraction rippled across her abdomen "Oh not my Lady Queen! I'm not worthy to have you attend me."

"Don't waste your strength with talk," said Avrille. "Today we are just women helping each other. Later we can be queen and subject."

"But My Lady…" Darilla tried to sit up.

Avrille pushed her back onto the pillows. "Do as I say now and everything will be fine." She loosened her shawl and rolled up her sleeves ready for work. "Elani, you stand by her head with a cool cloth. Hold her. Talk to her. You've been through this…" Avrille turned down the sheet and let her fingers probe Darilla's abdomen. The girl hardly had the strength to cry out as another contraction broke across the taunt flesh. Avrille probed deeper. The shapes did not make sense. She knew she did not have much time to turn the child. Was that a foot or a shoulder she felt? And what is this on the other side? Darilla's breathing came fast and shallow.

"Elani, help me turn her on her side. It will help her breathe."

"Oh mother," said Avrille to herself. "If only you were here. You would know what to do."

The hair on the back of King Frebar's neck bristled. He turned to confront his pursuer but saw no one. He started down the hall again but the feeling of being watched would not go away. His hand strayed to the dagger at his belt. He was almost to the archway between the hall and the royal apartments when a shiver as cold as death slithered down his spine. Frebar was no coward. He squared his shoulders, set his jaw with a determined clench of his teeth and returned to the library foyer where he first felt the intruder.

Everything was quiet. Most of the royal family had already retired. A few voices floated up from beside the fireplace in the great hall. There was nothing amiss in the oblong-shaped foyer. The candles burned steadily. The footprints recently crushed into the carpet Frebar knew were his own. He was almost ready to resume his walk back to his apartments when a flicker of movement caught his eye. He looked in the direction he had seen it but there was nothing. The door to the library was closed as it usually was. Frebar could not remember when he had last been inside. It had been years and years he was sure. He never liked the long stifling sessions with his tutors as a child. As for Tobar his brother the opposite had been true. He had practically lived in the library until he married Princess Analinne.

Another flicker. The large ornately-carved wooden door glowed, or was it only the candlelight? Frebar glanced at the sconce on the wall beside him. The candle burned tall and straight. He felt his hand reaching for the door latch. Why did he want to go in there? There was no answer to his question, yet his hand lifted the latch and pulled open the door. It was dark inside. He took the candle from the sconce and entered the room. The air was musty and stale. Dust was everywhere. Frebar wandered through the shelves of rotting, unused books. He now felt as if he were the intruder. His thoughts turned to his brother. They had been so different, almost as if they had lived in separate worlds. There had often been times he forgot he had had a brother.

At the far end of the room he came to a little alcove. There a desk was untidily piled with books, papers and spider-web encased dirty dishes. There was a stub of a candle in a wax-filled goblet. The essence of Tobar, his twin, lingered so strong that he could almost smell it. Again something flickered. He spun around to confront the darkness behind him. His spine was like ice. His knees shook. Gentle laughter echoed behind him. Frebar turned back to face the alcove.

Seated at the desk was the pale gray outline of a figure. He knew that line of slumping shoulders, that tangled mat of hair. The figure laughed again.

"I never thought to find you here, brother," said a thin frail voice.

"Tobar!"

"I used to be."

"But you're..."

"Dead? Yes, that I am. Soon you will be too. Two years is a long time for twins to be apart even ones as different as we are."

Frebar stood dumbstruck.

"Are you afraid of you own brother, or is it the thought of joining me in this ephemeral state that makes your knees quake and your dinner turn over in your stomach?"

Before Frebar could think of a reply a blue flame leaped up from the candle stub in the goblet. The one in his hand sputtered and went out. The blue flame danced high in the glass. It expanded until the room was filled with light like the blue of the midday sky. He was out of doors! First he was on the castle wall. He heard a disembodied voice give a command to hold. Then he was lying on his back looking up into the well of sky, idly watching carrion birds circling overhead. All around him black thunder clouds rumbled. In a brilliant flash a child's face shone like a golden beacon above him. Then the clouds rolled over him and he sank into the darkness.

Frebar hastily retreated along the dusty shelves toward the crack of light from the doorway. Once he was back in the foyer he took a deep gulp of clean, fresh air and bolted the library door behind him.

Lizelle swung her feet under the bench and made faces at the other children until they began to bore her. She slid down off the bench and wandered around the room, keeping an eye on the others lest they object to her exploring their territory. She stopped at the pot of hot water the serving woman had just lifted off the fire hook.

"Don't touch that missy or y'all burn yer fingers," warned one of the older boys.

Lizelle held her hands behind her back and peered into the pot. What she saw in the water was not her own reflection but a sight that sent her running unannounced into the birthing room.

"Grandma says two babies holding on. Poor littler one scared to let his brother go. Afraid a being left alone."

Avrille did not stop to question how Lizelle knew. "Can you talk to the babies, Lizzie?"

"Sure, Auntie."

"Careful, Lizzie," Elanille warned.

Lizelle shut her eyes and screwed up her face with concentration.

"Which way do they lie, Lizzie," said Avrille. "Help me turn one head down."

Lizelle put her tiny hands firmly over Avrille's hands and pushed. Another wave rippled across Darilla's abdomen.

"Push. Push, Darilla," Elanille chanted. "Breathe with me. Puff, puff, puff, pooh…"

Avrille and Elanille worked together at Lizelle's direction. The serving woman stood behind them, mutely holding the basin of hot water.

"Almost. One more push," encouraged Avrille.

Darilla screamed.

"Breathe. Breathe," said Elanille. "Push. One more time. Now!"

"I see the head!" Avrille cried. "You're so close, Darilla."

"I can't," the girl wailed collapsing back into the pillows. "I'm just too tired."

"We need pretty stars, Mommy," said Lizelle. "One for each finger like Grandma says."

"No time for stars," Avrille snapped.

"I can make them." Lizelle clapped her hands. "Poof, pretty stars! One-two-free-four-five." Lizelle twirled around. Five sparkling lights surrounded the bed. The serving woman gave a choked scream and backed out of the room, drawing a hasty warding on her breast as she fled.

"Good, her gone," said Lizelle.

Darilla's breathing accelerated. Lizelle held her hands. The stars glowed brighter. Humming filled the room. The first baby slid out effortlessly. The second one followed clinging to his brother's feet. Avrille picked up the lustily wailing infants, wiped their faces, then reached for her scissors to cut the cords but Lizelle stopped her hand.

"Me do it easy way," she said. "Poof!" The cords separated. Tiny red stars appeared on the infant's bellies where the umbilicus should have been. Avrille wrapped them in clean towels and laid them on Darilla's breast.

"What will you name them?" Elanille asked

"They already got names," said Lizelle before tired Darilla could answer. "Varan's the first one and Veren's the one that hanged on."

"Who told you that?" demanded Avrille.

"Grandma," said Lizelle with matter-of-fact confidence.

"They are good names," said Darilla with a weak but proud smile. "I will call them Varan and Veren, my star twins."

After Avrille and Elanille had washed their hands and picked up their baskets and shawls, the bedroom door creaked open. The younger children slipped quietly into the room to peer at Darilla's prize. The serving woman was nowhere to be found.

"What is your name?" the queen demanded of a girl about twelve.

"Nancie, Your Majesty," she said dropping a curtsy.

"Alright Nancie, you are in charge of the little ones. Darilla and the babies will be fine. Just let them rest. Since your servant has left, I will send one of my own women to help you.

Meanwhile…" She surveyed the wide-eye cluster of children. "I have a special command for each of you."

Soon Avrille had them sweeping, setting the table, stacking firewood and drawing water from the well. Nancie set out a simple supper of bread, cheese, broth and fruit. Avrille took a tray into Darilla's room. "Your house is in order," she assured the girl. "Just relax and enjoy these sweet moments. My woman will be here shortly. Keep her as long as you need her."

"Thank you, Lady Queen," Darilla reached out her hand. "You have done so much for me. I have no right to ask another favor but…."

"If what you ask is for the babies I will listen,"

"It is, but…" said Darilla, still hesitant. "Well I know the cards speak true to you and the babies well…Please, My Lady, I beg you…"

"You want me to do a casting?"

Darilla nodded.

"The birth was certainly unusual," said Avrille as she reached into her basket for her deck of cards. "You shall have it." Her hands trembled as she took them out. She was both curious and afraid to see the horoscope that would begin the star twins' path. She shuffled the cards. "Cut them twice, once for each child," she told Darilla. "The casting will speak for both." She shuffled the cards again. Lizelle edged nearer.

Avrille laid five cards face down on the quilt. "This shall be their birth sign," she said turning over the first card. A pair of silver stars rose up from the night sky of the card. Darilla watched awestruck as the stars eclipsed each other then fell as a single spark.

"You already knowed they were stars," said Lizelle. "I put them on their bellies."

Avrille laid the Star card back onto the quilt and drew the second card. "This will be the nature of their being." The card of Beauty blossomed, bringing visions of lost Allarion. Bright-colored birds caroled. The heady perfume of field after field of star flowers filled the room. The tinkle of a sunlit stream rang merrily. Lizelle picked up the melody, twirling trance-like, with her head thrown back and her arms outstretched. Avrille's heart ached for the beauty she and Will had tasted then lost. Reluctantly she lay the card down on the quilt beside the first. The magic faded.

"What will be their life work," Avrille asked the third card. Darilla shifted the now sleeping babies to the bed beside her and gingerly reached to turn the card. The silver moon shone over a quiet village. The scene receded until it was framed by a half-shuttered window. Behind them was the sound of rushing water and the unmistakable whine and squeak of a giant mill wheel.

"They will be millers like father," said Darilla obviously pleased.

Anxious to finish the reading, Avrille turned the fourth card. "What heritage begins and ends with this birth?" Darilla gave a startled cry then lowered her eyes. Avrille looked at her curiously before she turned her attention back to the card. The Black King! She stared in disbelief. These innocent babies from the Dark Lord? The card grew warm with life. She watched its painted face waver and change. The hair became soft and darkly curled. The eyes wakened to blue. The mouth turned up into a familiar grin. Will?

Lizelle's dance continued in the middle of the room. Her voice rose and fell with each revolution. "Starlight. Starbright. Two bright Stars in a night."

Will? Will and Darilla? That her foster brother, her husband could have fathered the twins was no surprise. Will spent a lot of time at Mabry's house. He and the girl had been friends of sorts ever since his apprenticeship. But Will as the Dark Lord? How could that be? He was the Child of Light! She knew him. She loved him. It did not make sense. One indiscretion did not make him evil. A dark and nameless fear churned deep inside of her.

She looked down at the card. It was the familiar painted face again. She glanced at Darilla. From the girl's downcast eyes and flushed cheeks it was obvious that she too had seen Will's face in the card. Avrille felt no anger, no jealousy, no sense of betrayal. The dark dread rising within her erased all petty emotions.

The last card lay in her hand, the seeker's card. What lay in wait for her? Fearfully she turned it face up. Lizelle crowded close to see, and then she laughed. The smiling face of Compassion looked up at them, wise and caring, loving unconditionally. For a moment she felt the tenderness of his embrace. Her thoughts cried out to the memory of her beloved Uncle Hawke. How she missed and needed him, especially now.

Avrille, Elanille and Lizelle finally started home. It was almost dark. Stars were beginning to appear above the silhouette of castle at the end of the street. As they neared Beck's tavern a familiar silhouette of Dell the Bard appeared at the door. "Hey Dell," called Avrille. "Are Mabry and my husband in there?"

"Yes, My Lady, they have been closeted together discussing some project or another since early afternoon."

"Then do me a favor. Go in and announce to all and sundry that Mabry is a grandfather and he should get himself home. Tell Will I won't be waiting up for him if he wants to tag along with Mabry."

Dell studied the queen's face for a long moment. "I think this sings like a bar room ballad."

"You make a ballad of this, Dell and I'll have your head decorate a pole on the castle wall."

"I'll tell them," said Dell with a formal bow and disappeared back into the tavern.

Back at the castle Avrille bid good night to her sister and niece at the door to their rooms and wearily headed down the corridor toward her own. But her feet passed the royal chambers without stopping. She wandered down the stairs, across the courtyard and into the guard house. The startled men snapped to attention as their queen rushed across the common room and flung open the door to the office of the Master of Arms. Rogarth looked up from his desk, then jumped to his feet. Queen Avrille fell sobbing into his arms.

Chapter 3

Queen Avrille tucked the napkin under her younger daughter's chin. It was a special occasion. The royal twins Arinda and Arielle were dining with their elders tonight to wish farewell to their cousin Kylie who was leaving in the morning to be fostered in Frevaria. The one-year-olds were propped with cushions into a large chair set between their mother and Linelle their nurse. Kylie sat in the place of honor to King Will's left. His sister Lizelle squirmed in her chair between her mother and Gil. Marielle's place was empty. She seldom stirred from her room of late. The family gathering was completed with the maiden aunts Cellina and Liella.

"Babies are so messy," declared Lizelle trying to divert some of the adult attention from Kylie and the twins.

"Look at yer own mouth, Lizzie," said Kylie waving his piece of meat.

"Kylie!" exclaimed Elanille. "Is that the kind of manners you are going to have at Grandpa's?"

The table was set with the good plate and everyone was dressed as if it were a state occasion. Roast venison and blueberry tart, Kylie's favorite foods, were on the menu. Only the absence of the damask table linens marked deference to the ages of the diners.

Arinda poked Arielle. The little princess gave an indignant squeal and bit her sister. "I'm not sure this was such a good idea," said Avrille separating them. She dipped two pieces of bread in honey and gave it to the twins.

"You will spoil those two," said Lady Cellina. "Giving sweets instead of swats, how can they learn right from wrong that way?"

"Aunt Cellina," said Will in his wife's defense. "This is a special occasion. Their moral education can wait until tomorrow."

"Tomorrow!" Lady Cellina exclaimed. "And what will this kingdom come to…"

Arielle squealed again. This time Arinda was trying to stand up in her chair, stepping on her sister in the process. Avrille jumped up. The table rocked and skidded back. Will caught the candelabra in mid air. "This is enough!" Avrille shouted. "I should have known putting them together would spell disaster. Linelle, take them back to the nursery and give them a bottle."

"Uncle King Will," said Kylie as he watched the nurse pick up the now shrieking twins. "Who gets to sit on the doffy chair when the twins are too big to share?"

"The what kind of chair?" said Elanille.

"The prince doffy chair," said Kylie amazed that his mother did not know.

King Will laughed. "You mean the prince dauphin, Kylie."

"Well what in Arindon is that?" said Cellina with a huff.

"Not in Arindon, dear aunt. In the land where I was fostered one of the names for a crown prince was the dauphin. Kylie and I were talking about that the other day."

"Well who gets it?" said Kylie with impatience.

"I hadn't really thought about it," said Will as he helped himself to another slice of venison. "I guess we will have to have two chairs."

Kylie fell silent for a while. He studied his bread, tracing his finger in the butter then licking it idly. The adults resumed their dinner and conversation. Gil and Will leaned in front of Elanille in a spirited debate about visitation rights of a fosterling's relatives. Elanille folded her hands in her lap and let them talk, her appetite lost in the confusion. Cellina conducted a mostly one-way conversation with the ladies on the proper rearing of royal children with all the zeal a forty-plus maiden aunt could muster, while Lizelle sulked, quietly sucking her honey-smeared fingers.

"Does Grandpa have a doffy chair," said Kylie suddenly.

Gil dropped his knife and looked to Will. Avrille caught their anxious exchange. "I don't know Kylie," she said filling in the silence.

"If he does," said Kylie. "Maybe he'll let me sit there."

"I'm sure your grandfather will have a special place for you Kylie," said Gil

After an uneasy silence the dinner resumed.

Elanille sat in the carriage with Gil. Kylie had insisted on riding up front with the driver. The ten miles to Frevaria were a short ride, but the finality of their separation once they reached their destination made it seem like the end of the world. Elanille remembered making the same terrifying journey in the opposite direction on her own seventh birthday. But now Arindon was her home more than Frevaria had ever been. The twin princesses, Analinne and Maralinne had become much more than foster sisters as they shared their daily lives and all their hopes and dreams. It was they and their royal aunts the ladies Cellina and Liella who arranged her match with gallant Sir Keilen. Elanille's eyes filled with tears. Now everything was changed. Keilen was dead. Analinne was dead. Maralinne was gone away with Jareth. Elanille felt very much alone. She did not know whether she was glad or sad that Kylie was leaving her too. She looked out the carriage window at the passing landscape and sighed. Gil patted her hand. Kind gentle Gil, she was glad he was riding with them.

The sun dappled the road between the trees. The river sparkled as it raced along beside them. Two peasant boys were fishing from a rock overhanging the water. They called and waved at the carriage. Kylie yelled something back to them. The cushioned seat of the carriage reduced the bumpy road to a dull, jostling rhythm. She leaned back and let herself drift. The warm sun patterns played on her closed eyelids as the carriage rattled on.

Cautiously the seeking touched her innermost thoughts. Elanille turned her head toward the right side window. Her eyes were still closed. The seeking persisted, calling in a voice both alien and familiar. Laughter swam gaily on the surface of her awareness. Elanille's eyes opened, searching for the voice. They were passing the silent, unmanned border gate between the two kingdoms. The woods here were tangled and thick. As she caught a glimpse of a pool behind the gatehouse the seeking stabbed through her consciousness, this time with clear unmistakable words. "Elani. Elani."

"Mother!" Elanille exclaimed aloud.

Gil jumped with the sudden sound. Elanille leaned out the window. Her eyes were wide and glazed. He touched her hand and called her name but she did not respond.

"Mother, where are you?" Elanille called to the receding landscape.

Gil gently pushed her back from the window and lowered the shade.

"Where are we?" said Elanille as if waking from a pleasant doze.

"About halfway."

"Was I asleep?"

"The sun is warm," said Gil opening the window on the opposite side. "Let's get some air."

"I feel so strange," said Elanille still leaning toward the right window.

Gil looked at her questioningly.

"Did you hear something back there?" She indicated the direction of the border gate with a toss of her head as she eased back into her seat. Her hands massaged her temples and her face was flushed.

"No," said Gil cautiously so as not to alarm her. "But there is something just about where we were when you woke up."

"Something good or evil?" she said with a fearful catch in her voice. She sat up straight again and looked pleadingly at Gil.

"The spring behind the gatehouse is believed to magical. When the border was manned the guards often reported hearing voices."

"But is it good or evil?"

"Water is elemental," said Gil. "It can be life or death."

Elanille looked straight at Gil. The deep Allarian blue of his eyes held her. "I heard Mother," she said knowing he would believe her.

"The Star Pool, as the place used to be called, is said to be the last place the gods touched the earth. It is also said that it is there that they will come when they return. Now it is just abandoned. The voices, if they really call there, have no ears to hear them."

"But I heard her. She called my name."

Gil nodded his agreement. After that they rode on in silence, past Frevarian fields golden in the late summer sun. Gil watched a group of farmers lift heavy buckets off their wagons and carry them along the rows of plants. It was hard work keeping the crops watered when the rains no longer came. King Frebar still refused to accept Will's idea of irrigation canals even after Frebar had inspected their construction in Arindon.

Above the clatter of the carriage wheels Gil could hear Kylie's excited questions and the driver's low replies. He looked over at Elanille. She had closed her eyes again.

"Lookee, Mommy! There it is, Grandpa's castle!" Kylie called eagerly from his perch up front with the driver."

Elanille reached for Gil's hand. She needed his gentle strength.

Maralinne put down her sewing. It was getting dark. Jareth and Jasenth would be home soon and supper had to be ready. She put another log on the fire and tied on her apron. The larder was almost empty. They had not taken the trip to Arindon market for a long time. There was just enough flour for one more batch of bread. Maralinne thought for a moment. There would not be time to bake regular loaves. It would have to be flat cakes. Yes, flat cakes and apples. The new apples were just starting to color. How she loved their sweet-tart flavor. She mixed the flour with water, added a pinch of sugar, broke two eggs into the bowl and set it aside. Then she settled back into the kitchen chair to peel and slice the apples. After the men came home she would cook them on the griddle until they were soft and top them with the batter. She was almost finished with the apples when she heard two deep voices outside. Who had Jareth and Jasenth brought with them? The door opened.

"How is the renegade princess?"

"Will! What are you doing here?" said Maralinne rising to meet her half-brother.

"Uncle King Will wants us to bring them here and…and," Jasenth began to chatter excitedly. Jareth tried to hush him but the boy chattered on. "Can we? Please, Aunt Mari, can we?"

"What's all this?" Maralinne asked as she ushered in their guest and scurried about setting another place at the table.

Will took his time answering. It was a pleasant relief being away from Arindon and he wanted to prolong it. "It seems my dearest half-sister, former princess, now happy peasant wife…"

"Please Will, just Maralinne. Now answer me. What's going on?"

Will grinned then continued. "I want to ask a favor of you and Jareth."

"Der's two babies and…"

"Quiet, Jayjay," ordered Jareth. The boy looked hurt but kept still. "Mabry's eldest daughter has given birth to twin boys. Magical events occurred at the birth. Each child is marked with the star sign. The poor girl is beside herself with no mother to help her and all the responsibilities of the rest of Mabry's brood. Their serving woman has gone mad and speechless since the event. So….." Jareth paused and waited for an indication of Maralinne's response to the news.

Maralinne took a long look at her half-brother and then at Jareth. Will would not meet her eye, confirming the paternity of the babies. "Does Avrille know?"

Will nodded.

"She delivered them with Lizzie's help," Jareth explained.

"Oh I see," said Maralinne with a touch of amusement at Will's distress. Then she shrugged her shoulders with a sight of resignation and said, "We would be glad to raise them here. And the girl can come too if that would help."

"Two babies exactly alike," burst Jasenth, no longer able to control his enthusiasm.

Maralinne turned back to the kitchen and poured batter for four apple flat cakes on the griddle while the men talked.

Elanille dismissed the serving maid. Too many confusing memories were crowding her mind to tolerate another person in the room. Her father had given her the queen's chamber for the duration of her stay in Frevaria. The room was changed very little from what she remembered as a child. The blue velvet draperies were pulled back to let in the sunlight just like her mother had done. In spite of the recent cleaning and airing the room felt musty with disuse and heavy with memories. She had been only four years old when she was told in this very room that her mother and baby sister had died. An untruth she would never forgive.

She began to loosen the laces of her gown, wishing momentarily that she had not dismissed the maid so soon. She tossed the empty shell of her traveling dress onto a chair and sat down on the bed in her shift. A pool of sunlight played on her lap. She turned her hand until her rings cast prisms of fireflies on the wall. Her mother had done that for her. Oh to recapture the childish delight in chasing those elusive rainbows! She thought of her own daughter and her burden of power. If only Lizzie could delight in such simple games. The sunlight felt warm and secure. She lay back across the bed and let her travel-weary body and troubled mind ease into sleep.

Kylie and his grandfather wasted no time. They went directly to the stables.

"Which one is mine?" Kylie asked hopefully.

King Frebar led his grandson to a large white horse with red mane and tail. "Tell me all you know about this horse," he said stroking the animal's sleek neck.

"It's big," said Kylie.

"And what else?" Frebar prompted.

"It's got two colors."

"And…"

"I don't know," Kylie whined impatiently. "Is this one mine?"

"Is it a mare or a stallion?" Frebar asked sidestepping the boy's question.

Kylie cocked his head and studied the horse. "I can't see underneath. The boards is in the way."

"Well it's a mare," said Frebar. He lifted the boy up and set him on top of the wooden gate. "Now what else do you know about this mare?"

"Its belly is fat!" Kylie exclaimed suddenly grasping his grandfather's line of questions.

"And that's because…"

"There's a baby horse inside," Kylie announced.

"That's my smart boy," said Frebar. "And when the foal is born it will be your horse. You will assist with the birth, feed it, groom it, teach it and someday you will ride it."

"When will my horse come out?" asked Kylie sensing the whole process may be quite long.

"In a few weeks if I am any judge of horses," said Frebar. "Frevarian men are all expected to be good horsemen. That is why I am giving you this horse."

Kylie was pleased with the gift but childish impatience made him ask, "When can I ride him?"

"Not for a long time, grandson," said Frebar, but sensing the boy's disappointment he added, "But until your horse is ready to saddle, maybe we can find another one for you to ride."

33

They walked on through the stables. Frebar named each animal. Kylie petted the less spirited ones and listened eagerly to his grandfather's tales.

The next several days of her visit were pleasant. Elanille tried to relax. Kylie spent every waking moment tagging along with his grandfather, taking care of "my horse's mommy" or watching the knights train in the practice yard. The castle rang with his laughter. Elanille had never seen her son so happy. Courtiers and servants alike were in awe of the child. There had been no royal children in the castle since Elanille's own departure sixteen years before. At first they were worried about upsetting the household routines and protocol. Then they began to whisper among themselves about the changes in their king's behavior. Some were as charmed by the boy as Frebar was, others held aloof, watching their king with caution. What would become of them and the kingdom if the child with such strong Arindian influences would be named heir? Cook, the unchallenged authority among the servants, had no doubts, however. After Kylie wandered into the kitchen asking how long until dinnertime, Cook ordered enough tarts and sweet cakes to be baked to satisfy a dozen royal boys.

Elanille spent the morning sewing with the Frevarian matrons, but soon grew tired of their prying eyes and limited conversation. In the afternoon she sought Gil's quiet company. They strolled into the gardens but soon were interrupted by King Frebar and Kylie.

"Grandpa is gonna take me hunting," Kylie shouted. "I'm gonna kill rabbits and squirrels and Cook will serve 'em up for dinner for everybody."

"How is my favorite daughter today?" said Frebar giving Elanille a warm hug.

"Fine, father," she said with a weak smile.

"Why so gloomy? Are you angry with me for stealing Kylie?" Frebar laughed.

"Of course not, father. Kylie is a big boy now," she said patting Kylie's shoulder. "He needs to learn how to live in a man's world. And from what I have seen here already, he will do fine."

"I promise not to spoil him too much," said Frebar laughing again.

"You have already done that," said Gil. "Your promise is already broken."

Frebar's smile vanished. "I have promised to give him the best education Frevaria can provide. Whether you trust me or not is irrelevant."

Gil chose to say nothing more and Frebar and Elanille were soon absorbed in discussing plans for visits and holidays.

"Come on Grandpa," said Kylie tugging at Frebar's sleeve. "We was gonna see the armory. We was gonna see the lances and swords."

"You must learn more than soldiering, Kylie," said his mother. "You must learn your letters too. Frevarian men write letters to the ladies they love."

"I'll write you letters, Mommy, an' draw pitchers too. I promise!" Kylie declared still tugging at his grandfather's sleeve.

Frebar allowed himself to be led away. When they were out of earshot Gil sighed with relief and Elanille sank back into her reverie. Giving up Kylie would be easier for her now that she knew he was happy in Frevaria. She tried to find joy in that, but the loneliness was closing in again. Her eyes blurred with tears.

Gil patted her hand. "Shall I order tea served here in the garden?" he suggested to distract her.

"What good would that do?" she sobbed

"It's pleasant here in the sunlight…."Gil began.

"Sunlight makes me feel worse," Elanille wept.

"Sunlight, your name means sunlight in the Allarian tongue. I wonder if Frebar knows."

"I'm sure father doesn't or he would have tried to get rid of me too."

"We all have our fears for ourselves, for those we love and for those for whom we are responsible. I dislike Frebar. I do not trust him but by Frevarian standards he is a good king."

"What do I care about kings and kingdoms when I'm so lonely and see nothing, nothing ahead…"

Gil took her hands in his. "You still have a daughter. You still must…"

"Gil, spare me the thought of Lizzie for these few days of freedom!"

They lapsed into silence after that, sitting by the lily pond until long past tea time.

Elanille went to her room and began packing for their return to Arindon the next morning. She had already dismissed her maid, kindly giving the girl one of her dresses and the scarf she had embroidered during her visit. "For your good humor and patience with such a moody guest," she had said. She was both glad and sad to be leaving. She tossed the shift she was folding back onto the bed and rummaged through her trunk for a dress to wear down to dinner. Finally she decided on a blue-gray taffeta with cream colored buttons and ribbons. She put it on then glanced in the mirror to check her hair. The glass clouded as she watched. She was drawn into the image in front of her. The sad blue eyes, the lips drawn tight, the cheeks unnaturally flushed, it was her face but not her face. The image looked older, sadder, and lonelier than she was. She watched the lips form words she could not hear. "Elani, Elani," they mouthed. She felt her heart answer. A sudden chill swept through the room, and the vision faded as quickly as it had come.

"I must be getting old," she chided herself, "I'm starting to see my mother's face in the mirror instead of my own"

With as much lightness as she could put in her step she descended the stairs to the dining room. They were having venison and blueberry tart for the second time that week. Kylie had ordered the menu for his mother's last dinner in Frevaria. He had also called for a storyteller to mark the occasion. After the plates were cleared and a second round of wine was poured, Dell the bard took his seat by the fire and began tuning his harp. King Frebar pushed his chair back from the table, turned it toward the fire and patted his knee for Kylie to join him. Dell treated them first to several nursery verses and a short country ballad. Then he looked at Kylie. "What song does the young master want to hear?"

"Tell the story about my daddy and his battle at High Bridge," said Kylie, his little chest swelling with pride.

Gil reached for Elanille's hand beneath the table.

"Your father was a hero, that he was," said Dell adjusting his harp and giving himself a moment to think. He cleared his throat and looked at the child.

"In the days and nights of long ago," he began.
"When men were greater than we now know,
The Delven curse rode out of the night
And brave Sir Keilen gave them fight.
Through the tangled wood he gave them chase.
On his snow white steed he kept the pace..."

"My daddy's horse was brown," whispered Kylie to his grandfather.
"In a ballad the hero's horse is always white," Frebar whispered back.
"Oh I know, the good guys is always white and the bad guys is always black. Right Grandpa?"
"Right Kylie," said Frebar turning his attention back to the bard's song.

"At the rushing river Keilen took a stand
To save King Arinth's lovely land.
He raised his sword and held it high.
'We fight for the Light' was his battle cry.
The swords did swing. The steel did ring.
They fought against the darkened tide.
The sun was high. Bright was the sky.
They fought with all Arindon's pride..."

Kylie sat enrapt in Frebar's lap, a cookie in each hand. Elanille looked at her son and blinked back tears of remembrance. Gil gave her a reassuring smile and retrieved her handkerchief which had slipped off her lap and fallen to the floor.

"Onto the bridge Sir Keilen rode
Over roaring flood
Sir Keilen's sword swung high and wide
And drank Dark Delven blood.
Step by step they fought them back.
Blow by blow they renewed the attack,
Til out of the wood screeched winged things

Birthed by the Dark with poisoned stings.
Sir Keilen fought with pride and skill,
But the Dark over came his life and will..."

Elanille choked back a sob. Gil poured her another glass of wine but she pushed it away. Her face was pale. Her eyes were glassy mirrors, red-framed and set above dark hollows of grief.

"The soldiers fell, first one then all.
Into the river they did fall.
Red with their blood the river ran
All the way through King Arinth's land,
That the people there should know
This darkened day, this tale of woe.
The tale is told. The song is sung.
But the fight lives on in Keilen's son."

Dell lay down his harp. Frebar began to clap.
"The last part is about me," said Kylie bouncing up and down on Frebar's knee. "Keilen's son, that's me,"
"You're right" said Frebar. "And you are my grandson. Dell must add that part to his song too, right?"
Dell nodded his head, but his harp was already tucked away.

The next morning Gil and Elanille left for Arindon. Dell was riding with them, perched on top of the carriage with the driver. Dell's tales were always welcome diversions in Arindon and his news and understanding of events often proved invaluable. He would sing at dinner to be sure. Then he and King Will probably would sit up most of the night talking. What news was Dell carrying this time to Arindon? What news would he return to Frevaria?

It was almost dusk when Jareth and Maralinne's horses galloped out of the woods. Little Jasenth held on tight to his uncle, thrilled with the speed of the ride and the excitement of their mission. As they neared Arindon they slowed down to a trot.

Mabry's mill loomed ahead. Lantern light glowed through the shuttered window cracks. The huge wheel groaned on the far side of the building.

"Ho Mabry," Jareth called as he dismounted.

The side door of the mill opened. Mabry motioned them inside. Maralinne was awed by the new interior of the mill. The huge stones were now connected to the wheel outside by cogs and smaller wheels. The long leather belts connecting the wheels to the large toothed saws were now slack and silent above a pile of newly cut lumber. Leaving the machinery, Maralinne's eyes were drawn to a quiet tableau in the corner farthest from the noise and dust. Darilla sat on a small stool holding one nursing baby while her sister Nancie patted the back of the other baby over her shoulder. Two small satchels lay on the floor by Darilla's feet. Jasenth stared at the two identical babies. He held his hands over his mouth enforcing his promise to be absolutely quiet.

Mabry took one grandson from Darilla. His eyes were full with emotion. His lower lip quivered as he passed the child to Maralinne. Darilla rose from the stool and adjusted her shawl. Her eyes did not meet her father's. Mabry embraced her and when he stood back, searching for words to express what ached in his heart, Nancie handed him the second child. Mabry looked long at the new life in his arms, then gave the child to its mother. He picked up the luggage and hurried to the door.

Outside behind the mill two horses were saddled and ready to ride. Mabry held the reins while Jareth strapped the luggage to one horse. Jareth helped Darilla up onto the other. One baby was tucked snugly under her shawl. Maralinne mounted her own dusky mare, cradling the second baby. With a nod of farewell to Mabry, Jareth swung Jasenth up onto his dark stallion then himself. Darilla did not look back. She could not bear to see her father and sister weeping in the lantern-lit doorway.

It was a warm gentle night. The full moon lit the narrow road even after it entered the woods. Jasenth squirmed in his seat. He looked at his uncle riding close behind him. "Can I talk now?" he whispered.

"You have been a very helpful and obedient partner tonight," said Jareth, "Yes you may talk but try not to wake the babies."

"They sure are cute," Jasenth said to Darilla. "I'm glad you're gonna live with us."

"Thank you, Master Jasenth," she replied.

Jareth laughed. "Don't call him that, Darilla, or it will go to his head."

The rhythm of the horse rocked gently. Maralinne held the warm, precious life in the crook of her arm. She was glad to bring more children into her life though it caused her to face again the sad fact that she and Jareth had none of their own. Jasenth poured out a barrage of questions. She tried to answer patiently. Yes, the babies could live with them until they were big enough to play with. Yes, someday they would sleep in the loft with him but for now they would sleep with their mother in the little bed near the fire. Yes, they were both boys.

Jareth reined his horse to a sudden stop and raised his hand for silence. At first Maralinne heard only the chirrup of tree frogs, but then she heard unmistakable hoof beats coming fast behind them. Jareth transferred Jasenth to the pack horse. The boy obediently put his hands over his mouth again, nodding his promise to be silent. Maralinne led the horses off the road and waited in the shadows while Jareth doubled back to meet their pursuer. After a few tense moments, "Ho Jareth," reached their ears. Rogarth? Maralinne thought she recognized his voice, but why would Rogarth be following them. Soon the two men caught up with them.

"King Will requests your presence at dinner tonight, Jareth," Rogarth was saying. "Dell rode back to Arindon today with Lady Elanille and Master Gil. This may mean news…"

"But I have the women and…" Jareth began.

"I am to escort them to the cottage and stay with them until you return," said Rogarth. He turned to the rest of the company. "Greetings, Lady Maralinne and Mistress Darilla."

"Me too," said Jasenth.

"And to you too, Master Jasenth," added Rogarth.

"Uncle says nobody is supposed to call me that or it will go to my head."

"Lady Maralinne's influence has failed to teach the child humility I presume," replied Rogarth holding back a grin.

"Jareth," said Maralinne. "If Will wants you to go, then you have to obey. But why do I have to be left with such an insolent protector?"

"I'm sure you will do just fine," said Jareth. "None can keep you safer than the queen's champion."

"And me too," said Jasenth.

Baby Veren started to cry when Maralinne leaned over to kiss Jareth goodbye. It was only a short distance to the cottage but the rest of the trip seemed endless. By the time they arrived both babies were crying and Jasenth was annoying everyone with his chatter. Rogarth performed his duties with silent precision. He rekindled the fire and cared for the horses. Then he sat on the porch guarding the door. Inside, Maralinne arranged the luggage, put on the teapot and battled the overtired, overexcited Jasenth until he finally agreed to go up to the loft to bed. She tried to comfort Darilla but the girl sat in the chair by the fire and sobbed quietly, tears falling on her nursing child. A cup of tea sat untouched and cold beside her. Maralinne looked at baby Varan already asleep in a pillow nest on the bed. She pulled his blanket up an inch higher and gently stroked his cheek. His tiny red mouth responded with sucking motions. As she watched him her mind reeled with the evening's events. She knew she could not sleep until Jareth returned.

Outside the window she could see Rogarth's bulk silhouetted against the moon-drenched clearing. With a reassuring glance at Darilla she slipped out the door.

"I heard tree frogs out here," said Maralinne. "I thought you might want some company."

Rogarth smiled remembering their battle with winged tree frogs at High Bridge camp so long ago. Maralinne would never let him forget how fear illusions fueled by his childhood nightmares had attack them that night. Though he said nothing in response he was none-the-less glad to share his vigil.

Chapter 4

"I be Princess Lizzie, fairest in a land," Lizelle declared as she surveyed her tiny night-gowned form in the darkened glass of the nursery window. "An' all the people, 'specially Kylie, must do as I say," she added with a lift of her nose and toss of her blonde curls. "An' I can have my very own story man, an' I can stay up all night, an' nobody can't stop me." She stamped her foot in four-year-old determination. "Nobody can't. Nobody can't."

As she twirled in front of the dark window the image clouded then grew larger. The wind outside rattled the pane. "Wishes three. Wishes five," the wind sang. "Wishes bright come alive," it tapped on the glass.

"Grandma! Oh Grandma!" Lizelle wailed to the wind. "Mama won't let me hear Dell the story man downstairs. She won't let me! I wish. ..I wish…"

The shadow in the glass grew taller. The voice in the wind rose again.

"Grandma, I love you so," said Lizelle. "I drawed magic stars for you but Mama made me scrub them all off. She won't let me do nothin'."

"Wishes five. Wishes three." The wind's fingers rattled the window latch. The shadow image quivered. "Light a wish and I will come to thee."

Elanille was exhausted. Dell's voice rose and fell lulling her into the pleasant netherworld between after dinner castle clatter and sleep. She was glad to be back in Arindon. The strain of the week-long visit in Frevaria weighed heavily. Her hand relaxed on her wine goblet. Jareth's quick reflexes shot across the table and caught it before it fell. He was exhausted too, but his mind was as taut as a bowstring. They had gathered for a quiet family dinner in the royal apartments. Afterwards they had turned their chairs toward the cheery fire for a few relaxed moments before retiring for the night. Jareth, Gil and Mabry exchanged news as they tossed down mugs of Frevarian ale, while Avrille and Marielle together with the royal aunts consoled Elanille and sipped their nighttime possets. The little princesses were asleep, Arielle on her mother's lap and Arinda on the hearth rug beside Linelle. Dell sang softly, more to himself than for his royal hosts.

Will picked up the ale jug. "Another round?"

Jareth held out his mug but Gil shook his head.

"Perhaps the ladies would like a drop more wine, Will sire," said Mabry.

"Ladies?"

Avrille looked around their little circle. "No thanks, Will, any more and we'll all fall asleep. It's been a long day."

"OK just one more song, Dell," said Will. "Then we can call it a night."

"What will it be?" said Dell caressing his harp. "My lady love here is in a melancholy mood. Shall I sing a song to cheer her or weep and share her sorrow?"

"Sing us a song of our new age," said Gil.

"The deeds of our young king and queen sing for themselves," answered Dell. "The people do not need me to make up praises. They sing in the streets and in the fields of what a good life these last two years have brought."

"Then sing the songs our people sing," said the queen.

Dell fingered an arpeggio. "This is one Cook was humming when I came down to his kitchen one night. It has no ending since I interrupted him, but…."

"Sing it anyway. I'd be interested to know what songs ring in Frevaria's kitchens," said Will.

"The Queen of Light,
Frevaria's own,
And the King of Night,
Make Arindon home.

She heals the land
With a gentle hand.
He makes us strong
With a sword sharp and long.
She bore him two daughters
And soon will bear sons…"

Avrille looked at Will. He gave her an ambiguous grin and looked away.

"To Avrille and Will
Let us our mugs fill.
To our Lady and Lord
Let us pound on the board,
And sing of the good times around us,
And sing of the good times to come…"

Lizelle was busy with her crayons again. "I don't care what Mama says. Stars is pretty. I'm gonna draw dem all again. One for each finger just like Grandma said."

When she finished Lizelle stood in the center of the room to survey her work. The wind howled louder outside. "Circle three, circle five," it seemed to say. "Circle stars, come alive." Lizelle traced a line connecting the five neatly crayoned stars. "Der it is, just like we used to draw, Grandma." She looked up at the window but the shadow image was gone. "Grandma where are you?"

Lizelle unlatched the window. The cold wind roared inside. The draperies waved wildly. Bedding, clothes and toys swirled around the room, smashing against the walls and furniture. The tapestry fell from its rod. The lamp rocked drunkenly on the night stand then crashed to the floor. The room burst into flames.

"Grandma!" Lizelle screamed. "Grandma, help!"

Elanille's head jerked up like a puppet. She gasped then slumped forward. Jareth reached her side first. "Help, she's been drained!"

"Lizzie?" Marielle exclaimed drawing a quick star sign on Elanille's brow. "What could she…?"

"I smell smoke!" Avrille screamed. The babies woke with a double wail.

Will and Jareth bounded up the stairs as one.

"Sound the alarms!" Mabry shouted. "Everybody out!" He sprang up onto the table shouting orders for people to go to the courtyard and for the guard to form a brigade to haul water up from the river. Gil hurried Marielle and the aunts out along with the servants.

"Will, Will, come back here!" Avrille screamed grabbing up Arielle and handing her to Linelle. "Take the girls and run!"

Linelle ran out to the courtyard with the others. A screaming, kicking child dangled under each arm.

"Lizzie! Lizzie!" Elanille wailed.

"Jareth will save her," Avrille promised. "Will! Will! Where are you? Come back here!" she shouted up the stairs. Avrille dragged her sister toward the gate, herding the servants along with them. "Take nothing, just get out!" she yelled. "Warn the village! Tell them to wet the thatch. Come on! Come on!"

Will reached the landing first. The hall was filled with smoke. He took one breath and started to cough. Jareth came up behind him and pulled him down to the floor. They crawled along toward the nursery, counting tiles to mark their progress. Ahead of them the fire crackled angrily. Timbers crashed. Flames engulfed the west tower and threatened to spread. The heat and smoke forced them back. Will coughed and gasped for breath. Smoke stung his eyes. He tried to mask his face with his sleeve. They fought through the collapsing timbers and intensifying heat, but they could not reach Lizelle. Elanille's screams drove them to try again and again.

Mabry swung open the heavy gate and herded the royal family safely outside. Then he ran back to help Will and Jareth. He fought blindly through the smoke making his way through the upper corridors until he found them. Will was limp, half conscious and wheezing for breath. They carried him down to the courtyard.

"We need a five," Will gasped between coughs.

"A what?" said Mabry as he helped Jareth ease Will to the ground.

"A five. Magic," he choked. "Me, April, Gil, Mother Marielle, who else, damn it, who?"

"Maybe four would work…" Mabry said trying to help.

"No it's got to be five," Will insisted. "Wait, I got it! Trebil! April's bird. Get her bird."

"We can't be thinking of saving pets now, Will," said Mabry. "We must…"

"He can help make the five. He's done it before," Will shouted jumping to his feet.

They raced back into the blazing west wing. The little bird's shrieks guided them to the right door.

"Help! Help! Raise the river!" Trebil trilled. "Help! Help! Rain! Rain!"

"That's it, raise the river," Will exclaimed as they burst into the queen's chamber. He grabbed the cage. "Trebil you're a genius!"

Behind them an enormous roar swept down the hall. The door exploded open. Flames leaped for the tapestries and bed curtains and whooshed across the carpet toward them.

"The servant's passage!" yelled Will. He dashed across the room, dodging the flying sparks.

Jareth tried to follow but the collapsing bed frame barred his way. He circled back and picked up a still intact chair. Using it as a shield he leaped through the flames toward the small archway. His shirt sleeve burst into flames. Before he had a chance to react Will tackled him and rolled him to the floor. Smoke poured into the passage. Will kicked the door shut and helped Jareth to his feet.

They felt their way along the unlit passage and sprinted down a smoke-filled stairwell. Trebil jabbered and squawked with every step. They ran through the kitchens and out through the gardens. At last they reached the gate. "April! Gil! Mother Marielle! Where are you?" Will cried as they emerged from the smoke. "Quick, no questions. Grab hands," he ordered. "Now, Trebil. Say it now."

"Raise the river. Rain! Rain! Raise the river. Rain! Rain!" They chanted Trebil's simple spell. The villagers and servants picked up the words. "Raise the river. Rain! Rain!"

The smoke billowed black. The flames licked out of the windows. The heat tried to force them back but they held their ground and continued to chant. Marielle lifted her arms to the sky. Gil stood behind her, his arms supporting hers. Marielle's voice rose above the others. She grew taller, rising in scintillating blue brilliance until she seemed to touch the sliver of the moon half hidden in the seething clouds above. A jagged fork of lightening skittered across the sky, followed by another and another. The roar of thunder shook the ground. Large drops of rain splattered down on their upturned faces. The fire sizzled and spat. The people cheered and renewed their chant with vigor. "Raise the river. Rain! Rain!"

A wall of water rose from the quiet river and swirled above the flaming castle. The fire hissed and steamed. Smoke boiled upward. The people cheered, heedless of their cold, wet clothes. Marielle shrank and collapsed into Gil's arms. He picked her up and ran, shouting to the villagers to bring blankets.

"Trebil wet!" said the little bird trying to hide his head under his wing.

"Yes, Trebil," said Will. "Let's get these people inside somewhere and dried off.

Mabry opened his home to the royal family giving them the entire second floor. He huddled his own brood in the tiny back room behind the kitchen with instructions to both keep out of the way and to immediately serve their royal guests if they should require anything.

Lady Cellina was in an uproar. She worried about her possessions back in the castle. She worried about her appearance. She worried that her chamber maid was nowhere to be found. When Lady Liella assured her that their "girls" were probably safe with their families, Cellina remarked, "Well, what are they doing there?" Liella tried to calm her, but in vain. Cellina trotted up and down the stairs until she was so out of breath she collapsed into a rocker by the fire.

Sensing one of their guests was in need, Mabry's twelve-year-old Nancie cautiously approached. With a deep curtsy she said in a small but clear voice. "Would Your Ladyship care for a cup of tea?"

Cellina started with a harrumph, readjusted her position in the creaking rocker, then looked at the girl. "You're the first one to show some sense around here."

"I'll fix it straight way," said Nancie bobbing another curtsy.

The kettle was already boiling over the fire. Nancie selected mint for upset stomach and chamomile for nerves from the canisters and carefully lifted down the teapot and one of the best cups. When the tea had steeped she carried the cup to the now dozing Cellina.

"Your tea, Your Ladyship, and do you take sugar?" said Nancie trying to bow and not spill at the same time. Cellina took the cup and held it while Nancie measured out three spoonfuls of sugar. Cellina eyed her carefully.

"What is your name, girl?" she asked.

"Nancie, Your Ladyship."

"How old are you?"

"Twelve, thirteen by midwinter."

"Hum..." said Cellina draining her teacup. "You will be my personal servant while I am here. You will take care of my things and do as I say. Do you understand?'

"Yes, Your Ladyship," said Nancie. "Would you like more tea?"

"You are a bright little girl," said Cellina holding out her cup. Nancie poured and added three spoonfuls of sugar without being told. Mabry smiled at his daughter from top of the stairs.

The door burst open. Will and Avrille arrived soaking wet. "Did Linelle get here with the twins alright?" demanded Will. "Are my babies alright?" said Avrille pushing past him.

"They are upstairs and already in bed, though I'm afraid not asleep," said Mabry coming down to greet them.

"And my aunts are fine too, I see," said Will taking in the little tableau with Nancie and Cellina.

"My sister and Marielle?" said Avrille breathlessly.

"Master Gil is attending both royal ladies," said Mabry.

"Come on then April," said Will turning back to the door.

"You shouldn't go out again, my Lord and Lady. Let me at least get you something..." Mabry began.

"No Mabry, we are OK but there are still people out there that have no place to go. We got to see that everyone is safe.

"You need dry clothes..."

"Later Mabry. What I need from you now is to guard my family and see to their needs."

"With my life I..."

"All we value is in your hands, Mabry," added Avrille.

Lady Cellina set down her tea cup with a clink. "Well if you two won't be sensible, just go and do whatever business you must do. I will be fine here."

Will laughed his goodbye as he and Avrille headed back out into the rain-filled night.

The young king and queen worked their way through the village, knocking on doors, hurrying along groups of stragglers to shelter, and shouting encouragements. Avrille picked up a lost child and carried him to the nearest house. Will checked with the soldiers who were erecting tents and distributing blankets in the market square. The stable boys and kitchen staff were tumbling all over each other trying to follow orders in the makeshift camp.

Avrille lost sight of Will. She stood on tiptoe and looked for him first one direction then another. Finally she saw him heading down the street toward the steaming debris that had been Arindon castle. "Will! Will!" she called. "You're not going back there again tonight." She picked up her skirts and ran after him.

"I got to secure the gate," he said when she caught up with him.

"Everyone is out. We counted. We got all the names," she panted.

"Except Lizzie."

"The child could never have survived, Will. Even my sister accepts the fact."

"The gate still needs to be secured." Will insisted.

Avrille looked up at him through her streaming hair. She tried to push it back out of her face, then gave up. "You think the fire was set then?" she asked as they trudged down the muddy street.

"The whole place tingled with power long before we called the rain. You felt it. You must have."

"I was too scared to feel anything."

Will grinned at her. "You look like a real mess, April," he said with a laugh. "Not very queenly."

"You're not a very pretty sight yourself, Willy." said Avrille giving him a shove. Will shoved her back and they both laughed.

The rain let up a little as they walked hand in hand toward what had been their home.

"Support me April," said Will when they arrived at the darkened husk.

"Like Mom and Uncle Hawke?"

"Yeah, I wish we could really work together like they did," Will said more to himself than to her.

"They loved each other," said Avrille. "That was their strength."

Will did not meet her eyes. Instead he looked down the street to the village. The weight of the kingdoms made his shoulders droop and his face taut. Avrille searched her heart to find the little brother she had grown up protecting, but too much had come between them in the lifetime of the past four years. Tonight they had worked together as partners, as parents, as king and queen, but not for each other.

He turned to her. His face was saddened. He seemed older than his seventeen years with his hair plastered to his skull and his sodden clothes clinging to his slumped shoulders.

"For Lizzie," he said. "Help me seal the gate for her."

Avrille slipped behind him. She placed her arms underneath his. Her face pressed against his wet shirt. "For us," she said as they raised their arms together toward the ragged hole that had been the gate. Blue fire splayed from Will's fingertips. The gate exploded into millions of multicolored stars. The air sang with a shrill electric sizzle.

"That should keep what's out, out and what's in, in," said Will.

Avrille collapsed with exhaustion. Will picked her up and staggered with uneven steps toward Mabry's house.

Chapter 5

A caravan arrived from Frevaria just before dawn. King Frebar himself drove the royal carriage. "Where are my girls?" he shouted as he raced into the village square. There he was directed to Mabry's house. He burst through the door without knocking, waking Mabry's exhausted household. He swooped up Avrille and Elanille into a fervent embrace and announced to everyone that they were coming to live with him in Frevaria for as long as there was a need.

Soon the royal ladies and sleepy children were bundled into carriages with their belongings. At Mabry's insistence Gil carefully wrapped Marielle in the household's warmest quilt. Elanille rode with her, silent in her grief. Gil paused before he closed their carriage door.

"It's alright, my love," whispered Marielle. "The next journey we will take together."

Gil kissed the fingertips of the pale hand she offered, then tucked it back beneath the quilt.

Frebar insisted that Avrille and the twins ride with him. With a word, he ordered the caravan to move. Avrille popped her head out of the window to shout, "Be careful," to Will. Frebar settled back into his seat and reached for one of the twins. "Now which little lady are you, Arielle or Arinda?"

At Lady Cellina's insistence Mabry personally helped her and her sister into the third Frevarian carriage. "I just look a sight!" Cellina complained. "I would give just about anything for my hairbrush."

"Now Celli…" began Liella.

"This just has to be the worst, I mean the worst thing that has ever happened to us."

"And by far the most exciting," said Liella.

"Exciting!" Cellina exclaimed with a disapproving glare as she squeezed her skirts to fit on the narrow carriage seat.

"You know we haven't gone out anywhere, much less to Frevaria, for ever so long."

When the royal aunts finally settled into their carriage, Mabry lifted Nancie up onto the running board. She clutched her small bag of belongings tightly in her hand. In her eyes was a mixture of fear and excitement. Mabry kissed her forehead and told her to be a good girl. Nancie took her place beside Lady Cellina's voluminous skirts. She waved silently to her younger siblings standing in the doorway as the carriage pulled away. Recent events were taking a heavy toll on her twelve tender years.

While the last wagons were being loaded with what few household items they had salvaged, Rogarth galloped into town. Jareth had ridden home to the cottage with the news as soon as everyone was safe. Rogarth returned immediately to Arindon to secure the village and organize the honor guard to Frevaria. Soon the tired soldiers were sent back to their camp to catch some rest before the dreaded cleanup operation in the days to come.

The sky was clear with no trace of last night's rain clouds. The road was still muddy, reflecting the sky in blue ribbons of water along the wagon ruts. The air was still crisp but with a promise of warmth. It would have been a beautiful morning but for the heavy odor of ash hanging in the air and the heaviness of their hearts.

Gil and Mabry stood with Will at the blackened monuments that had been Arindon gate. Each man was silenced by his own memories of the life that was lost here and of recent memories haunted by flight and terror. How had this happened? What will happen now?"

"What a mess!" said Will.

"Let's get started," said Mabry as he unhitched the horse from the salvage wagon to let the animal graze where the grass was still green.

The wardings Will and Avrille had placed around the broken walls were still intact. No curious villager had risked fate with lure of plunder, which said much about their love of their sovereigns.

Will sent out a probing. In a shower of stars the warding breached momentarily to let them through. They spent the day sifting through years of history. In the family quarters much was damaged by smoke and water but those items which had been in chests or armoires were still intact.

Will picked up his wife's jewelry box. From a small, velvet-lined drawer he took out the diamond pendant he had given her as a wedding gift. Beside it was a simple knotted kerchief containing a chain of dried flowers he had made for her the day they played in the pool in Allarion. His mind churned with memories and half-understood emotions. He took a deep breath. The smoky air rasped his lungs.

On strict instructions from Lady Cellina Mabry recovered as much of her personal effects as could still be useful. He loaded her trunks onto the wagon while Will stacked his own by the gate for the next load. Others would complete the salvage in the days ahead, but they had to be the first to see and feel the loss.

Those things that had been protected by wardings, such as the cask with the crowns, the thrones, and Arinth's sword were untouched by the catastrophe. Gil felt each artifact call like a beacon until it was recovered from the debris. Eventually he made his way up the stone stairs to the nursery where Lizelle had slept. The heavy door was gone. He stepped through the arch fearing the worst but he was unprepared for the sight. The place still tingled with the powers that had been unleashed there. "Will, I found some answers," he called down to the courtyard.

Gil waited until Will and Mabry joined him before he explored the room. There was no charred body of a child as they all had feared. Instead, a huge black hole gaped in the center of the fire-ravaged room. A faintly glowing circle surrounded it. Will shuddered as he looked into the depths of the abyss.

"Look at this," called Gil from a point along the circle that glowed brighter than the rest.

Will and Mabry picked their way along the rubble-strewn floor. Gil pointed to a faint but unmistakable star drawn by a childish hand. They followed along the edge of the hole to find four more magic stars. Where did the blackness lead? Who had abducted Lizelle, or who had saved her?

Agreeing without need for words Gil and Will positioned themselves on opposite sides of the dark star sign. They began to chant the home spell, hoping against all hope to draw the child back. But before they had finished, the earth beneath the castle began to shake. Will was thrown against the stone wall and everything went black.

The next thing Will knew he was lying in the courtyard. Gil's face hovered above him. His head throbbed. A moan escaped his lips. Gil bathed the gash on Will's head with a cool cloth. Mabry was lying beside him with his left leg splinted.

"What happened?" asked Will.

"Look," Mabry pointed.

The whole west wing of the castle had collapsed. Dust was still rising from the fallen debris.

"The star sign?"

"Gone," answered Gil.

Armon Beck's tavern was open for business again by noon. A hollow-eyed Will with a crudely bandaged forehead and Mabry with his leg splinted and propped up on a stool presented a sorry sight. After their grave morning's business, Gil left to join Marielle in Frevaria, but they had sought comfort here. Dell the Bard sat tuning his harp. When Will ordered food and drink, he called out for Dell to join them.

"We missed our talk last night, Dell," he said. "But then last night's news is old news now I suppose."

"Not so, my king," said Dell testing a chord. "Today's news is old for everybody knows it. But yesterday's news is new for no one knows what has not been told."

"Then sing it now or must you whisper it over a mug of Armon's ale?" said Will.

"I need the ale whether I sing or say," said Dell with a yawn.

Will motioned to the innkeeper. The large apron-skirted man filled the bard's mug and set the pitcher down on the table. Armon Beck ran a good house. He was sensitive to his patron's needs whether they were royal or peasant. He knew when to talk and when to listen and especially when not to talk and when not to listen. He tidied the tables on the far side of the room. He carefully guided other patrons to take tables near the kitchen, allowing Will and his company their privacy.

With half a mug down and half left to ease his throat as he spoke, Dell began. "Some say Frebar is bewitched." He waited until Will's eye brows lifted and fell before he went on. "Some say it is but love for the child that has so changed him, but all agree that Frebar has not been known as an indulgent, loving man until now. Though none speak ill of the child's mother, fair Elanille they still call her, they question her blood. None have forgotten that she is the child of the witch queen Janille. They cannot fault young Keilen, a true Frevarian lad they say, but they whisper about his fey sister." Dell took another sip of ale. "The thing that should concern us most is that they question your judgment in sending 'an Allarian spy' as escort to Lady Elanille and Master Keilen."

"They still whisper against Gil?"

Dell nodded. "And they spoke none too kindly for your own lady queen with her 'healing arts'."

"So I may have just sent my family into the jaws of death and I sit her with my bandaged head all fuzzy with ale?"

"They only whisper, My King. It is not Frebar we must watch but the whisperers who have his ear and wait upon his needs. It is they that spoke to me with more than words. There were the nods, the looks, and the sleight of hand doing their warding signs behind their better's backs. None see a simple bard when he doesn't sing but a silent bard sees everything."

"Will you come with us to Frevaria, Dell?"

"No, I would rather stay here a while unless you command me otherwise. The folk could use a few songs before these times are through."

"Do whatever you want, Dell," said Will. "And have another mug for your tale."

But the bard declined pleading need for sleep more than refreshment. With yawn he nodded his respects and curled up on the bench by the fire. Taking his cue, the innkeeper arrived at Will's table with a platter of cold meat and bread. Will and Mabry fell to their meal with good appetites.

At last Will rose and asked for two villagers to assist Mabry to the wagon waiting for them outside.

"I feel so useless with only one leg," Mabry complained, his face reddening with embarrassment.

"Come with me to Frevaria," said Will. "With April's gift of healing…"

"I can't leave my family with both Darilla and Nancie gone," said Mabry quickly to mask his distrust of anything magical. "I won't feel so useless at home," he said as two brawny villagers hoisted him up into the wagon seat beside Will.

"I need you Mabry," said Will driving toward the mill.

"I can serve you best here, My Lord," the man begged. "If I remain then you would have a place to come to if you needed it. In Frevaria there is no escape from the eyes and ears."

"You are right as always, Mabry. But will you come if I send for you?"

"You need only to command…"

"Thank you, my friend," said Will as he pulled the horse to a gentle stop in front of Mabry's house.

In the two weeks that followed, Arindon's royal household settled in at Frevaria. The ladies spent mornings sewing and gossiping in the east sitting room. At first the conversation was strained but Avrille played her role as visiting queen as best she could. She smiled and exchanged pleasantries with the dour Frevarian matrons. She praised the beauty of the sunny room where they worked and other features of her father's court. She asked her aunts and cousins about Frevarian genealogy and traditions, trying hard to ignore their raised eyebrows and furtive whispers. When small talk lagged Avrille concentrated on her knitting. She was making matching caps for the twins. She had already started a white one with pink flowers for Arinda but she asked her companions for advice in selecting colors for Arielle.

Elanille kept to herself. The ladies clucked about such a pretty young thing wasting away in her grief and speculated which knight or nobleman would be a good match for her after what they assured each other would be an appropriate time.

It was Lady Cellina who fit in most easily. Her Frevarian lineage gave her the proper introductory credentials despite the fact that she had left to live in Arindon more than thirty years ago. Her outspoken manner reassured rather than intimidated the ladies. Cellina's fingers flew as fast as her tongue as she embroidered Frevarian sunbursts on a pinafore for Nancie while the girl worked quietly on her sampler beside her mistress.

"You should have seen this dear girl's father," Cellina was saying one especially bright morning. "He worked side by side with King Will to design our marvelous mill. Thank goodness that beastly fire didn't destroy the mill too. It's on the other side of the village, further up the river you know." She stopped momentarily to wet a thread and tie it in a knot. "There," she exclaimed. "Now for a bit of pink to soften the design." She began rummaging through her workbasket. When she had located the right shade, she threaded her needle and resumed her chatter. "If it were not for this girl's brave father who rescued all my personal effects from that beastly fire, I would have lost everything."

"Celli, be still," Lady Liella complained. "These ladies are bored to death with your constant babble."

"I suppose you would rather babble about parties and balls like a girl half your age," her sister retorted.

"And why not?"

Their morning was interrupted just then by King Frebar himself. Liella blushed from head to toe. She had been quite taken with Frebar ever since he announced that since there were so many charming ladies in the house, the old custom of having balls and tournaments should resume.

"Avrille, daughter, when do my favorite grandbabies finish their nap? It's a beautiful day outside."

Avrille jumped up, eager to get away from the sewing circle. "I'll go have Linelle get them ready, father. We could take them for a stroll in their pram. I could use a breath of fresh air myself."

With a formal adieu to the ladies Frebar exited with Avrille on his arm. Soon they were out in the garden. Avrille dismissed Linelle when Frebar insisted on pushing the pram himself. They wound through the paths of roses and passed the lily pond. Frebar picked a bouquet of flowers for Avrille. All the while Arinda and Arielle angelically munched the sweets grandpa had given them. As they passed Cook's kitchen herb patch, Avrille bent down to pluck a few basil leaves. She crushed them between her fingers.

"I do so love the scent of basil," she said. "Don't you?"

Frebar stepped back. "I guess you would know your herbs with your healing and all?"

"Basil is for cooking, father. You eat it all the time." Avrille tried to laugh.

"Well I will have none of your herb business while you are here. Do you understand?"

"Whatever you say, father," said Avrille. Then she added, "I cannot change what I am, but I will respect your wishes while I am under your roof."

"And while you are mothering my little sunbeams here," he said giving the twins more sweets. "At least you bred true in spite of your Allarian witch blood." Then realizing he may have offended her, he gave Avrille a hug and teased her with a sweet.

"Stop it, father. You don't want me to get fat." She laughed to reassure him, but the warnings her husband and Gil had voiced would not be silenced with sugared fruit.

When they reached the gate, clangs from the practice yard greeted them. The men were hard at work preparing for the upcoming tournament. Frebar pushed the pram over the rough ground. The twins squealed with delight at the bouncy ride. A group of young Frevarian men had just finished their fencing lesson. The instructor pulled off his mask to greet his royal visitors.

"Sire, Ladies," said Rogarth sweeping into a ceremonious bow.

Arinda took one look at the giant in practice gear and let out a shriek.

"Now look what you've done," exclaimed Avrille, but Frebar soon quieted the child with another sweet and promise of a ride on grandpa's shoulders.

"Where is that husband of yours?" said Frebar. "He should be out here sizing up the competition. He shouldn't let all the glory go to Rogarth here."

"Will has a lot to do in Arindon, father. With Mabry the miller injured, Will has been doing most of the supervisory work himself

"I offered him anything I…"

"I know, father, but Will has a lot of thinking and planning to do too. Sometimes that comes easier when the body is busy."

"Well if I were he, I wouldn't leave my pretty young wife alone too long."

"Now father, I am certainly safe here with both you and Rogarth to protect me," she answered with a 'help me' look at Rogarth.

"That grandson of yours will soon make a fine pupil," said Rogarth changing the subject. "It's seldom that a boy so young has such dedication."

Kylie sat astride the cream-colored pony his grandfather had given him to ride until his foal was big enough. He clutched his little wooden sword and shield as he watched the knights ride with their lances to take the ring from the practice machine. The child was obsessed with martial arts. Every morning he asked Cook to pack him a lunch for his saddle bags. Then he would be off to the stables or the practice yard where he tagged along with the grooms and pages, absorbing the gallantry of military life. In the evenings by the nursery hearth he would re-enact the day's adventures with his toy soldiers.

Frebar strode along the fence toward Kylie with Arinda still perched on his shoulders. Avrille and Rogarth exchanged a look and a smile. Then Rogarth returned to the fencing arena and Avrille hurried after her father.

"Ho, Kylie!" called Frebar.

Kylie turned to them with a big smile but his face fell when he saw his little cousins.

"Here, Kylie, let's put Arinda, or are you Arielle, on a real horse. Grandpa's shoulders are getting tired."

Arinda shrieked and kicked but Frebar laughed and boosted her up onto the pony in front of Kylie. "Now hold her tight with both arms," he ordered Kylie, taking the reins from him.

"Careful, father," warned Avrille.

Kylie held the wiggling, whining baby. Frebar did not seem to notice Kylie's clenched fists or diverted gaze as he led the pony along the fence chatting with the grooms. Then the ultimate happened. Warm wetness began to spread along the saddle back toward Kylie. He wrinkled his nose.

"Pew, Grandpa! Take her away."

Frebar roared with laughter, but he did lift a very wet Arinda off the pony and gingerly handed her to Avrille. Kylie inched back from the wet spot. Tears of anger welled in his eyes.

"I think it's time to get the twins back to Linelle," said Avrille. She moved Arielle aside to make room for her twin in the pram.

Kylie bit his lower lip as he watched them leave. His little brow was knit in a dark scowl.

Gil and Marielle's room had an excellent view of the practice yard to the south and the river to the east. Gil had seen the royal drama below and did not have to hear the conversation to know what had transpired. He stepped back from the window and looked at Marielle. She was sleeping. Her health was failing rapidly since the ordeals of the fire and the move to Frevaria.

Frebar had graciously offered them anything they required but except for extra quilts and the simplest of foods, they asked for nothing. Instead, they cloistered themselves in their small tower room and nourished each other with love and lost memories. United at last after years of service to the Light in Arindon, they sadly faced age and change.

Chapter 6

"Hurry, Mama, hurry," shouted Kylie. "I hear trumpets. We'll be late. Grandpa won't want us to be late."

"We are just in time," Elanille assured him.

Queen Avrille walked elegantly on King Willarinth's arm. Nurse Linelle followed wheeling both princesses in their pram. The cheering crowd parted as they threaded their way to the royal box. King Frebar and most of the other noblemen had been at the arena since dawn overseeing the preliminary games. Now for the final tournament and parade the seats were filled and the rails on all five sides were crowded with the entire populace of the Twin Kingdoms.

Frebar orchestrated the larger event as well as the smaller, but none the less complicated, task of arranging the seating in the royal box. Elanille was to sit on his right and Avrille on his left. Linelle and the infant princesses were to sit behind them. King Will was on Avrille's left and Kylie was to have his own little stool beside his uncle. The boy took his seat quietly. He bit his lip when he saw his grandfather reach back to the pram to lift Arielle onto his lap.

The trumpets sounded again.

"It's such a pleasure to be in the company of not one but four lovely ladies all at the same time," said Frebar.

Will patted Kylie's knee but the boy pushed his hand away.

The gates on the far side of the arena opened. Out marched the heralds trumpeting boldly. Drummers and dozens of banner bearers marched behind them. Everyone leaned forward trying to be the first to see the knights ride in. One by one the armored horses circled the arena then stopped before the royal box to raise their lances in salute.

Avrille untied a red ribbon from her dress. Frebar smiled at her and rose to address the participants. "The royal ladies wish to honor the knights with their colors," he announced.

"Who shall it be little daughter," he said to her.

"Rogarth of course," she said stretching to place her ribbon on the tip of his lance. Will looked away as the queen's champion tied the token on his sleeve.

There was a disturbance in the aisle behind the royal box. The ladies Cellina and Liella arrived breathless and apologetic, followed by Mabry the miller carried in a chair by two sturdy serving men. Little Nancie bobbed along behind them, self conscious in her new blue dress. Cellina loudly directed their seating and the placement of Mabry's chair.

"Am I too late to give my token?" Liella asked as she sank into her chair.

"No, no, my dear," said Frebar. "My knights but await your honor."

"Celli, is that the blond young man we were admiring at dinner?" Liella whispered to her sister. "There, the one with the blue striped helmet?"

"How should I know?" Cellina retorted with a harrumph. "Those gruesome helmets all look alike. Don't disgrace yourself, Liella. You're far too old for him."

Frebar leaned across Avrille and Will to smile at Lady Liella. "The young man is waiting," he said.

Liella fumbled with her pink ribbon. Sir Anton of Frevaria humbly dipped his lance to receive it.

"Is everyone done now?" said Frebar. "What about you Elanille dear?"

"No, no, I can't," she said looking down at her hands gripped in her lap.

"Of course we are done," said Cellina. "Let's see some action. Enough of this childishness!"

King Frebar lifted his arms and the knights filed out. Kylie sat quietly swinging his feet, kicking the bunting that draped the railing.

"Let me carry you to the window, my love, so you can see the banners," said Gil.

"No, I have seen them many times," Marielle replied. "Why don't you go to the games, Gil? You don't have to stay because of me."

"I have seen the games many times, my love. My place is here with you."

Gil left the sunny window to sit at Marielle's bedside.

"Poor, poor, Gil," chirped Trebil. "Love games, love lady, love both. Poor, poor, Gil."

"Little friend, you are simple but wise," Marielle said raising her hand for the bird to perch.

Gil was glad Avrille asked them to house the mirror bird in their quarters when they moved to Frevaria. He agreed with Will that his association with Allarion should be minimized. They also agreed to use no magic during their stay. Frebar's welcome was generous, even extravagant. His concern for Marielle's health was solicitous, but Gil still felt uneasy. The staff had been instructed to treat her with courtesy, though they did so with obvious reserve. No one denied that this frail, ailing woman possessed powers they distrusted and feared. Gil tended her with his own hands to spare her their eyes and to ease the aching of his own heart. Little Trebil was Marielle's constant companion. She often sat for hours by the window or with her mirror, seeing with Trebil's eyes, what scenes Gil did not know or ask, but he was grateful for the pleasure it brought her.

"Poor, poor, Gil," chirped Trebil again.

"Come, little fellow," said Gil holding up some of the dried fruit Marielle kept handy for him. "Entertain us both this time."

"Trebil see games for Gil? Fly back, tell story? Gil have games and lady too?"

Before Gil could reply the little bird flew out the window.

Lady Liella clapped her hands daintily as Anton of Frevaria nodded to the royal box. Her pink token fluttered on his sleeve. The gold and blue of his shield gleamed in the bright sunlight.

"Will, hail that vendor," said Lady Cellina. "Kylie needs a sweet. Don't you young man?"

"Sure, Auntie," said Kylie brightening somewhat.

Will waved the vendor to the box. Cellina spread her handkerchief on her lap and heaped it full of fruit and candies. Kylie picked out a popcorn ball on a stick.

"Take two, take two," Cellina prompted. Then she turned to Nancie. "Don't be shy, girl, pick what you like."

King Frebar tossed the vendor a purse of coins and ordered him to leave his entire tray. In spite of Avrille's protests he fed baby Arielle a sugared fruit. Seeing her twin enjoying something she did not have, Arinda squirmed out of Linelle's grasp.

"Help! Help! Get them off of me!" Frebar laughed dodging sticky fingers as his granddaughters wrestled in his lap. Linelle hauled the squalling babies back into their pram.

The cheering crowds soon drowned out the royal princesses as the final contestants were announced. Anton of Frevaria had just won the last joust and would be the one to challenge Rogarth of Arindon, long time champion. Avrille stood up and cheered.

"What will you wager, my boy?" said Frebar to Will.

"Since all I own is at your mercy," Will answered sourly. "Arindon can only wager its pride and today there is very little of that."

"Don't be such a spoil sport, Willy," said Avrille.

"Now children," said Frebar trying to be humorous. "Let's not squabble on such a glorious day." He looked out into the arena then back at Will. "I have it. Daughter you will be the prize. You will favor the winner with the first dance at the victory feast tonight."

"Then we will both lose," Will grumbled. "Rogarth always has the first dance and the second..."

"Shut up Willy."

Frebar laid a hand on Avrille's shoulder. She folded her arms, slumped back into her chair and glued her eyes to the joust. Will leaned over to talk to Kylie.

The contestants met in the center of the arena. Rogarth's red and silver contrasted with Anton's blue and gold. They saluted each other then retired to opposite sides of the arena.

"Do horses ever get hurt in the joust, Uncle Will?" Kylie asked.

"A good knight does not let his horse get hurt," answered Will.

"Then my horse is gonna joust with me when it grows up."

"Just like your father did."

"Yep," said Kylie swelling with pride.

King Frebar raised his arms. The knight's visors clicked down. Their horses pawed anxiously. "Begin!" he shouted.

The crowd cheered as the combatants charged with lances held steady and even. The clang of metal on metal echoed from wall to tower to wall. Neither knight faltered as they met again and again. Young Anton was light and quick. His mount danced along the track. Rogarth rode his powerful steed with strength and control. Over and over they charged but neither one could unhorse the other. The crowd was in a frenzy. They stood on their seats wildly waving their flags. Their shouts and the heat of their excitement matched the blazing noonday sun. Neither horse tired. Neither knight wavered in purpose as the joust drove on. The combatants seemed oblivious to the chaos surrounding them. They were caught in the repeating time loop of the joust.

Brilliance! Exploding light! The sun leaped from shield to shield, from gold to silver, then ricocheted across the arena. The noise stopped in a timeless moment. The air tingled with power. Elanille screamed and fell back in breathless sobs. The noise of the crowd erupted again. When the dust of the arena had settled both knights lay on the ground deathly still. Queen Avrille leaped up and over the rail.

"April, come back here and sit down," ordered Will. "You're making a fool..."

His words were lost as she fled across the field to where Rogarth lay motionless. Squires rushed in to steady the horses. The track surgeon and his crew arrived with stretchers. The queen held Rogarth's head as they lifted him. "Please, dearest friend," she wept. "Please don't leave me. I need you. You promised me. Remember?" Tearfully she followed as the fallen knights were carried out of the arena.

The royal box was in an uproar. Princess Elanille had fainted after her outburst. The royal aunts were clucking over her while King Frebar shouted orders for her maids, orders for some wine, orders for Avrille to come back at once, orders for the games to stop and for everyone to go home. The royal babies were screaming. The only one silent was Kylie. He stood dazed beside his uncle's chair, holding tight to his popcorn ball.

The knight's tent behind the arena was in a panic when the casualties arrived. The surgeon yelled for everyone to stand back as they lowered the stretchers. He removed Sir Anton's helmet. The face was slack and ashen. The eyes were blank. Anton of

Frevaria was dead. With a look of resignation the surgeon turned his attention to Rogarth.

"Don't touch him!" Avrille screamed flinging herself across the body of her champion.

"Please, My Lady," the surgeon said gently.

"Get away! Get away from him!" Her wild eyes searched the room. "You, and you," she said pointing to two bystanders. "Take him to my chambers. Now! I command you!"

Disregarding the surgeon's pleas to calm down and be sensible, Avrille and Rogarth's appointed entourage headed toward the castle.

Will bounded down the corridor to his wife's rooms and flung open the door. "April...!" he shouted then stopped when he saw the silent tableau inside. Gil and Avrille held hands across Rogarth's chest. Five tiny stars hovered around the man's head.

"Lend us a hand," said Gil without looking up.

Will marched into the room. "We agreed not to do magic here."

"Lend a hand or this man dies."

Will stood at the foot of the bed, staring at the irregular rise and fall of Rogarth's chest. He tried not to watch the deep stain spreading across the sheet. Avrille's knuckles were whitened. Her eyes were closed as she searched deep inside herself for the power to staunch that crimson flow.

"Am I in time?' said a frail voice from the doorway. Marielle clutched a pale blue robe around her wasted form. Trebil was perched on her shoulder.

"Now's a Five. Now's a Five," chirped the little bird.

The glowing stars surrounding the bed brightened. Marielle took Will's hand. "Join me, son."

"All I know is the fire spell," he muttered.

"The fire of life is what we need here," said Gil.

The room pulsed as they chanted the song.

"Light and Death are one,
Love and Dark are one."

Time weighed between each labored breath.

"Truth and Time but move,
Eclipsing each other in tune."

Rogarth groaned. They renewed their effort. Their chanting rose and fell with their own breath, willing their friend to live.

"We live and are of Earth.
We die and are of Fire."

Gil glanced at Marielle. Alarmed by the strain he saw in her face, he let Avrille's hand slip from his hold. The tone of the stars shifted pitch. Will turned to Avrille and the star song rose with renewed vigor. This time they all took hands in a circle, resuming their chant, not only for Rogarth but for all life.

"In the Air we fly free,
In the circle of Time,
To our birth in the Sea.
None can change what we are.
None can change what we must be."

Slowly the fallen warrior's breaths became regular and deep. The red stain beneath the sheets stopped spreading.
"Trebil treat now?"
They all relaxed with a laugh of relief. Gil caught Marielle and quickly helped her into a chair. "You shouldn't have..." he cooed over her.
"OK you got your lover back," Will sneered. He stalked out of the room and slammed the door.
Avrille sat down quietly beside the bed as if she had not heard.
"Avrille, dearest lady," said Gil. "Will you look after Marielle? Your sister, Lady Elanille, is not well and I must go to her."
"Elani!"
"Events in the arena affected much more than the lives of our two knights. I will explain everything as soon as I can."
"Then go, Gil. Do what you must do," said Avrille. "We women will look after Rogarth and each other."

Trebil flew out the door after Gil. His plaintive chirps, "Treat? Treat?" echoed down the hall.

The victory banquet that evening would not be the festive event they had all looked forward to. With one hero dead and the other gravely injured, King Frebar thought of canceling the occasion, but since the preparations were already made he announced that, "At least we all can eat a good dinner."

Will was on his way to the banquet hall when Gil caught up with him.

"May I speak with you privately, Sire?"

"What message is April coward to deliver now?"

"This is not about the queen. It is about her sister," said Gil taking two steps to Will's one.

"Well, what about her?"

"Privately, sire."

"What is this?" said Will stopping abruptly.

"A matter which may be of great importance," said Gil.

Will debated a moment then with a nod he accompanied Gil to Elanille's room. A worried serving girl answered their knock.

"Master Gil, she has been calling for you."

"What's the matter with my sister-in-law?" said Will pushing past him.

"Your Majesty!" said the girl dropping a formal curtsy. "The Lady still calls for her little one, the one that died in the fire. She says the child came to her and spoke to her."

Gil thanked and dismissed the servant then turned to Elanille. She was feverish. Her eyes were glassy. Gil sponged her forehead talking softly. His fingers busily wove a calming spell.

"Are we here to play nursemaid or what?" said Will.

Gil would not be rushed. "Sit down, sire"

Will continued to pace.

"Please," Gil added. "Trebil went to the games to see for me."

"Trebil good boy," said the little bird from his perch on the bed post.

"His report was most unusual," Gil continued.

"I was there. Why..."

"Please sit down, Sire."

70

"OK. OK." Will threw himself down into a chair and assumed a dramatic "listening" pose.

"The easiest way is to let Trebil show you what he saw," said Gil. "Come here, little friend." He tipped Elanille's boudoir mirror toward them. "Trebil, tell us only the part from the last charge."

The mirror clouded then brightened with the dazzle of the tournament arena. The horses charged. The sunlight struck first Sir Anton's shield then Rogarth's. It arched once, twice, three, four, five times across the arena before it winked out.

"OK so we all saw that," said Will.

"Now Trebil," said Gil. "Tell it again, but very slowly this time. Will, watch closely at the spot just between the two shields."

The scene replayed. The sunlight struck and leaped from gold to silver.

"It's a face!" Will exclaimed.

"Now listen."

Elanille screamed, "Lizzie!" The face was definitely a child with rosy cheeks and golden curls. At Gil's request Trebil replayed the scene yet again, this time slower still. The child's mouth unmistakable formed the word "Mother".

"How come we didn't see that this afternoon?" said Will.

"Did you see it now until Trebil slowed it down? In the excitement of the tournament and the brilliance of the sun, only the person for whom the vision was intended was able to see it."

"So Lizzie isn't dead, she's just off somewhere calling for her mom. Lost kids do that," said Will with a flippant toss of his head. "Wherever she is I hope she stays there. If it weren't for her I'd still be king in Arindon and not licking my father-in-law's boots in eternal gratitude."

"Where else could we have gone after the fire?"

"Enough of your interference! Enough of your fatherly advice!" Will yelled.

"Sire, calm down. You will upset Lady Elanille."

Will started to answer then glanced at the bed. Elanille was sleeping fitfully. Gil stroked her forehead. He drew a small star sign and she relaxed again.

"No magic in Frevaria, Gil," mocked Will.

"The agreement had purpose when we made it," Gil replied still calmly stroking Elanille's forehead. "Even though this afternoon's events caused us to change that agreement, it was and still is a good idea."

"So little things the ignorant Frevarian's won't notice like secret healings and secret bird reports are OK?" snapped Will. Gil opened his mouth to speak but Will gave him no opportunity. "I'm not afraid of His Majesty King Frebar," he said pacing the room with gigantic strides. "He is a pompous ass and his generosity stinks. If he is afraid of magic, he should be." With that he turned as if to leave, gave Gil a malicious smirk, and with an arrogant gesture traced a fiery star sign in the air. Elanille cried out.

"There, dear sister-in-law, that should keep you safe," said Will and stalked out the door.

Try as he would Gil could not dispel the fiery sign. Torn between protecting Elanille and rushing after Will, he set five singing stars to guard her bed. He waited until she sank back into her pillows and closed her eyes, then he turned to go down to the banquet hall. The sign flared as Gil skirted its domain. He stopped at the door and looked back. The sign was moving! It began slowly. Then it accelerated with purpose as it crossed the room. The darkened mirror in the corner opened like a hungry mouth to suck in the writhing fire sign.

Queen Avrille was glad to be alone at last. Dinner had been a disaster. She kicked off her petticoats and removed her earrings. She was still angry, or was her anger only a disguise for her growing fear? Will had been surly and disrespectful to her father all evening. At first Frebar seemed unaware of Will's intent. When it finally became obvious, Frebar nobly tried to dismiss Will's behavior as stress from recent adversities. That had only accelerated Will's attacks. She grabbed her hairbrush and pulled vigorously through her lacquered curls until they frizzed up with static. She had tried to calm Will, first with teasing, then with direct confrontation. She threw her hairbrush down on the bed and started to pace, gritting her teeth as she relived the humiliating scene. Will had called her a witch and slapped her in front of everyone! Right now she hated Will. The empty, lonely hurt she had tried to hide was now open and raw for all to see. She knew Gil had tried to work calming spells on and off all throughout dinner. They had affected Frebar and even herself to some degree, but on Will they had no effect. Instead Will challenged Gil's interference, but the aging Allarian said nothing in response.

What would happen next? Avrille was too exhausted to care. Her eyes rested on the basket beside her on the night stand. Her cards, dare she ask them the truth of recent events? She reached for the basket. If ever she needed to know the future it was now, yet she hesitated. Was she afraid to know? So many dreams had been lost already. Would it really matter what she knew or did not know? Breathing in the courage, she took out the cards. They felt warm in her hand. She shuffled once, but before she cut the cards to shuffle again, she decided not to ask the questions for herself but to ask them for Will.

"Who is this man that I call both brother and husband?" she said turning over the first card. She half expected it to be a dark card, but the White Knight looked up at her, glowing with Willy's cherubic smile. She laid the card beside her on the bed.

"What is the nature of his being? What force drives him?" she asked, turning the second card with quick confidence. She was unprepared this time. The Black King leered up at her from his icy throne. His face was distorted and cruel but definitely Will. She pushed the card away from her, trying not to remember when she had last drawn that card. Darilla and her twins had almost been forgotten with the onslaught of recent events.

"What will be the task that is set upon him?" she asked the third card. The Star twinkled up at her, glittering first silver, then gold as it rose up from the card. A glowing star? She was puzzled yet could sense no ill in it. She laid it next to her then drew the fourth card.

"What place will his life and work have in the history of the kingdoms?" She was suddenly overwhelmed with loneliness. The Fountain card pictured one of the abodes of the gods. The scene before her was a bubbling, sun-dazzled pool. Three women frolicked in the water. One was old, one was young and one was but a maid. There was happiness and contentment there. The flowers, the trees, the caroling birds were all beautiful, but Avrille felt no part in it.

"What is for me?" she said to the last card, the seeker's card. She turned it quickly, hungry to know her own truth. She saw a peasant couple tilling the earth and scattering seeds. They sang as they worked. "No, not me!" Avrille declared as she slid the Earth card back under the deck. "Fertility! Not me. Not again! Once was double enough!" She threw the cards back into her basket. It was all too much to think about now.

Gil stood quietly in the doorway. It was several moments before Avrille sensed his presence and looked up.

"I have a favor to ask," he said.

"Anything, Gil. Just name it."

"Marielle has spoken of fond memories tonight, of floating down the river on the royal barge..." He paused and stared at the floor.

"Yes, Gil..."

"I want to take her on one last holiday if you..."

"But Gil," Avrille said, her face full of concern. "Wouldn't that be too much for her?'

"Nothing I can do is too much for her...now," he said with a tremble mounting in his voice.

Avrille gave him a puzzled look. "Anything you want," she said with a sympathetic smile. "I will order the barge to be readied. When do you want to go?"

"At dawn," he said without looking up.

"At dawn!" she exclaimed. "But Gil, it will be too cold..."

"I will keep her warm," he said barely above a whisper.

Avrille caught his hand and looked into the tear-filled blue of his eyes and understood the nature of their journey. "Anything and everything you wish for her, Gil," she said embracing him.

It stormed during the night. Dawn broke with black clouds still churning in the west. The royal barge pitched and tossed on the choppy water, pulling at its moorings. The canopy was draped in Marielle's pale blue colors. A couch piled high with furs and blue silks replaced the royal chair. Gil arranged a basket of flowers and set a small table near the couch. He gave the boatman a coin and dismissed him.

"But Master Gil, who will pole the barge for you?" said the man.

"I will take the pleasure myself," said Gil.

"But who will assist you with the Lady Queen Mother?"

"That I will do also," Gil assured him. "Go now. You have served me well."

The boatman reluctantly obeyed.

Avrille watched from her chamber window. She saw Gil emerge from the quay gate with Marielle cradled in his arms. A gust of wind whipped her gown as he stepped out onto the dock. Lovingly he adjusted her shawl and tucked her head against his shoulder as he carried her to the barge. With tenderness he placed her on the couch and wrapped the thick quilts around her. He kissed her as he placed a flower in her folded hands.

Will joined Avrille at the window. He put his arm around her but said nothing.

Gil untied the ropes and poled the barge away from the dock. Avrille started to wave but Gil's gaze was already down river. Avrille and Will watched in silence until the boat was about to round the last bend. Suddenly the sun broke through the storm clouds. A brilliant rainbow leaped across the river gorge. The speck of the boat sailed through the prism of colors and vanished.

Avrille and Will stood at the window a long time, each with their own thoughts, sharing the emptiness. They held each other more like two frightened orphans than rulers of the world.

"We might as well go down for breakfast," Will finally said.

"Soon, but not yet," said Avrille.

After another long silence she looked up at him. "Will, let's run away. Let's be free. Let's be April and Willy one more time before we grow up. Say yes, please," she begged.

"Don't be silly. Where could we go?" said Will. "We can't…"

"Oh I know none can change what we are. None can change what we must be," she said with more regret than sarcasm. "I don't mean forever, just for today. One day just for us."

Will looked down the river. Avrille could not read his thoughts.

Chapter 7

Queen Avrille removed her jewelry. She pulled the pins out of her hair. The heavy braid fell down her back. This was going to be so much fun she told herself. She rummaged through her trunk until she found a plain brown shawl. She tied it over her oldest day dress, smacked a kiss to her reflection in the mirror and stole out into the hall of her father's still sleeping castle.

Will was waiting in the stable as they had agreed. A bulging knotted cloth was tied to his belt.

"Did anyone see you?" Avrille said giving him a quick hug.

"Cook I think, but it's OK. He looked my direction once and laid bread, cheese, and a whole peach tart on the table. When he left I grabbed it all," said Will patting the bundle at his side.

"Can we trust him?"

"April, he was whistling 'Romantic Rendezvous' as he left."

Will boosted Avrille up onto the gentle brown mare. He swung up behind her and they went galloping off through the village and out across the fields. A few early rising folk stared as they sped by but no one recognized the royal pair.

The air was fresh and cool and clear. Avrille lifted her face to the wind and breathed in deep. A few miles beyond Frevaria the farmsteads grew farther apart. Will slowed the mare to a trot as they skirted the edge of the woods.

"It's so wonderful to be free!" Avrille cried.

Will gave her a hug and slid his fingers teasingly down her sides.

"Don't tickle Willy! Don't! Don't!" she squealed with delight.

They topped a small hill. Will reined the horse to a stop. The waking land spread out before them. A patchwork of greens and browns dotted with farm buildings stretched all the way to the gleaming ribbon of river. Smoke from breakfast hearths curled lazily to the pale pink sky.

"Where shall we go? Name the direction," said Will with a sweep of his arm. "All the land you see is mine and I will give it to you, my love, for a simple kiss."

"If you only meant that Will," Avrille said with a sigh.

"Come on April. This was your idea. Don't spoil the fun."

She grinned over her shoulder, then leaned back against him. "I know a secret place," she whispered.

"Secret?"

"Yes, a little spring. Gil said it was the last place the feet of the gods touched when they departed long ago. It would be cool and lovely and…"

"Private," Will added with a wicked chuckle.

"Will!"

"Which way to this arbor de amour?"

They trotted along the fence rows and through a little arm of the woods that reached from the forest toward the river. Soon they arrived at the bend in the river near the gate house, halfway between the kingdoms. The morning was still chilly when they entered the serene little glade. Will helped Avrille dismount then turned the horse out to graze on the lush grass. They found a sunny log beside the pool and opened their breakfast picnic.

"I'm starved!" Will declared.

Avrille found she had quite an appetite herself. They said little as they ate. When Will finally leaned back in the now gentle warm sunlight she tied up the remaining food in the cloth. "I wish we could always be like this," she said.

"Well we can't," said Will. "We got this damn stupid kingdom to rule and repair."

"And four children to rear," she added.

Will shot her a look of alarm.

"I know, Will. I know village girls don't give birth to star-marked children without…"

"Are you accusing me?"

"The cards tell truth. They do not accuse."

"You knew!" Will shouted. "You knew and acted if nothing had happened all this time."

"Will, I know we are all pawns in some perverse game of the gods. My twins are girls and Darilla's twins are boys. This all must mean something, some master plan beyond our control."

Will shifted his weight on the log but said nothing.

"My life just drifts," Avrille continued. "I can't feel anything anymore."

"Except for your champion."

"Now who is accusing?"

"People talk, April. It does no good for the stability of the kingdoms to have people talking."

"Rogarth is my friend, no more, no less. I'll admit to some hero worship way back that time when we traveled to Allarion, but since then, Will, since we're married and all, he is just my friend. He is a calm, dependable friend. With all the confusion in my life I need him. You can't fault me for needing someone to talk to." She adjusted her shawl and brushed back her hair. A breeze waved the trees above them and rippled the pool at their feet.

Will took her hand. "I guess it is hard on you April."

"You have everything, Willy," she said picking up a stick to throw in the water. "You have freedom and power and a strong friend like Mabry and…and…" She hesitated to say it all, but decided to go on. "And you have all the kitchen maids and village girls to give you love."

"I do not love Darilla," Will said emphatically. "She is a sweet kid, a sweet starry-eyed kid. Mabry just put her in the right place at the right time. And it was only once. Believe me, April, it was only once."

She looked away from him, but he turned her face back.

"Look at me, April," he demanded. "What more do you want me to say?"

She grabbed his wrists and pulled his hands away from her face. "Tell me how much you enjoy the kitchen maids both now and back in Arindon."

"How can you be jealous of wenches?" He gave a hollow laugh.

"I'm not," she said with calm regret. "I'm just lonely."

"We can't afford to do this, April. We have responsibilities to the kingdom, to the cause of the Light. We can't argue over selfish things when our world is falling apart around us."

Avrille silently dug her toe into the grass.

"We have got to work together," he continued. "We did at first, you with your healing and teaching, and Mabry and I with the mill. What happened? Who changed?"

"My twins were girls. That's what changed you." Avrille stared straight at him.

"Nonsense!" Will stood up.

"You know it's true, Will. And now that someone else gave you sons it's more than true."

"April this is stupid nonsense." He walked away then turned back. His pale face was blotched with red. "We have got to work together, if not for ourselves and the kingdoms, then we must do it for our children, all four of them."

Avrille started to sob silently.

"Cut it out, April. Don't pull this crying thing on me. I'm willing to work. Why won't you?"

She continued to sob. "If you only loved me." She smeared a fist across her wet cheeks. "If only someone loved me like a real husband should."

"This no time for story book romances. This is real life." He tried to sound firm but there was a catch in his voice too.

She looked up at him. "You said you loved me when we were in Allarion. Do you remember?"

"By the pool?"

"Did you mean it?"

"If I said it, I meant it."

"Then say it to me again, now."

Will looked at her long and not without tenderness. It was not fair to either of them. The words of the Song of Life raced mockingly through his mind. "None can change what we are. None can change what we must be." He took his time to answer. "I would like to let the meaning of the word love grow beyond wife, and sister and queen, April. Light and love mean the same. That's why we're here. That's why our children are here." He stopped a moment. He took her hand. Then his words came out with a rush. "Will you work together in love with me?"

Avrille studied the face of the man she called husband but loved as her little brother. "I will try," she said because there was nothing else to say.

"Let's drink to that," he said kneeling down to the pool.

Avrille knelt beside him. Together they drank the cool, pure water from the cup of each other's hands. The quiet glade came alive. Birds caroled from tree to tree. Sleeping flowers opened to the warm sun. The rippling pool glittered with rainbows. They lay back on the grass and absorbed the refreshing beauty. Avrille watched Will's eyes slowly close as the healing sun soothed him. Cautiously she moved her hand toward the water's edge. Will's never-sleeping sixth sense caught the movement.

"Splash me and you go in head first," he said without opening his eyes.

Splash! She let him have it. Will pounced. They rolled over and over in the soft grass. Their laughter rang throughout the glade.

"You're going in. You're going in," he teased pinning her down.

"Not with all my clothes on. Will, please," she begged. "People would talk if the queen came home all soaking wet." She wriggled free only to let herself be caught again. This time face down on the grass she lay submissive as Will undid the fastenings of her dress. His hands felt warm and wonderful. He kissed the nape of her neck, her shoulders and her hair. She rolled over on her back and slid her arms out of her sleeves. She kicked free of her skirts and reached for him.

"Thanks for helping, April," he laughed dodging her arms. "In you go!"

"Not without you!" She twisted, grabbed his ankle and toppled him precariously close to the water's edge.

"Wait! Wait!" he said still laughing. "Let me get mine off too."

"Are you sure you know how?" she teased straddling his middle. Will struggled halfheartedly. "Poor little boy, look at your shirt," she exclaimed. "You buttoned it crooked. Must your big sister dress you in the morning?"

"My wife has to start undressing me right now," he said helping her to hurry the process.

She drew him to her and they tumbled laughing into the warm bubbling pool.

Avrille woke in the grass beside the pool. She eased her arm out from beneath Will's head, taking care not to wake him. She smoothed her dress and sat up. The sun slanted low through the trees. She knew it was getting late but made no move to rouse Will. She was reluctant to part with the delicious oneness that filled her. She looked down at him. A faint smile flitted across his lips. His long dark eye lashes fluttered a moment then lay still. She felt a strange yet strengthening presence deep inside her.

"I will try," she silently mouthed the words. Will stirred and rolled toward her. His shirt was buttoned crooked! Avrille was more than puzzled. The memory of their lovemaking was still warm and beautiful, yet now they were fully clothed. Her long thick hair was dry. What had happened? How could Will's shirt still be buttoned crooked? Her questions soon turned to fears. She drew a quick star sign on her heart, but before her fingers finished the practiced gesture her whole hand tingled. The shape of the sign danced in front of her in a rainbow of tiny stars. It rose to hover between her and Will for a moment, then as it drifted toward Will it began to change. The sparkling colors darkened. Black smoke swirled from its center trailing into five groping fingers. She froze with terror unable to help as they threatened to engulf Will.

Will coughed and sat up. The dark sign vanished. "Wasn't it wonderful, April? Everything was as it should be."

"Yes, it was."

"This glade was transformed!" Will exclaimed spreading his arms wide to encompass the scene.

"The sunlight and the birds were…"

"I don't remember any birds, but this pool…"

"Yes, the pool." She laughed and gave him a hug.

"All this brush was cleared and the stone wall made everything neat and that statue…" his voice trailed off as he shrugged off her embrace.

"What statue?" she said. Her fear and confusion returned abruptly.

"In the middle of the pool."

"I didn't see any statue."

"The one with three women, one old, one young and…"

"One but a maid," she finished for him.

"Yeah, that one."

"I didn't see it," she said. Her heart raced as she recalled the Fountain card she had drawn last night.

"You were here right in the courtyard," Will insisted. "The walls were almost finished."

"What are you talking about?"

"Our castle!" cried Will jumping to his feet. He glared down at her.

"Either you are crazy or you are more poetic than I ever thought," Avrille exclaimed.

"Crazy? Poetic?"

"Will, did you or didn't you see this place change when we drank the water?"

"Yes and…"

"Did you or didn't you make love to me here at the edge of the pool?"

"Now who's crazy?"

"Will!"

"April, I've had enough of your romantic nonsense. Running away for a picnic when there is work to be done was crazy enough. I shouldn't have listened to you. And now when I have a vision, a plan for our future, you talk crazy and won't help me."

Avrille took a step toward him. Her fist clenched. She thought of slapping him but instead she heaved an exasperated sigh. "What plan? What vision? Will, why are you doing this to me?"

"Just shut up and listen. We saw it, the same castle I saw the first day we came to the kingdoms. Remember when we were on the hill top with Mom and Jareth and Uncle Hawke? I saw it in the clouds across the river and we saw again here, today. I knew it was a prophecy that first time. Now I am king and I can fulfill it. I can build that glorious castle, so what do you want to talk about? Romantic slush…!"

Avrille jumped to her feet. She brushed the grass off her skirt with an angry sweep and tossed her braid back over her shoulder. "You shut up, Will! We're finished! It's over! Everything!" She stamped toward their horse and grabbed the reins. Before Will could stop her she hitched up her skirts and swung up into the saddle.

"April, come back here!"

"Never!"

"You can't leave me here."

"Yes I can. Just try and stop me," she said letting the horse dance just out of his reach. "Give it up, Will. You're on your own now." She dug her heels into the horse's sides. "Next time you want it go to the kitchen. My door will be locked!" she yelled back as she galloped away.

"Damn! Damn you, April! Damn everything!" Will snatched the picnic bundle off the log and threw it into the pool. He had seen it. They both had seen it. The pool was cleared and contained in a stone wall. The courtyard was paved with a mosaic of colored stones and lined with flower beds. The walls were yellow Frevarian sandstone and the towers pure white Arindian gypsum with sparkling glass windows. This was the castle he was born to build and she wanted no part in it. He picked up a stone to skip across the pool. It sank. "Damn!" he said again, this time with less enthusiasm. He remembered it all. April was there. He knew it. What was happening to them? He was angry and confused. He didn't want to think about her. Instead he thought of Mabry. Mabry would listen to his plan.

The sun was sinking fast. It was five miles by the road to Arindon. He took a step toward the road then stopped. A surge of power filled his veins feeding on his anger. With a flourish Will drew a star circle around himself and pictured Mabry sitting at Beck's tavern. The air blazed silver then darkened along the sign he had drawn. The fabric of the universe lurched.

Armon Beck let the dish towel drop. King Will had just appeared out of nowhere right in the middle of his establishment. The innkeeper took an unsteady step backward. His hand groped for the security of the bar behind him.

"Where's Mabry?" Will demanded.

"Here, Sire," said Mabry sitting at a corner table with his injured leg propped up on a chair.

Will sauntered across the room. "Two ales and whatever you got to eat," he ordered.

The innkeeper's gaping mouth snapped shut as he hurried to obey. Mabry tried not to look surprised. Will yanked out a chair and almost upset the table.

"Easy there, Sire," said Mabry with a nervous laugh.

"Things are going to be different," Will announced.

"So I see."

"We no longer need to kiss my father-in-law's ass in Frevaria." Will lowered his voice and leaned forward to Mabry. "I have seen a vision of the future."

By the time the innkeeper brought their meal and filled their mugs Will and Mabry were deep in plans for building the castle of Will's dream.

Chapter 8

Kylie stuffed an extra apple turnover into his jerkin pocket and asked to be excused from the dinner table.

"What's your hurry, young man?" said Lady Cellina who was just settling back into her chair after a more than adequate meal.

"I got to say goodnight to my horse's mommy," said Kylie as he slid down from his chair.

"Spoken like a true Frevarian," said Frebar. He clapped the boy on the shoulder. "Horses first, then all other obligations. Go grandson, do your duty."

Kylie took the little lantern Cook let him keep by the kitchen door and headed across the garden to the stables. It was very dark, with no moon and no stars. He swung the lantern as he hurried across the open space, wishing its warm yellow circle stretched farther. He fumbled with the latch on the stable door. Inside he could hear excited voices, then feet running toward him. The door burst open before he could step aside sending him sprawling into the dust as two grooms raced to the castle. He groped for his lantern, but it had gone out and he could not find where it had rolled. His forehead hurt and so did his arm. Slowly he sat up. Shouts were coming from the stable?

"Where's the king?"

"Did somebody go for Frebar?"

Kylie peered into the stable. Lanterns were hung around his horse's stall. His face broke into smiles as he started to run. "Is my baby horse coming? Is my horse coming?" he cried.

"Get that kid out of here," yelled one of the grooms.

"It's my horse," exclaimed Kylie.

"This is no time for you," said the stable master. "Go back to your mother."

"It's my horse," Kylie insisted. "My horse."

The mare was whinnying and snorting. Frebar rushed into the stable. "Step aside," was all he said to Kylie as he pushed past and entered the circle of lantern light.

The grooms closed in behind him shutting Kylie out. "My horse," he said again, but no one heard him. His eyes spilled over with tears. His forehead throbbed and his arm began to hurt in earnest. He sank down in the straw and cried. The excitement in the mare's stall increased. Frebar shouted directions. The mare kicked and screamed in agony. Kylie covered his ears and wept.

At first he did not feel the hand on his shoulder. It was the music of Dell's voice that finally touched the rejected child. Dell called him a hero's son as he wrapped his arms around him.

"It's my horse," Kylie sobbed.

"Your horse has been a hero too," said Dell rocking the boy gently. "But what was meant to be has taken toll of all our dreams to set the creature free."

"Whatcha mean 'set the creature free'?" said Kylie wiping his nose on his sleeve.

"Your mare is dead," said Dell as gently as he could.

"But my baby horse is OK?" said the boy jumping to his feet.

"Kylie!" Dell tried to stop him but the boy was too quick. He climbed up the wooden gate of the stall. The grooms rushed to cover the gruesome sight but the child had already thrown himself onto the body of the misshapen foal lying in the blood-soaked straw.

"It could have never lived, grandson," said Frebar pulling the boy back. The grooms picked up the lifeless two-headed foal and carried it away. "Shame for the mare though, she was a good one," he added wiping his hands on his breeches.

Kylie broke away from him and ran out into the night. No one tried to stop him. Dell slipped out of the stable too. Words of a new ballad danced in his head. He sang softly.

"One head of silver,
One head of gold,
The kingdoms are one,
So I've been told."

The starless night gave no witness, yet the truth of Dell's song would not be stilled.

"The loins are joined,
Were never apart,
But reason and wrong,
Have divided the heart."

Somewhere far off a beast howled. Was it a wolf or just a farm hound crying for the return of the moon? Dell opened the kitchen door. He was glad for the warmth and light.

Cook was warming a mug of milk and honey for Kylie. He had already set out a plate of turnovers and cheese. "Something for you too Dell?" he offered taking down a mug. "Ale? Spiced cider?"

Dell shook his head.

"Shame about the mare," said Cook. "The little master here was putting all his lucky cards on her foal." He patted Kylie's head. "He's trying to take it like a grownup, aren't you laddie?"

Dell looked kindly at Kylie who seemed at the moment much smaller than his seven years.

"Guess Grandpa couldn't decide to give the baby horse to me or to the twins," he said staring into his mug,

Cook raised his eyebrows. Dell returned his puzzled look. "Why don't you take your mug and plate up to your room, Master Kylie, my boy," said Cook. "The king and his men will be coming in soon for their ale. Be a good laddie now and I'll be sure there is something special for your breakfast in the morning."

Kylie did as he was told, but what Cook did not notice was that the boy took all the turnovers and the rest of the wedge of cheese. Nothing escaped Dell's eye, however. The last lines of another ballad touched his lips as he watched the boy head up the stairs to the royal apartments. "The fight lives on in Keilen's son," he sang to himself.

"What song is that?' asked Cook as he sliced thick chunks of meat and bread.

"Just something that's not quite finished yet," said Dell as he slipped out into the night.

Mornings in Frevaria had a certain golden quality that guests from Arindon had rarely experienced until now. The windows of the king's study were open, letting the light in with the cool morning air. Frebar, Will and Mabry had breakfasted heartily at first light. When the remains of their meal had been cleared away Will spread out his plans on the table. At first Frebar listened with the slightly amused attention a parent assumes when a creative child explains his drawing or nursery game. Building a completely walled city was an impractical fantasy, but gradually he began to listen more carefully. Walls made of Frevarian sandstone, towers of Arindian gypsum, a strong five-sided star shape with river access as well as an internal water source had many social-political as well as tactical advantages. He began to have a glimmer of admiration for his outspoken, headstrong son-in-law. And the man Mabry was indeed a genius of practical advice. It could be done. A new central castle could be built. Frebar gradually found himself agreeing that it should be built, yet he remained cautious.

"This technology you found in the land where Kyrdthin had you fostered," Frebar carefully framed his question. "Tell me about it again."

"It's not magic if that's what you're asking," said Will, trying not to sound too condescending. "It's based on laws of the real world. It can be seen, touched, taken apart and reassembled by any man if he has been properly trained."

"Then why don't we have this technology here?"

"Does a child know all about farming and milling when he eats his morning porridge? Does a court lady know all about mining and smithing when she clips a gold pin in her hair? There is no need for one person or a whole kingdom, for that matter, to know everything. They need only what is relevant to their lives. We did not need this technology until now."

"I see," said Frebar slowly.

Will paced to the end of the rug back again. "I know only a little about that land," he said. "I was just thirteen and wasn't done with school yet, before I had to come back here and claim my heritage."

Frebar opened his mouth to reply then thought better of it.

Will continued, "Mabry and I want to take a trip back there to learn more and to get some tools for the project at hand."

"Then I will outfit the expedition," said Frebar a bit too suddenly.

Will shot Mabry a quick glance. "I am grateful for your offer," he said with as much tact as he could. "But what I need most from Frevaria is what you have already provided. That is housing for my family and support for my plan. A small scouting party would be much less conspicuous in a land where customs are different. I believe Arindon's coffers, depleted as they are at this time, will still be sufficient to outfit us. When construction actually does begin then I may ask for your help, but not now."

Frebar did not press the issue. He leaned back his chair and fingered the trim on his jerkin.

The door flew open without ceremony. "Father, have you seen Kylie?" cried Elanille breathless from hurrying up the stairs.

"Not this morning, daughter," said Frebar. "Will and his man here have kept me busy since before breakfast. Kylie's probably out in the practice yard," he said rising to greet her with a hug.

"No, father, I have looked everywhere." Elanille's face was flushed from her efforts. "He is not in the castle. His pony is gone and his bed has not been slept in."

"Then he has gone off on a jaunt." said Frebar giving her another hug. "He's not a baby any more."

She pushed away from him. "Father, this is serious!"

"He'll be back home in time for dinner, Elani dear. I guarantee it."

"The last person to see him was Cook and that was last night. Cook also said some food is missing."

"Then he won't starve until dinner." Frebar laughed and put his arm around her. "He'll be alright. Seven-year-old boys do these things and most live to grow up. Stop worrying and go down stairs to your ladies."

Elanille let her hands drop to her sides. She looked from her father to Will then left with a sigh of resignation.

When his sister-in-law had gone Will said, "I'm sure the boy has run off to grieve for his mare and foal."

"Shame for the mare," said Frebar. "I hate to lose a good mare for a worthless foal."

"I'm sure Master Kylie doesn't think of it as worthless, Your Majesty," said Mabry.

"Of course not," said Frebar. "That's all the more reason to go off alone for a while, away from overprotective womenfolk."

Avrille felt awful. The very thought of breakfast made her stomach retch anew. The sunlight glittered on her jeweled mirror, bathing the room in patterns of rainbow light, but she did not care. She sat on the edge of the bed and hugged her stomach. Her hair hung in matted clumps. Her nightgown was wrinkled and stained.

She was so miserable that at first she did not hear the soft knock at her door.

"Sister?" Elanille called knocking louder. "Surely you're awake, it's long past breakfast."

"Go 'way. Lemme alone."

"Avrille, are you alright?" Elanille called again. "Please let me in."

"It's not locked," Avrille muttered easing back into bed.

"Oh you poor darling!" Elanille exclaimed seeing her sister's condition. "Why didn't you call someone?"

"Nobody would care."

"Oh sweet sister, here I was coming to you with my own troubles," said Elanille pouring water from the pitcher to the washbasin. "Where is your face cloth?"

"I don't know."

"You poor, poor dear!" Elanille cooed as she splashed her sister's face and tried to smooth back her tangled hair.

Avrille turned her face away. "Just tell me what you came for, then leave me alone".

"Kylie has run away. I am almost frantic. He never slept in his bed last night and his pony is gone. He took some food along and…" Elanille burst into tears. "And father doesn't even care," she wailed. "He laughed at me and Will along with him."

"Don't talk about Will to me," Avrille growled.

"They all said he'll be home for dinner," Elanille went on. "I just know he's in trouble. I just know it."

"I'd like to help you find him, but I can't do anything right now. I'm so sick."

"I'm so sorry I bothered you," said Elanille rummaging through Avrille's trunk for a clean gown. "Is there anything more I can do for you?"

"Just lemme alone."

"Someone has to care for you. Should I send for a maid?"

"No, no…"

"Then I'm staying. You need me." Elanille sat down on the chair beside the bed with an emphatic plop.

"Whatever…"

Elanille sat by her sister for what seemed a long time. Her mind churned with recent events. Someone had to find Kylie. Someone had to take care of Avrille. She could not do both. Her sister was curled in a tight ball on the bed. Her eyes were pinched shut, but she was not asleep. Elanille stood up and started to pace. The anxiety from just sitting doing nothing had become too much. "I was going to ask you to reads the cards for me, for Kylie that is," she said looking back to her sister.

"Damn the cards!" said Avrille. Her head hung over the basin.

Elanille turned away and held her own stomach. "If I draw just one card can you tell me what it means?" she persisted.

"They're in my basket. Help yourself," Avrille mumbled without looking up.

Elanille shuffled the cards. Her hands shook with fear. She held the deck as far away from herself as she could and drew the top card.

"Well, what did you get?" said Avrille rolling over and trying to sit up.

"The White King, what does that mean?"

Avrille rolled back again. "I don't know." Her words were muffled in the pillow. "Go away and lemme alone."

For Dell it turned out to be a long night. After he left the castle kitchen, he walked the streets and alleyways of Frevaria until his feet ached. He thought and thought, trying to make sense out of the night's events. At last he found himself at the gate of a small farmstead at the edge of town. He knocked on the door of the cottage and begged a place by the fire and a warm drink in exchange for a song. Dell told stories to the clutch of rosy-cheeked children before the farm wife bundled them off to the loft. Afterwards he sat quietly by the fire while the man smoked his pipe and the wife busied herself tidying up the kitchen.

"Well how's life inside the great one's walls?" said the farmer.

Dell picked up his harp, adjusted a string, then laid it back down in his lap. "It is hard times when songs are in the making," he said.

"Hard times it is then?" said the farmer blowing a smoke ring toward the fire.

"Only heads are crowned, not hearts," said Dell.

"So that's the way of it?"

With sudden resolve Dell turned to him. "Have you a beast you could lend me for a ride to seek the advice of a friend?"

"Well now I..." the farmer began with hesitation.

"To be returned on my word though I cannot name the hour or the day?"

"We be chicken farmers not the king's stables. There's only the donkey for pullin' the cart and he's no prize I'm tellin' ye." The farmer clenched his sparse teeth around the stump of his pipe and stroked the stubble on his chin.

"But will you?" Dell pleaded.

"Well now I don't rightly know what to say....even a poor beast has got a price." The man drew back on his pipe, exhaled a cloud, then spat onto the hearth. "What value have you got to leave me until the deal is done?'

Dell took a long, deep breath. "I have my harp, but it is my livelihood, my one true love, my very life..."

"Then you'd be sure to return my beast," said the farmer exhaling with a satisfied grin.

Dell stroked his beloved instrument. With resignation he wrapped it in his cloak and handed it to the man. "I'll have no more songs until tonight's work is done, with or without my harp, I fear. Keep her safe."

"I'll put it in the woman's pile of sewing. The little ones won't get at it there."

The farmer shook Dell's hand and gave him a half loaf of bread and said, "I hope that keeps ye, there's no more till she bakes in the morning."

With only a frayed blanket for a saddle Dell rode along the dark track of a road. The going was rough. There was no moon. Fog hung low over the fields. He guided his reluctant mount along the road by sound alone, thankful for the fence row along the ditch. A faint yellow glow appeared ahead. Dogs barked as he approached the next farmstead. He whistled a nervous tune as he passed. The dogs did not attack. It was slow traveling. He counted the farm lights and the crossroads until he came to the edge of the woods. There he stopped and dismounted. He led the donkey into the brush just inside the first line of trees. There was no way he could travel farther into the woods without a light. He gave the donkey an affectionate slap on the rump and tied the beast to a tree. He kicked leaves into a pile, spread out the saddle blanket and slept curled up tight against the dampness.

Moonlight awoke him. Dell stretched his cramped legs. The fog still flowed in ghostly eddies across the fields under the scattered stars. He looked up at the sky then back across the fields toward the silhouette of Frevaria and figured it was about an hour before dawn. He folded his blanket, remounted the donkey and headed into the forest by the faint moonlit track of road. Just as the sky was beginning to pale above the trees he came to the edge of a clearing. Smoke curled up in welcome from Jareth's cottage.

Elanille spent the remainder of the morning running between her sister's room and the kitchen. No one in the household seemed concerned about Kylie's absence besides her and Cook. She knew the boy often liked to play by himself. She knew he often asked Cook for a lunch to take along to the practice yard or to his favorite tree in the fence row just beyond the gate. He was none of these places now. He had never gone away before without telling someone. He had never been gone so long. Only Cook was sympathetic. He blamed himself for hurrying the boy out of the kitchen last night when he was so troubled. Elanille assured the man he was not to blame, but did encourage sending the kitchen staff out to look for him while Cook busied himself baking small cakes to celebrate the child's return.

By noon Avrille had recovered somewhat. She let her sister help her bathe and fix her hair, but she still felt weak from her morning ordeal. By afternoon she let Elanille persuade her to take tea in the garden. Cook set them up on a bench beneath the apple tree, now mottled green and red with fruit. There they sipped their tea in silence, each occupied with their separate tragedies until approaching hoof beats interrupted them. Shouts arose from the stables. The gate clanged open and the arriving party strode across the garden court yard.

"Jareth!" Avrille and Elanille exclaimed at the same time. "Jareth, Kylie is missing!" Elanille cried rushing to greet him. Dell followed in Jareth's wake looking tired and more disheveled than usual but happily caressing his recovered harp.

"Slow down, My Lady," said Jareth taking Elanille's hands and leading her back to the bench. "Tell me this from the beginning."

Both women tumbled out the tale, Avrille taking over when her sister's tears choked her voice.

"I should have stayed with the boy," Dell declared blaming himself. "I saw how upset he was about the foal. I saw him take the food too, but I just thought he needed time alone and meant to hole up in his room for a while."

Cook called from the kitchen doorway, "Any news of the little master?"

Elanille shook her head.

Dell gathered up their tea things as Jareth and the ladies headed back into the kitchen.

"Where would the boy go?" Jareth mused aloud.

"He's not in the castle. Everyone has looked. And he is at least not obvious in the village. We have everyone looking there too," answered Avrille.

"He's been gone for hours and father doesn't even care," Elanille wept.

Avrille put her arm around her sister.

"He took his pony," said Jareth still talking more to himself than to anyone else. "That means he planned to cover some distance, farther than the village....now where would a boy go to seek comfort, perhaps guidance..."

"To his father," said Dell.

Jareth and Avrille stared at Dell. Kylie's father was dead. What on earth did the bard mean? Elanille lifted her head from her sister's shoulder. She understood. "To High Bridge," she said.

Jareth nodded. It was possible. "Would he know the way?" he asked.

"There is only one main road," said Dell.

King Frebar was already in the dining room. "Greetings, daughters. Greetings, gentlemen," he called. "Has my wayward grandson turned up yet?'

"Father, I think he may have gone to High Bridge and Jareth agrees," Elanille told him.

"Why High Bridge?"

"He plays his father's battle with his toy soldiers so often that..."

"Gone to be a hero like his father has he?" Frebar reached for her. "Quite a spirited grandson you have given me, Elani love."

"Please, father, this is serious!"

"Alright, it's nearly dinner time and he isn't home. We'll send someone out to look for him."

Frebar summoned his guard and sent riders to question the villagers door to door and to all the farms along the road as far as High Bridge. When that was done he tickled Elanille as if she were a troublesome toddler to be pacified and said, "That will fetch the royal rascal. Now go and pretty yourself up for dinner."

Elanille ran from the room. Avrille started to follow her then stopped to speak to Jareth.

"There is an item of some importance I need to ask your advice about," she said. "Please accompany me to my sister's rooms."

Frebar raised his eyebrows but let it pass. Dell settled down in his favorite place by the fire still caressing his harp in happy reunion.

"To my room instead, both of you," said Avrille when they had caught up with Elanille and were safely out of earshot from the dining room. "This morning I was too sick to care about the cards when you came to me, Elani, but now..."

"What did they say?' asked Jareth.

"She drew just one card."

"It was the White King," said Elanille.

Avrille put her finger to her lips. Mentioning the cards in Frevaria castle too loudly was not wise. When they arrived in Avrille's room the deck of cards was still on the nightstand. The White King was face up just as Elanille had drawn it that morning.

Jareth picked them up. "Let's see what we get now," he said ready to shuffle the cards again but the White King began to pulse with a pale yellow light. Jareth held the card steady as Avrille and Elanille crowded close to see. The royal figure sat on a chair carved with the symbols of both kingdoms. The scene was out of doors in a springtime field. As they watched the flowers and grasses withered and a black mist slithered over the land. The figure shrank until it was the size of a small child dwarfed by the massive chair. Jareth's hand trembled. Avrille reached to steady the card, but when she touched it the vision faded and the lifeless, painted face of the card stared up at her.

Elanille was terrified. "What do we do, Jareth? What do we do?"

"Dell came to me on a hunch last night," said Jareth. "You know he is more in tune with the way of things than most men."

"Like you are," said Avrille.

"We both are detached from the routine of the kingdoms. Perhaps that makes us more perceptive, though in different ways," Jareth agreed.

"How does this find Kylie," Elanille said impatiently. "Yes, father has finally dispatched searchers but he should have done that hours ago. I'm sure he is at High Bridge and yet they will stop at every house and gatepost before they get there. Avrille, can't you send your bird to see if he is there and alright?"

"It's almost dark, Elani. He'd never make it but maybe there is something he can do," said Avrille. "I can send him to find Rogarth. If anyone can find Kylie and bring him home safe, it's Rogarth."

Dinner was silent and tense. Dell pleaded not to sing until he could sing the lad's adventures so Frebar did not insist. Elanille only picked at her food. Avrille suggested they have a tray fixed for them to take to her room. Elanille nodded her agreement and they headed upstairs. Jareth excused himself from the table and followed.

"Everyone is leaving me," Frebar bellowed. "You would think that I had sent the boy away."

"You were sure in no hurry to find him," said Lady Cellina between mouthfuls of roast duck.

"But I didn't think..."

"That's about the size of it," Cellina accused. "Kylie is a sensitive boy. One minute he is all but heir apparent with his grandfather showering him with gifts, and the next his twin cousins have moved in to steal his place. Then to top it off his horse dies. No wonder the child has run off."

Frebar did not answer. The household continued the meal with only the occasional clink of plate to punctuate the silence. A log rolled off the andirons with a shower of sparks. Dell kicked it back from the edge of the hearth and sat back on his bench. He fingered his harp but did not play. The words of his newest ballad ran through his head.

"The loins are one,
Were never apart,
But reason and wrong
Have divided the heart."

"I thought you weren't singing tonight," said Frebar.

Dell had not realized he had said the words aloud. "Just something I've been working on," he said. "I'll sing it when the tale is done."

Elanille could not sleep. Avrille and Jareth tried to keep vigil with her but soon Avrille was slumped across her sister's bed. Jareth tried to talk to her but all Elanille could think of was Kylie. The wait dragged on. If only Maralinne were here, he thought. That was it! He turned to Elanille.

"I can't just sit here," she was saying.

"You don't have to," he announced. "Why don't you come with me when I go home tomorrow and visit Maralinne? News of Kylie can reach us quicker there and you can be away from all this confusion."

"Splendid!" Elanille exclaimed and immediately started packing.

Jareth helped her drag out her trunk. "Nothing fancy now. You know Maralinne and I live simply," he cautioned as her pile of clothes on the chair started to topple.

At last she decided on a cream-colored riding dress with a matching jacket to wear on the trip and a blue day dress and shawl to wear after she arrived. She folded the dress neatly with her lingerie and tucked them into a satchel. She added her mirror and hairbrush and snapped the latch shut. "If I need anything else I guess I can borrow it from Maralinne."

"My horse will be grateful that you have agreed to travel light," said Jareth with a laugh. "You won't be too inconvenienced to ride double with me will you, My Lady? If we took time to outfit a carriage we would not be away until noon."

"Then let's leave now!" she said picking up her satchel. Then she stopped to listen.

Outside galloping hoof beats bore down on the gate. Shouts were exchanged and the heavy gate creaked open. Jareth leaned out the window to see.

"It's Rogarth!"

Avrille stirred and sat up.

Soon the queen's champion was pounding on the door to Elanille's room. When Jareth let him in, Trebil was proudly riding on Rogarth's wrist like a miniature blue falcon.

"Trebil good boy. Bring Rogarth," said the little bird. "Treat?"

"Did you find him?" asked Avrille ignoring Trebil.

"I found his pony tied to a tree at High Bridge camp. I found his knapsack and saddle blanket by a small campfire. It was still smoldering." Rogarth stopped and looked from Avrille to Jareth.

"What else? Did you find him?" Elanille asked her face pale with fright.

"Nothing."

"What do you mean nothing?"

"There were many footprints and signs of a scuffle but no other clues. I could not follow their trail in the dark, but they seemed to head upstream, Jareth...."

"What kind of footprints?" Elanille demanded with a thin shrill voice.

"Boots," said Rogarth not looking at Elanille. "Delven boots."

Avrille grabbed her sister and held on tight. "We will find him. Jareth and Rogarth will find him," she promised. Elanille sobbed and sobbed. Trebil flew to her shoulder and sobbed with her, his treat forgotten.

The next morning Will was up early. He was heading down the hall when he heard a door stealthily creak open. He hid behind a pillar to find out who else was busy at this hour. Mabry emerged from Lady Cellina's room carrying a tea tray. He limped away as fast as he could, as if he was trying to put as much distance as he could between himself and his rendezvous with the lady regent. Will watched with amusement but not without concern for his friend. That Mabry was ambitious was no news to him, but Mabry courting Aunt Cellina! This would be interesting to watch. Perhaps a thirty-some-year-old widower with a family to worry about would look differently at women. But why did an intelligent man need to get mixed up with women at all, especially dangerously powerful ones? Will shrugged his shoulders and took the back stairs down to the kitchen.

Avrille was standing in the kitchen doorway between two satchels. He stopped when he saw her. She looked so tired and sad. Where was the caring big sister he loved? Where was the capable, if a bit feisty, wife he admired? This small forlorn woman was like a stranger. What had gone wrong? What had he done to her? Was she really pregnant again? With his child? What had really happened that day at the Star Spring?

Sensing his presence, Avrille turned to face him. "I'm going home to Arindon, Will."

"Don't be crazy. Where would you live?" he said hopping down the last two steps.

"I'm taking a house in the village," she said with a toneless calm in her voice.

"What about the girls? You can't just…" He tried to grab her but she avoided him.

"Linelle will bring them to me in a few days…as soon as I get things settled."

"April, you can't just leave me!" Will pleaded.

"That is exactly what I am doing," she said turning her back on him.

A carriage arrived at the garden gate. Tad and Tam, Mabry's ten-year-old twins, were in the driver's seat. Rogarth opened the carriage door and climbed out. The boys hopped down and ran to help Avrille with her luggage. When they had secured her satchels on top, they fought to assist her into the carriage, but it was Rogarth's hand she took. She leaned toward him and said something in a low voice. Will strained his ears, but he could not hear what she said that made the big man blush. The queen's champion bowed and kissed his sovereign's hand. Then he lifted her up and climbed in beside her.

Tad flicked the reins and his brother cried, "Giddyap!"

Will watched them go until the carriage was but a mere speck on the road between the fence rows.

Chapter 9

Jareth stood at a respectful distance. Princess Elanille had much to think about. It was here at High Bridge four eventful years ago that she had lost a husband and now perhaps a son as well. Jareth let her have the time she needed. The spot held memories for him too. He let his thoughts drift back to his flight with Maralinne and their daring leap across the river just up stream. He shook his head as he recalled returning to the carnage here at the bridge after their escape through the Delven caves. He looked at Elanille. After a brief but sweet reunion with Maralinne at the cottage, she had insisted on coming here.

At last she turned to him. "Show me where they found his pony and pack," she said. Her face was mask-like. Her eyes were dry.

High Bridge camp had been abandoned since Belar's fear spell destroyed Sir Keilen and his men and almost dealt the same blow later to Rogarth. Jareth led Elanille to the three-sided rock shelter where the fresh remains of a small campfire and the trampled moss and leaves told of recent visitors.

"Can you follow his trail, Jareth?"

"I can and will, but first I must take you back to Maralinne."

"No, I am going with you."

"My Lady, with respect," Jareth objected. "Maralinne was a foolhardy maid when we entered those caves. She was accustomed to strenuous adventures, but you could not endure such hardships."

"If Kylie is in the caves, then I must go there. Please, Jareth," she begged. "If I die in the attempt what does it matter. My life is nothing. The Dark Delven have taken my husband. They have taken first my son's joy of childhood, and now they have taken what is left of him." She stared ahead biting her lip. "And for all I know they may have taken my Lizzie too."

Jareth looked at the generous picnic bundle Maralinne insisted they take with them. He thought of her passionate kiss goodbye. Had she known what decision they would make here? He let the image of his last sight of her linger. The fire of her loosely braided hair burned bright in his memory. Only the fire within her heart could match that beautiful flame. He fingered the little leather pouch on a thong beneath his shirt. A lock of Maralinne's hair clipped on their first night together laid inside it, next to his heart. Something more than Elanille's grief drew him to re-enter the realm of icy dark. A tide he could not name pulled him toward the caves. The need grew stronger, irresistible. Elanille bravely followed him up the rocky path to the falls.

Queen Avrille felt the calling. She laid down her book to listen but her ears heard nothing. She tried to resume her reading but she could not concentrate. The lamp flickered, threatening to go out, though she felt no breeze. Everything was quiet. She felt suspended in the moonlight slanting through her bedroom window. The cold light beckoned to her. She threw a cloak over her night gown and went downstairs, but she stopped herself at the door. The High Queen could not go wandering outside in her night clothes. She had met enough scrutiny when she had moved herself and the twins from her father's castle in Frevaria to take a house in Arindon village. Will had objected, but had not forbid the move. Later she begged him to join them but he refused.

She opened the door and looked out. The street was empty and dark. Even Armon Beck's door was closed and his besotted patrons had been sent home. She drew her cloak tighter against the chill. She breathed in the peace of the early morning hour, yet the faint calling still pulled her. When she turned to go back inside the calling intensified, pulling her out again into the night. "Who are you? What do you want?" she asked the half-darkened moon hovering above the sleeping village.

As if in answer a meteor streaked across the sky, falling from sight just beyond the black ruins of Arindon castle. With a sudden wave of panic she detached herself from the scene, hurried back into the house and bolted the door. A shiver of fear ran through her. Upstairs she could hear the twins whimper and the soothing cadence of Linelle's reply. She poked at the fire and put on another log. The insistent calling inside her head would not stop. She wandered out into the pantry. Nothing looked appetizing. Her stomach did an odd flip-flop so she cut a slice of dry bread and carried it to her chair by the fire.

"April, April, help me!" This time the voice was clear.

She rushed to the window. At first she saw nothing. Her eyes strained in the dark. Her heart beat faster. Then she saw a small, dark figure limping through the ruined gates of the castle. Part of her wanted to rush out, to heal the need of the caller but her feet refused to move. A dread darkness drove the shadowed figure toward her. She waited until she heard the knock at the door. Against her will she felt herself sliding the heavy bolt and stepping back to let him in.

"Gods, Will, what happened?" she exclaimed when she saw him in the light. His clothes were dirty and torn and soaked with blood. A deep open gash ran across his forehead and the way he cradled his arm she knew it was broken.

For the next hour she worked silently, washing his wounds and binding them with clean linen. She summoned all her skills to knit the severed flesh and bone and to ease the pain. She touched the familiar body of the man who was her husband yet recoiled from a cold strangeness she could not name lurking inside of him. Patiently she listened to his tale of how he had experimented with place-crossing using star signs like Kyrdthin had done. First he learned to cross from place to place about the kingdoms with Mabry's reluctant assistance, but when he proposed to venture to the land where Kyrdthin had hidden them as children Mabry begged to have no part of it. He pleaded for his injured leg and for obligations to his family, but Will knew it was the magic that stopped the man. What Mabry did not understand he feared. So Will decided to go alone. Avrille listened intently as he described his tempestuous crossing.

"I almost lost it," he confessed. "But I did get to Five Oaks, or what's left of it." Will rubbed his injured head. "Why don't you get Trebil to help me tell this? My head hurts too much to think."

"Bad, bad, Will," chirped Trebil as Avrille uncovered his cage. "Will hurt. Poor, bad Will."

Ignoring the little bird's remark, Will took his wife's hands. Together they stared into the fire and let Trebil weave his magic.

Avrille drifted into the dancing flames. It was morning. She saw through Will's eyes as he walked about what had been their childhood home. The trees, all five of them, were nothing but charred trunks. Two were dead specters but the rest were venturing a few new leaves. A powerful magic had torched those trees and showered sparks onto the cottage roof. Will looked at the blackened shingles on the part of the roof that had not collapsed. He wondered what it had been like inside that terrible, flaming circle. That it had been used for a crossing was obvious, but by whom and to where? Two year's time and nature's healing had hidden the evidence.

Their mother's garden was only a patch of weeds. The cottage door stood open. Will entered and slowly picked his way through the house. The furniture was gone. The shelves were bare. Windows were broken and obscene signatures of vandals were scrawled on the walls. Rain had fallen unchecked on the now moss-covered floor where part of the roof had caved in. He made his way to the remains of his room. The bed frame lay there broken and rusty. Everything else was gone. He almost turned to leave when on an impulse he reached far back into the closet shelf. There where the drywall did not quite meet the stud was an open space where he had hidden his childhood treasures. Yes, it was still there. He pulled out the coffee tin trailing dust and cobwebs. Inside was a Swiss army knife, only slightly rusted, two small model cars, an assortment of shells and pebbles and a small leather bag. He opened the bag and pulled out a tightly-rolled wad of bills, a five and nine ones. Fourteen dollars, he thought, not much, not near enough, but it was a start. He put the knife and the money in his pocket and went back outside.

Will broke Trebil's spell to ask Avrille for a drink of water.

"You're feverish," she said. "Maybe you should stop for a while." She reached to soothe his forehead. Her fingers started to send a calming but he pushed her hand away.

"Just get me a drink," he growled.

He drained the cup, hiccoughed then took Avrille's hands again. "Keep going, Trebil."

With a chirp of objection the little bird complied. This time Avrille let herself sink deeper into the tale, touching Will's emotions as he relived the scene.

Will headed for the garage. The car was gone, but Hawke's old van was still there with one wheel jacked up.

"Skip the repair scene, Trebil," Will interrupted. "Get on to where I get it running."

Avrille felt his frustration and helplessness before Trebil shifted the scene. Then Will was behind the wheel of the bucking, lurching van. She shared his elation as well as his terror. The engine sputtered. He shifted down a gear and let out the clutch with a jerk. The van roared and took off down the highway toward town followed by a black cloud of exhaust. He braked at the stop sign but forgot to push in the clutch.

"Damn!" he shouted as the engine died.

Already motorists were rudely honking their horns. He groped for the two live wires under the dash and pinched them together. Nothing happened. He thought of pushing the van to the side of the road to try starting it again but he was afraid someone would stop to help and seeing his hot wire job, think he had stolen the vehicle. The honking grew louder.

"Start, damn you, start!" he yelled pounding the steering wheel. Anger and frustration surged through his body, exploding through his fingertips. Blue fire jumped from his fist to the engine. The van roared and took off. He had no control! The possessed vehicle streaked wildly down the highway. His foot wasn't even on the accelerator. He jammed on the breaks. The van did not slow down. He twisted the wheel then jerked it back, narrowly missing several cars. Both feet stamped on the brake. He skidded around a curve almost crashing head on with a pickup truck.

Avrille clutched Will's hand so tight that he cried out in pain. Mile after mile he fought the wheel and the magic he had unleashed. Then he saw the bridge, the detour sign and the right angle turn. It was all in slow motion, the rushing approach of the barricade, the crash, the turning, the tumbling, falling, and finally the impact of cold dark water. "April, help!" Will screamed.

With a rush Trebil's spell ended. Both Avrille and Will breathed out a long deep sigh of relief.

"Next thing I was lying in the castle courtyard hurting like hell."

"I heard you, Willy, but I didn't know who it was," said Avrille.

"Next time I go back I won't use magic to start a car." Will tried to laugh.

"Next time! There will be no next time Will Arinth!"

Will did not answer. He laid his bandaged head on her lap. Avrille fingered his dark curls, relieved that he was safe. She drifted with him until sleep took over both of them. When she woke up the next morning Will was gone. Where was he? He was injured. He wasn't fool enough to try to go back there again, or was he? Avrille started to panic.

Lady Cellina was emphatic. Under no circumstances would Mabry go to any far off land to help King Will gather materials for a castle no one needed anyway. Mabry had obligations to his motherless family. She spoke for the welfare of little Nancie her maid. That she had no authority to forbid Mabry or King Will to do anything was not a case in point. King Frebar smiled to himself, but only to himself, as he was confronted by this mountain of female force.

"My dear Lady Cellina, your point is well taken," Frebar began with care. "The dangers of such a journey as King Will proposes may be great and Mabry is a valuable man to his family as well as to the kingdoms."

"Invaluable," Lady Cellina agreed.

"I understand why King Will wishes such a capable man to accompany him," Then he hastily added. "Yet, your concern is not unfounded."

"Then what are we going to do about it?"

Frebar bought time to think by pouring another glass of wine. He offered Cellina a refill but she would not be distracted from her cause.

"I simply forbid it and so must you," she decreed waving her empty glass.

"My dear Lady Cellina, one king cannot forbid another king, no matter how much he differs with him. To do so would mean war."

"That headstrong boy will have a war with me if Mabry sets one foot outside the kingdoms."

Frebar stifled a smile. "Perhaps you could influence Mabry the Miller yourself. Your Ladyship's powers of persuasion and practiced charm no doubt could discourage the man from such a venture as we have discussed."

Lady Cellina drew her handkerchief. "Why I put myself through all this for the sake of a mere serving maid I don't know. But Nancie is such a dear child and…"

"And Mabry is an intelligent, creative, irreplaceable man," Frebar added again smiling to himself. "Yes, that he surely is," she agreed as she returned the lace handkerchief to her cleavage.

"Then I can count on your speaking to him?" said Frebar pouring another glass of wine for both of them. This time Lady Cellina did not refuse.

In the days that followed all hands that could be spared from both kingdoms were working at the star spring. The Arindian peasants and villagers sang as they worked, happy to serve their beloved King Will. The Frevarian workers were less enthusiastic but worked willingly. Except for the honor guard left at Frevaria castle and a few scouts about the countryside, the entire joint military force was at King Will's command to put his project into action. Brush was cleared. The pool was dredged and walled. All trees except the five old oaks surrounding the site were cleared and the land was leveled. Stones were cut, dressed and piled ready to lay in the courtyard mosaic Will had designed. Surveyors marked the perimeters where the walls and towers would be built.

Will paced the site with nervous energy, stopping occasionally to consult Mabry and their sheaf of diagrams and plans. Mabry had set up an awning over his table near the spring. They still needed to find a way to obtain enough stone for the walls and towers. Scouts were dispatched to the old mine sites in the hills but the men returned with feeble reports. Will knew it was fear of the Delven depths that turned them away, not the condition of the shafts or the ancient equipment. Again his thoughts turned to magic. Could he transport building materials and modern equipment between worlds? Could he use magic to cut and transport stone from the mines to the building site? His mind churned with questions and ideas. Mabry helped in every way he could, but his advice was practical, not theoretical. Mabry showed Will how to prepare the ground for laying the foundation. He showed him how to mix mortar, how to measure and fit the stones, but when Will talked of using magic Mabry held back. Will did not push him. He respected his long-time friend and mentor. He also knew he needed him. If magic were to be used he would have do it alone and secretly. His boot heels dug into the soft earth. The urgency to complete the project drove him. Will soared with his dream.

Trebil lit on Avrille's shoulder. "Trebil good boy. See Rogarth. Get treat now?"

"What would I do without you, my little friend?" said Avrille as she stroked his breast. "Tell me what Rogarth said."

"Treat?"

"Tell me first." She kissed the top of his blue-feathered head and turned to her mirror. The glass clouded then cleared to a view of Rogarth's quarters. The Queen's champion was at ease before dinner. Avrille saw him look up. Then he reached for a bowl of dried apple slices.

"Rogarth give good treat," chirped Trebil.

"Does he have you spoiled or what? Tell me what he said."

The scene in the mirror shifted. This time the view was of the Frevarian gardens from Trebil's perch on Rogarth's gauntlet. They stopped by a rosebush with peach-colored blooms. Rogarth carefully picked a half-open bud. "Show this to my lady." He kissed the rose and tossed it into the pond. The flower floated a moment as the concentric ripples sparkled in the sunlight. Queen Avrille sighed a deep lonely sigh.

It was raining. Will paced impatiently up and down the corridor. He had argued with his father-in-law, but Frebar firmly refused to order his men to work in such weather. Will chafed at the delay of his plans, but without Frevarian support there was little he could do. As the day wore on, the rain let up a bit but Will's temper got worse.

Just after noon a scout galloped to the gate shouting for Frebar. "Delven...legions of them...edge of the forest...riding hard," the man gasped.

"Sound the alarms!" Will shouted one step ahead of Frebar. He ran toward the gatehouse buckling on his sword as he went. He bounded up the stairs to the castle wall two steps at a time.

The gray clad farmland stretched to the hills. Dark clouds rolled across the sky. He shivered in the drizzle. Below the guard filed out the gate two by two, Arindian swordsmen and Frevarian bowmen side by side. Banners of red and silver flapped beside blue and gold. In the distance the thunder rolled, drowning out the clamor of arms below. Will strained his eyes until he focused on a thin dark line emerging from the forest. Frebar saw it too. Without a word both kings climbed down from the wall to join their troops and ride against their common foe.

Thunder boomed again. Wave after dark wave of Delven horsemen poured out of the forest. The groom steadied a sleek back mare for King Will to mount. Wind tore at the red banners raised in a semicircle to his right. The rain began to fall in earnest. Will fingered the hilt of his father's sword at his hip. His heart raced for action. He glanced at Frebar and the men on his left. A jagged fork of lightening set their golden armor ablaze. The black storm clouds boiled and spit great tongues of fire. The menacing black lines advanced. The fields darkened with their presence. Will and Frebar held their position and waited.

A small party of six riders broke away from the line, galloping straight for the castle. The thunder spoke again and again. Frebar raised his hand, but he did not give the signal to advance. The ground shook. The air sizzled with power. The leader of the six riders fell back beside the second, much smaller rider. Will inched his mount forward but he also withheld the command to charge. The oncoming party carried no banner. Will watched as the smaller rider took the lead. He was waving and shouting, but the thunder drowned out his words. The sky fell in torrents. The wind lashed at them without mercy. Frebar looked to Will and nodded. Together they advanced in slow, stately defiance. Their armies still did not charge. The small fore-rider waved frantically.

"Grandpa!" his high-pitched voice floated on the wind.

"Kylie!" Frebar spurred his horse. The heavens opened with a fiery explosion. Frebar's gold-armored silhouette was etched for a moment in blue fire against the sky. Time stilled one long, ozone-heavy breath until the earth shook with a deafening clap. King Frebar's limp body splashed into the mud.

Will shouted, "Charge!" His horse flew ahead toward Kylie. The armies behind him split to surround and cut off the advancing black horde. When Will approached, Kylie's five escorts stopped. Their horses reared and retreated at full speed. The armies of the Twin Kingdoms galloped after them. Will bore down on Kylie's horse. Without slowing down he reached out, snatched the child from the saddle and galloped with him back toward the castle. Frebar's horse stood statue-like beside his fallen master. Will caught the reins and swung Kylie onto the horse's back. "Hang on! Ride home...Go!" Will ordered. He circled once then charged back to join the bloody melee in the fields.

Side by side Arindian and Frevarian fought and fell. Will raised Arinth's sword high shouting challenge. "For the Light! For the Light!"

Wherever the silver light of the sword fell, the dark tide faded into the fog. Will held it high, dispelling the evil that threatened to engulf them. His challenge echoed with every clash of sword and shield, with every twang of bow and hiss of arrow across the field. "For the Light! For the Light!" Will drove his silver light into the dark mass, carving a swath before him. The army of darkness retreated to the hills, dispelled by the power of Will's challenge. The thunder clouds rolled away behind them and the rain stopped. Will looked around him. The muddy field was full of death. He signaled to retreat. The sun broke out as he rode toward the gate. Kylie sat frozen in terror astride his grandfather's huge stallion. He had not fled. Both he and his mount stood guard over the spot where Frevaria's king had fallen.

Will dismounted. Frebar's lifeless eyes stared up at him. Will took a step. The golden sword lay within his grasp. He could take it and raise it. Who would challenge him? He was already High King. He did not need a figurehead on Frevaria's throne. He looked at his army. Frevaria's defense huddled in disarray, watching him with suspicion. Will reached for the sword. Several Frevarian noblemen stepped forward. Will did not heed them as he turned to Kylie. Sunlight danced on the child's golden curls. His eyes were wide. His mouth was pinched tight trying not to cry. Will raised the golden sword to catch the sun, then turned the hilt toward Kylie. "Hail Keilen, King of Frevaria," he shouted. "I salute you with your grandsire's sword."

The tension broke. A cry rose and carried like a springtime flood from the field to the village, to the castle walls. "Hail Keilen, King of Frevaria!"

The procession was grandiose. King Will had sent out a summons. Every person of royal blood, every lesser noble and land holder, even the guildsmen and the merchants were ordered to attend the event. The great hall was packed when the trumpets blared, "All hail King Willarinth and Queen Avrille, joint rulers of the Twin Kingdoms."

Avrille waited nervously in the atrium. She had chosen to wear a flowing red velvet gown today. Her hair was piled high, entwined with pearls and chains of silver filigree. Her jeweled braids encircled her head in a glory no crown smith could match. The great doors opened. Where was Will? She took a step. The people began to cheer. Her eyes searched the room. She smiled and nodded, greeting her subjects. Where was he? The red and blue banners waved. The voices rose then stopped abruptly. King Willarinth stepped out from a tapestry behind the thrones. Avrille's feet kept walking. The image the cards had foretold took shape and moved toward her. Will was dressed entirely in black from his silk under tunic and hose to his lacquered ceremonial breastplate and shield. His face was pale beneath his dark curls. He wore no crown, no rings of state as he stood on the dais with hand outstretched to receive his queen. Avrille walked in silence. The long carpet stretched like an eternity before her. Who was this man? Where was her husband? Where was her little brother? When she arrived at the dais, she took Will's hand without meeting his eyes. When the trumpets blared again, Avrille sank gratefully into her chair.

The herald announced, "Representing her nephew, Prince Jasenth, son of Prince Tobar, younger brother of the late King Frebar of Frevaria and the Princess Analinne, elder daughter of the late King Arinth of Arindon." He paused for a breath. "The Princess Maralinne!"

Maralinne had chosen to flaunt her reputation as a renegade princess. She wore a simple tan peasant dress. Her bright hair swung in a single braid down her back. She walked quickly to her chair. The ring of her boots drowned out the whispers in the hall.

"Princess Elanille, elder daughter of the late King Frebar of Frevaria," the herald announced. The doors remained closed. Again the hall was filled with whispers. The herald repeated the announcement. Still no one entered.

Maralinne rose and addressed King Will. "May I speak for my foster sister?"

Will nodded.

"Princess Elanille fled from her grief to the company of myself and my consort Jareth at our cottage in Arindon wood. She insisted that Jareth take her to High Bridge, the scene of her losses. They departed fifteen days ago. Since then neither of them has been seen nor has anyone received sign of their whereabouts."

Without comment King Will signaled the herald to proceed with the announcements. Maralinne sat down again. Avrille whispered a word to her then turned her attention to the next arrival.

"King Keilen, son of Princess Elanille of Frevaria and the late Sir Keilen, Chief Bowman of Arindon."

Kylie appeared at the top of the grand staircase tightly clutching Lady Cellina's hand. With rehearsed care he descended the stairs to the landing. He looked childishly awkward in his blue silk tunic and gold trappings. A quickly crafted miniature of his grandfather's sword was belted at his side. His blond curls were unadorned. All eyes looked up with anticipation.

The herald's trumpet sounded one more time. "King Keilen will be attended by the Lady Cellina, sister of the late Queen Veralinne of Arindon.

Cellina swooped majestically down the stairs. Her gown exploded with sapphires. Kylie tripped along like a puppet trying to keep up with her. When they reached the dais Cellina pushed Kylie forward. She pulled his tunic a minute bit straighter and whispered loud enough to be heard throughout the hall. "Now stand tall."

Will gestured for Cellina to be seated. She plopped her bejeweled bulk into her assigned chair beside Maralinne, giving the princess's rustic attire a disdainful glare.

Dell the Bard retrieved his vantage point at the top of the stairs now that all the players were on stage for the drama below. King Will had choreographed the first act for maximum impact with much success. Would the second act fare as well? Dell peered through the railing as Will began to speak. He listened as Will carefully brought forth all claimants to the Frevarian throne. Little Jasenth did have a strong case but Maralinne set it aside stating that as guardian for her sister's orphan she would continue to rear him in the school of the land and the values of the common people. She said that when he reached majority, should he wish to press his claim, he would then know the true heart of the people and they him.

Queen Avrille stepped forward. A murmur swept through the Frevarian noblemen. Dell strained to hear the queen's low voice.

"There are some who would suggest that as my husband has assumed the duties of kingship in Arindon as well as High King of both kingdoms that I assume the same duties in Frevaria through my claim as younger daughter of the late King Frebar." She paused for the restlessness in the hall to subside. "However, I feel that my nephew Keilen has a stronger claim being male and the son of my sister, King Frebar's elder daughter. I support Keilen's claim above myself and my daughters, the princesses Arinda and Arielle."

Will waited. Dell admired his skill. Timing, suspense and dramatic effect all were dealt with calculated precision. Will let his gaze sweep the room. He drew in a long, slow breath and stood up. "As High King of both kingdoms recognized by our father-in-law the late King Frebar, we have the power to create lesser kings or to eliminate them."

The Frevarian faction was on their feet. King Will paid them no notice. He drew his silver sword. The blade caught the light. The room filled with voices like the rush of a great wind. "On the fields of Frevaria I named Keilen king. Would any here dispute his claim?" The hall fell silent. Will let his gaze rest on each occupant of the room in turn. No one moved. He lowered his sword. "Then what we need to decide here is who will act as regent to advise young King Keilen until he comes of age."

Dell was taken by surprise along with the rest of the assembly. No one expected Maralinne or Avrille to assume the role. Most agreed that even were Elanille restored to them she would also decline. Again King Will let his audience speculate before he spoke.

"We will support our nephew King Keilen now in his infancy and later in his majority. Yet there are conflicts of interest both real and accused for ourselves to assume a larger influence in Frevarian internal affairs." He let the whispers subside then continued. "We are pleased to have observed both formerly in Arindon and continuing here in Frevaria that one person has remained an advocate for young Keilen. This person is of Frevarian noble blood, though fostered in and subsequently resided in Arindon. This person is educated in courtly affairs and mature enough to provide parental as well as political advice." Will turned to Kylie. "King Keilen, will you name your regent?'

Kylie walked to the edge of the dais and said in a loud, clear treble, "Lady Cellina will help me rule."

The hall rang with shouts of approval. Both Frevarian and Arindian were on their feet. Lady Cellina remained seated as she blushed and nodded her head first to Kylie and then to her supporters.

With a glance to his new regent the new little king raised both his hands. The noise subsided. "Now that I'm king, I got some decrees," he said holding himself as tall as possible. An amused but respectful titter rippled across the hall. "First we got to honor Grandpa. Everybody's got to wear black and not have fun until Equinox. That's when I get my cor...coronation." He paused and looked to Cellina. "Auntie, are all these people gonna stay for dinner?"

This time it was a wave of laughter that spread across the hall.

"If that is your wish, Your Majesty," Regent Cellina replied.

"Then I decree a feast for my Grandpa and for me an' all these people are invited."

Shouts and cheers for King Keilen's long rule rang loud. Dell slipped away singing to himself, "...and the fight lives on in Keilen's son."

Chapter 10

Jareth lay in a pile of dirty rags on the cold, stone floor of his cell. In the smoky torch light of the corridor he watched the Delven guard eating his dinner of bread and ale. Jareth had refused to eat since his capture, though his strength was failing. He needed the purity of the fast to activate his plan. The guard brushed the last crumbs from his tunic and wiped his moustache on his sleeve. Slowly his eyes began to droop. He leaned against the wall. His hand loosely grasped his blade. After an uneasy silence punctuated by a belch from the dozing guard, Jareth began his work. He took a loose chip of masonry from the far corner of the wall and started to draw on the floor. First he drew a circle and then five evenly-spaced stars. When his drawing was complete he sat inside the circle of stars and chanted quietly, barely mouthing the words.

"One for Five
Five for One
Hie thee home…"

The home spell began to light the crude star sign with a faint silver glow. He drew in a deep breath. He did not dare to break his concentration, not even to glance at the guard. He continued to chant, creating a mental picture of the cottage securely nestled among the giant trees of Arindon wood. He drew on memories from his childhood, the smell of apple blossoms beyond the door, and more recent memories of Maralinne's apple pies and apples eaten out of hand and shared with Jasenth. The star sign blazed brighter. The guard woke up but Jareth did not notice. His parched voice rose chanting his anguish and desire.

"Hie thee home
Home to Love"

There was a sudden wrench, a sudden weightless cold. He rushed along the time stream, tumbling backwards until at last, the sense of movement stopped. He opened his eyes. Yes, he was at the cottage, but what had happened? The fire was cold. The shutters were closed. The floor where he sat was strewn with debris. Where was Maralinne? He was too exhausted to let panic take over. He had escaped the Delven dungeons. That was enough for now. There was nothing he could do to rescue Elanille until he could think. He curled up on the floor and let himself drift off to sleep.

When he awoke sunlight was streaming through the crack between the shutters. His eyes wandered around the room. That the cottage had been ransacked by vandals was obvious. When he should have been asking himself the questions, why and by whom, it was the strangeness that dominated his thoughts. The place looked familiar but wrong. Where were Maralinne's red-checked curtains and the twins' cradle by the fire? Where was the partition he built to screen off the bedroom and the railing to keep Jasenth from falling out of the loft? And why was it so cold? He stood up slowly. Giddy with hunger, he took a tentative step. When he was assured of his balance he crossed the room and opened the shutters. A light snow was falling. No wonder it was cold. But this was late summer! He forced his senses to tell him the answer. This was the cottage where he had lived with his mother but... Jareth stopped. He was afraid to accept what his heart told him was true.

There was his mother's chest beside the bed with its lid thrown open. He had moved it to the loft for Jasenth's things. And there was his old toy bear beneath the over-turned rocker. He picked it up and cried silently, overwhelmed by loneliness until his empty, aching stomach roused him. He rummaged through the shelves but found nothing. He could not stay here. He had to find food. He had to find the way home to Maralinne. When he threw open the door a raw wet wind lashed at his weakened body. With his last ounce of strength, he slammed the door shut again.

Avrille and Maralinne bounced along in the open carriage. They were glad to be leaving Frevaria and the formalities of court behind them. The day was clear and warm. Rogarth sat aloof in the driver's seat, occupied with his own thoughts and respectful of the ladies' need for privacy. At first they did not speak but suddenly as if a dam had broken, the women hugged each other and poured out their loneliness and fears. Afterwards, amid embarrassed laughter, they dabbed their eyes with their handkerchiefs. By the time they reached Arindon they had all the details planned out for a holiday together. Avrille and her twins would come along to the cottage to keep Maralinne company until Jareth and Elanille returned.

When they arrived at Avrille's house, Linelle greeted them at the door with a twin on each arm. Maralinne swooped up both her nieces, babbling about how much they had grown. Rogarth carried Avrille's trunk inside. Then he sat silently in the doorway until he was needed further. In a flurry of excitement Avrille directed the packing of the twins' clothes and toys. She threw open the lid of her trunk and tossed her court finery on the bed.

"What does a lady wear in Arindon wood?" she said laughing as she surveyed her closet. Maralinne helped her pick out two plain day dresses. Avrille changed into one of them and stuffed the other along with a handful of undergarments into a satchel. "That's enough I'm sure," she said.

"You'd better take a shawl and your sturdiest footwear," Maralinne advised.

"This is going to be so much fun!" Avrille sang as she danced around the room.

"Trebil fun too?" said a plaintive voice from the cage by the window.

"Shall we take him?" said Avrille.

"He may be useful," said Maralinne. "And besides, he is your friend. Aren't you, pretty bird?"

"Treat?"

"Here, pack his canister of nuts," said Maralinne. "I have plenty of fruit, but I know these are his favorites."

Trebil fluttered his wings noisily, screeching at the top of his voice. Avrille picked up the bird cage with one hand and her satchel with the other. Then she called to Rogarth to carry the children's luggage to the carriage.

"Are you sure you won't need me, Lady Queen," asked Linelle for the hundredth time as she handed the twins into the carriage.

"No, I said you deserve a holiday too. We'll be fine. Go home to your family. I will send for you when we return."

Baby Arinda clapped her tiny hands and called, "Bye-bye. Rindy go bye-bye," while her sister Arielle sat pouting quietly, saving her wails until they were too far away to return. Rogarth cracked the whip and they were off at a spirited trot through the village, past the mill and into the wood.

Jareth shivered in the snowy, late afternoon twilight. He searched the cottage for warm clothing. The vandals had left little of value. He poked through the tiny memory-filled room. He climbed the ladder to the loft. It was empty. As he climbed back down something caught his eye. Protruding from behind the chest where it had fallen was the bearskin rug his mother used to spread out on the chest to make an extra seat for guests. Jareth quickly wrapped himself in the fur. He considered staying at the cottage but his hunger drove him out into the approaching winter night. He had to find food. He looked up at the apple tree swaying gaunt arms beyond the door. It looked much smaller than he remembered. He spied a few high fruits the wind and deer had not claimed. Dizzily he climbed the rough trunk of the tree. He picked the fruits that were in his reach and dropped back to the ground. He leaned against the trunk of the tree and disciplined himself to eat slowly. When he finished the second apple, he stashed the rest in his pouch and tried to think what to do next.

He started down the road that should eventually lead him out of the woods to the farms and to Arindon. When he had walked about a mile, he noticed a flicker of firelight off in the trees to his left. He hesitated to leave the road in the darkness but he was drawn to the fire. He approached with caution until he could see a lone figure standing with a staff raised toward the blaze. Dancing shadows leaped in the oak-ringed clearing. The fire was built atop a pile of stones and the fuel was not wood but human flesh. Jareth's stomach did a twist as he watched this funeral rite. Numbness gripped him as his mind's eye separated from the scene to view it from the opposite side of the clearing. He felt an intense terror, like nothing he had felt since childhood. He was certain he had witnessed this same scene before. He remembered crouching in the bushes watching Kyrdthin the magician honor what the Delven Dogs had left of his mother.

His mind snapped back to the present when a clash of arms and rough voices burst into the clearing. He knew his childhood self had run away at that sound. The terror he felt even now as an adult warred between his heart and his feet, immobilizing him. He fought the bonds but he was rooted to the spot. The soldiers held back a moment when the magician turned toward them. Their leader shouted, but before the men could respond Jareth's invisible restraints were suddenly released. Weaponless except for his battle challenge, Jareth sprang into the clearing. Kyrdthin the magician's voice rose. A surge of power leaped from his staff. His robes fell away. His body transformed into a towering pillar of white light. As the soldiers fled, Jareth felt the backwash of power surge through his own body. The weight of his bearskin cloak became part of him. His limbs shortened and thickened. His head grew heavier. He opened his mouth to cry out but he growled with a bear's voice.

The blazing pillar that had been the magician gradually dimmed, then it winked out with a shower of stars. Kyrdthin looked at him with a quirk of a smile, nodded then walked away. Jareth had no choice but to follow him.

Avrille took Rogarth's hand and climbed out of the carriage. Her legs were stiff from the long ride. She set Arinda down on the ground with a sigh of relief. Holding a wiggly eighteen-month-old for over an hour had been an ordeal. Maralinne, with Arielle still in her arms, was already hugging Jasenth. Darilla stood in the doorway of the cottage. Her twins were behind her on a quilt spread out on the floor. Arielle kicked until Maralinne put her down beside her sister. Jasenth immediately commandeered his aunt's attention. Jareth had still not returned. The boy was both afraid and angry at what his elders did not know or could not explain to him.

They all trooped into the cottage. Sunlight slanted across the floor. Darilla's infant boys looked up with identical, small, pale faces set beneath their thick dark curls. There was no question that Varan and Veren were King Will's own.

"Baby! Baby!" Arinda cried darting in front of her sister. She pounced on tiny Veren with a ferocious hug. Arielle, caught in mid-stride, wobbled but did not fall. "Baby!" she cried in imitation of her sister and toddled to Varan. The light in the room suddenly grew dim. Had a cloud strayed across the late afternoon sun? Avrille stopped in the doorway. Everything in the room began to waver and shift. Both pairs of twins clung to their counterparts, poised in a suspended moment. Her stomach did a flip-flop. A scarcely audible hum vibrated through the air. All four babies squealed and toppled together in a heap in the middle of the quilt. The sun broke through again in a shower of gold. Dazzled for a moment Avrille could seen only a single pair of babies. Then all four were crying. Darilla rescued Veren from Arinda and Maralinne picked up Varan from where Arielle had pushed him. Darilla sat down to nurse one squalling infant and Maralinne filled a bottle for his brother. Arinda and Arielle turned their attention to Jasenth who was dragging out his toy basket to entertain them.

"This venture may prove more than interesting," said Maralinne.

"I'm afraid it will," said Avrille with a quick glance at Darilla.

All the while Rogarth hovered uneasily in the doorway with the luggage. When the children were finally content he said. "If the ladies are settled in I should be returning…"

Maralinne jumped up. "But you will stay for supper?"

"Please, Rogarth," added Avrille. "I need you."

Rogarth hesitated, looking very much uncomfortable.

Then Jasenth chimed in, "Please stay. You can sit in Uncle Jareth's place until he comes back."

Rogarth reluctantly let himself be persuaded.

When Avrille took down Maralinne's apron from the hook in the kitchen, Darilla jumped up. "My Lady Queen you cannot…" the girl began to say as she disengaged sleeping Veren from her breast.

"No Darilla," Avrille commanded. "You hold your child and I will cook."

"As you will, Lady Queen," said Darilla flushing with confusion. "I have soup ready in that pot. It only needs reheating. There's bread and…."

"Blueberries, lots a blueberries," said Jasenth.

Avrille struggled with the heavy soup pot. Rogarth took it from her and hung it on the fire hook. "Allow me, My Lady," he said.

"Stop it! Stop it both of you!" Avrille stamped her foot. "I came here to get away from 'my lady this' and 'my lady that'. Maralinne is the only person in this stupid world who treats me as an equal. I don't want to be queen, here or anywhere." She sank down into a chair and buried her head in her hands. "Please just call me Avrille," she sobbed. "I am a person, not some, some...I don't know..."

Maralinne exchanged a quick look with Darilla then set Varan down on the quilt with his bottle. "Alright, the captain of the guard is on kitchen patrol,' she said with a forced laugh. "This is a loaf of bread and this is a knife. You slice while I whip some cream for the berries." She stopped when a squeal from Jasenth erupted in the corner where the boy was desperately trying to both share and repossess his toys. "Jayjay, be a big boy and set the table. I will lift down the bowls and you can do the rest. Count out five big spoons for the grownups and yourself and two little ones for the girls."

Arielle screamed. Arinda was hitting her with Jasenth's wooden sword. Avrille picked her up and probed her head for injury. She tried to send a calming spell through her fingers but found she had none to give.

Jareth followed Kyrdthin through the snowy woods. Unaccustomed to his new body and on-all-fours perspective he soon was completely lost in spite of his heightened senses. His thick fur turned both the cold and the dampness. For that he was grateful. They must have been traveling south because soon he heard the roar of the river. When they reached the steep embankment Jareth peered over the edge to try to see exactly where they were. The wet, loose ground suddenly gave way. He flailed at the bushes with his forepaws but he could not stop his slide. Down, down he plunged to the icy river below.

The water closed over his head. He pawed franticly toward the surface, his lungs bursting for air. The current tore at him, dashing him against the rocks. It took all his strength to conquer his panic but he managed to get his head above water long enough to gasp a breath before the current pulled him under and dragged him along the bottom. Again he pawed his way to the surface. At last the river took mercy on him and cast him into a small eddy near the far bank. Jareth hauled his bruised body out onto the rocky shore far downstream from where he had fallen in. Glad to be alive, he almost laughed as he shook himself dry and peered across the water for Kyrdthin. Finally he saw him about a quarter mile upstream. Jareth stood up on his hind legs and tried to wave. Kyrdthin vanished in a shower of stars and reappeared beside him.

"Now that's what I call taking a short cut!" said Kyrdthin laughing heartily. "Let's get you back to human form before you try something really dangerous." He raised his staff. Again Jareth felt a surge of power but nothing changed. Kyrdthin looked perplexed. He tried again, but again nothing changed. Jareth was still a bear! "I don't know why it isn't working on you," said Kyrdthin shaking his head. "Well, come on we can worry about it later.'

"Later!" Jareth tried to say but out came a growl instead. He followed Kyrdthin along the faint mossy trail. By now he knew where they were and where they must be headed as they picked their way upriver toward the roar of the falls. The wet rocks were slick. Jareth lost his footing more than once, but at last they ducked through the spray to the narrow ledge behind the falls. Kyrdthin traced a star sign in the air. In the faint silver light he examined the face of the rock wall.

"Where's the latch?" he said clearing away a clump of ferns. "Ah, there it is." His fingers touched the inlaid circle of stars. The rock slid back to let them pass.

The small guard room inside was more recently occupied than the one Jareth remembered from his trips with Maralinne and Elanille. Kyrdthin started a fire and put on a kettle of water. Jareth settled his exhausted body on the hearth. His wet fur steamed. Kyrdthin left for a short while to return with two fish flopping in a basket. Jareth seized one from him, and gulped it down alive and whole. Not caring whether it was his own hunger or the bear's instincts that drove him, Jareth felt the food fill and begin to strengthen him. Wearily he rolled over on his side.

When all five children were finally asleep, Rogarth stood up to take his leave. Avrille carefully laid Arielle on the bed and walked him to the door. Maralinne also rose from her chair. She put a hand on Rogarth's arm. "Thank you for staying, my friend," she said smiling at him with a special meaning.

He smiled briefly and pulled away.

"It has been a tense but non-the-less good evening for all of us," said Avrille.

Rogarth smiled again, this time sadly. "Such friends we are! Such a circle of triangles!"

Maralinne raised her eyebrows. "The queen's champion speaks in metaphors?"

"Sometimes a metaphor speaks gentler than direct truth," he said staring out into the darkening woods. "The first lady was mine, but I did not love her until I had given her away. The second lady was a child, but I did not love her until she was grown and another had taken her away."

"Here without Jareth and Will, we remember and wonder what might have been," Maralinne tried to help him conclude.

"We're together, but none of us are free," said Avrille looking back at the children bundled in the bed and Darilla slowly rocking by the fire.

Rogarth, Avrille and Maralinne held hands in a silent circle. Time flowed around them until Maralinne broke the spell. She bid Rogarth goodnight. Avrille walked with him out into the twilight toward the empty carriage. He stood a moment, idly stroking the horse's cheek. She waited until he reached up to climb into the driver's seat. "Don't leave me, please! Please!" she begged flinging herself into his arms.

"My little lady Avrille…" he began.

"Please stay, please."

"You are here with friends. You can send the little bird to me and…"

"Everything is out of control!" she wailed. "Will is awful! I'm so mad at him! Why wasn't it me? Why did some other girl have to give him sons?"

Rogarth held her and patted her hair.

"Nothing is right! All this stupid magic spoils everything. You saw it when the twins met. I know you did…" She buried her face in his sleeve. "When will it all stop? I just want to be an ordinary person." She sobbed. "I miss my mom, but she's gone. Uncle Hawke's gone. Gil and Queen Marielle, my sister and Jareth, everyone is gone but you."

"Dearest little lady, I have vowed to keep your true self safe beneath the weight of the crown. That I will do. But here...." He stopped a moment then continued. "Here I fear losing my true self. I cannot stay. Princess Maralinne and your children will protect you here."

"I could command you."

"And I would have to obey."

She tightened her arms around his neck and pulled him down to her. "Then go if you must, but first kiss me goodbye."

He smiled kindly and reached to disengage her arms.

Maralinne watched discretely form the doorway. Her own heart ached for Jareth. She shared Avrille's anguish and longed for release from the forces that toyed with all their lives.

Jareth was awake before he opened his eyes. He sensed Kyrdthin kneeling beside him. He felt a tug at his neck.

"What do you have here?" said the magician holding a small leather pouch on a thong about the bear's neck.

Jareth growled possessively and pulled away.

"No offense, my man, but since my skills cannot free you for the moment at least, I thought to look for a clue as to whom you might be."

Jareth let him untie the thong. When Kyrdthin opened the pouch the firelight caught the lock of Maralinne's hair inside.

"The New Age is not far from us when a maid of Arindon is crowned with hair like this," said Kyrdthin with reverence as he returned the pouch and sat down beside Jareth on the hearth. He pulled a pipe from the folds of his robe. Thoughtfully he lit it and leaned back to enjoy the strong, sweet aroma. "Since we can't talk like men, by some perversity of fate, we will have to improvise. You can understand me, right friend?"

Jareth attempted to nod his large bear's head.

"There must be some purpose for you being here, some purpose for keeping you in your present form." He drew on the gurgling pipe. "Perhaps it's a disguise."

Jareth tried to nod again.

"With ourselves out of immediate danger, it's Cara's lad I'm worried about. That's the son of the woman whose pyre I was tending when we met so abruptly. He's dear to me, like a nephew you'd say. I did what I could for them. She insisted on living here to be near to the boy's father." His eyes grew wistful with the memories of what was a much longer, sadder tale. "But Belar's Dogs found her...." His voice trailed off as he puffed on his pipe. "We may have scared them off but they will be back. The King of Darkness has no tolerance for half-Allarian brats. We have to find the boy. With this new snow falling he will be easy to track, if we only knew where to begin.

Jareth raised his snout and sniffed loudly. Kyrdthin looked puzzled for a moment then broke into a grin. "So you think you could sniff him out?'

Jareth raised and lowered his head.

"Let's get going then," said Kyrdthin knocking the ashes out of his pipe. "The boy's a sharp one but he is only seven and probably scared to death."

Avrille almost enjoyed the next few days with Maralinne. The freedom of life at the cottage was wonderful. They joyfully shared the housework and the barn chores. Caring for the children was tedious at times but still a relief from castle life. Even living in Arindon village after the fire she had a royal role to play, but here she could almost be herself.

For Darilla the situation was not so pleasant. The girl, who was already quiet by nature, withdrew from Avrille and Maralinne's company until she hardly spoke at all. She vacillated between jealously guarding her sons and deferring to Avrille as if they were her queen's children, not her own.

One especially hectic morning Avrille openly challenged Darilla's silence. "I'm sick of your sulking insolence!" she yelled.

"Avrille!" Maralinne intervened. "It's been a trying morning for all of us and I know you aren't feeling well...."

Avrille would not be stopped. "To think I delivered the babies of my husband's mistress with my own hands! I should have refused and let you suffer alone," she raged.

Darilla burst into tears.

"Avrille, enough!" Maralinne ordered stepping between them.

Avrille's temples throbbed. Her stomach rolled with a wave of nausea. She steadied herself on Maralinne's arm but would not stop the tirade she had begun. "Do you love my husband?" she demanded.

Darilla cringed.

"Answer me."

"As...as my king. My Lady, please. Only as my king."

"Avrille, back off," Maralinne warned.

Avrille silenced her with a commanding glance and turned again to the cowering girl.

"So you slept with him only because he commanded you?"

Darilla mustered enough tearful pride to defend herself. "The king seemed pleased with how his childhood acquaintance had grown. So my father told me to go to him if His Majesty asked for me."

"And did an inexperienced child please the king?"

Darilla answered with a clear, sad voice. "He was gentle and patient but he did not speak of love to me, not even as he fathered these sons."

Avrille's breath hissed inward, then she let it go. Her strength was fading and with it her anger. "But you do love him?" she asked in a gentler tone.

"Only as my king," said Darilla. "He's not the same boy that once worked for my father."

"You loved the boy he was?"

"I don't know, Lady Queen," said the girl shaking her head. "Does it matter now that he is a man and my king?'

Avrille doubled over with a wave of sickness and ran out to the porch to retch over the rail. Maralinne followed her and stood with a hand on her shoulder until Avrille sank to the floor exhausted.

"Why don't you go back in there and tell Darilla what you're really upset about."

"Lemme alone."

"Tell her you are afraid because you are pregnant to a man who is lost to you. Darilla's certainly the one person who could understand. Tell her how lonely and confused you are."

"Go away."

"She will understand, Avrille. And she will be noble enough to forgive you."

Avrille got up slowly and let Maralinne guide her back into the house. Maralinne busied herself putting on the teapot. For a long time, Avrille hung her head and leaned against the doorframe, lost in her misery. Nothing was right. Nothing was fair. Why? Why did she have to get pregnant again? She didn't want another baby. She hated Will. She hated herself. She hated everybody. Why was all this stupid magic controlling them when they had enough trouble controlling themselves? And then there was Darilla... She looked up, and humbly took Darilla's waiting, outstretched hand.

Chapter 11

Elanille lay at the edge of consciousness. The sibilant whispering had stopped but its awful "pretty, pretty" echoed over and over in her exhausted mind as she drifted back to sleep. The darkness of her prison enclosed her mind as well as her body. She and Jareth had threaded their way through the subterranean labyrinth in search of Kylie. Numbing cold drove her on though her legs ached from the unaccustomed exertion. They descended long, slippery ramps and winding stairs, the stale smoky air tearing at her lungs. Jareth tried to help, first with words of encouragement and then a supporting hand, but their progress became slower and slower until finally she collapsed. Then he carried her until she woke again. Elanille recoiled from the terrifying encounter of tight sticky strands wrapping around her, pulling her out of Jareth's grasp, the sweet, sleepy smell, the whispering voice in her ear, the jolting pain of being half dragged along the cold, stone floor away into the dark.

Now she tried to move but only her head was free from the binding webs. She was afraid to call out for fear that her whispering captor would hear and return. Where was Jareth? Had he met the same fate? Did this horror also hold her Kylie? She thrust the thoughts far back into her mind and tried to concentrate on the present. Her eyes strained in the darkness but she could see nothing. Faraway she could hear water dripping, dripping, dripping. She tried to shut out the sound but the dripping, dripping, pretty, pretty, pretty, tormented her until she felt the repulsive presence of her captor hovering over her.

"Pretty, pretty, Spida's gotsa pretty. Spida gotsa pretty, he does." Padded footsteps circled her. "Nassy Watcher not gonna taka dis pretty. Spida gonna keep it. Keepa pretty, pretty, pretty."

She could feel its breath as it leaned over her. It smelled nauseatingly sweet. Her head swam. She let the smell waft her back into unconsciousness.

* * * * *

"Try again, Trebil, try," Avrille begged. The little mirror bird was reluctant to show her what he said was a "sad, sad story". Avrille held the bowl of water to catch the sunlight. The sparkling surface danced in a rainbow of colors then quieted to reflect a picture of a familiar room in Frevaria. Rogarth was sitting on his bunk. His head was bowed. In his hands was a small, red silk scarf.

"My token!" she exclaimed.

The queen's champion thoughtfully fingered the scarf until a knock on the door interrupted him. He quickly tucked the scarf up his sleeve then called, "It's open."

King Will stalked into the room. His dark expression matched the dark fabric of his clothes. "So this is where you've been sulking."

"At you service, sire," Rogarth answered with a deferring nod.

"I ordered you to report to the construction site."

"I am a warrior, sire, not a common laborer."

"You are whatever I say you are," Will fumed.

"I did not mean to challenge your authority, sire, but…"

"If you won't follow my orders, then you are confined to quarters until further notice," Will commanded pulling his short stature up as tall as he could. "You will communicate with no one, especially not my wife." His eye caught a small blue flash duck behind the window curtain. "Go home Trebil," he roared. "Tell your whoring mistress that her Lord King sends his love."

The scene blanked. Avrille set the bowl of water back on the table. She kissed the trembling little bird. "My sweet, loyal, little friend! Will is such a meanie. Here, you can have some of Darilla's cake." She sliced a piece and crumbled it onto the table.

Avrille walked out to the yard where Darilla and Maralinne were hanging up laundry.

"I thought your morning sickness was over," said Maralinne when she saw Avrille's face.

"Trebil just came back from Rogarth," she said reaching into the laundry basket to help. She pinned up a diaper and reached down for another.

Maralinne listened without comment as Avrille related Trebil's tale.

"What am I going to do?" Avrille concluded.

"We are more alone now than ever," said Darilla.

"No offense to you Darilla, but how dare Will accuse me when he's the guilty one?"

"Your baby is the king's?" Darilla half stated, half asked.

"I'd give anything if I weren't pregnant to anyone right now, Darilla, but this," she patted the small round outline of her abdomen. "This is one of the few moments of marital happiness I have shared with Will..." her voice trailed off.

Maralinne pinned the last tiny nightgown on the line and picked up the basket. "We had better get back in there before the darlings tear up the house," she said trying to ease the tension with a laugh.

"Only Jayjay and Rindy were awake when I came out and they were content with Darilla's cake," said Avrille.

"Then it's guaranteed to be a mess."

Elanille woke to the clank of metal and rough voices. Fear gagged her throat.

"No dinna, dinna!" her captor was insisting. "Spida dinna help a man escape. No! No!"

"Enough of your lying," said a brusque voice followed by squeals and a scuffle.

"Donna hurt a Spida."

"Then tell us where the prisoner is."

"Spida donna know. Sold ugly man 'cause Spida donna want it. You had it. You lost it"

"Maybe he didn't do it," said another voice.

"Prisoners don't just disappear," said the first voice.

"Donna poke poor Spida wida nassy knife. Spida donna have a ugly man."

"Let him go," said the second voice.

"I still think we should search his lair."

"Not me. You can go in that filthy hole. I don't want to know what he's got wrapped up in there."

There was another scuffle and two sets of boots echoed back into the welcome silence. Elanille sank back, but before she could relax, she heard the whimpering of her captor nearby.

"Stinkin', stinkin', Delven Dogs. Stinkin' stinkin'..." His feet padded back to where she lay. "Won't take a pretty. No. No.

Spida gotsa secret. Nassy Delven Doggies donna know Spida's secret."

Delven! Elanille's hopes of rescue and escape shattered. Her voice had failed her, refusing to let her cry out to the rough voices. Now she was glad she had not, but her captor...

"Pretty, pretty, pretty. Spida gotsa pretty."

The padded footsteps circled her. The sickening sweet smelling air closed in on her again.

"Aunt Mari, come quick!" called Jasenth.

All three women dashed back into the house. Jasenth stood on a kitchen chair. In front of him was the bowl of water Avrille had used to mirror Trebil's tale.

"Look! A dark lady inside the water. Look!"

Maralinne lifted Jasenth down from the chair. Then she stared with Avrille into the water, but only the calm, clear reflection of their own faces looked up at them.

Jasenth tugged at his aunt's skirt. She lifted him up and held him over the bowl. "Do you still see her, Jayjay?"

The boy looked again. "Nope."

"What did you see? Tell us exactly."

"A lady wearing black clothes."

"Anything else?"

"I think she was old."

"What was she doing?" said Avrille.

"Just lookin' at me."

"Did she look nice or mean?" said Maralinne.

"Dunno. Maybe mean. No, crying. I think she was crying."

"Jayjay, you are a good boy," said Maralinne giving him a kiss. "Be sure to tell us if you remember anything more or if you see this lady again."

Jasenth nodded solemnly, then at his aunt's suggestion he went out on the porch to play. Arielle toddled after him. Avrille stood a moment watching him drag the boot rug from the doorway to the step. He sat down with his little bow and quiver on his lap and announced to the woods beyond the yard in a clear defiant voice, "I'm man of dis house till Uncle Jareth comes home." Arielle sat down beside him. "Unca Jareth come home," she mimicked.

Avrille looked at Maralinne. "I think we need to get out the cards."

Darilla held back at first. Then she inched forward to see as Avrille shuffled the deck.

"Let's each cut, since we all are involved in this," she said placing the deck on the table. She took the first cut, reshuffled and passed the cards to Maralinne. After the third shuffle she handed the deck to Darilla. "Go ahead. Just take some of the cards off the top. Don't turn any over yet." Avrille reassembled the deck saying, "Five for the Future?"

Maralinne nodded her agreement.

Avrille drew the first card. "Who seeks us?"

"The Black Queen? Of course that's it, but who is she?" said Maralinne.

Darilla took a step back obviously shaken, but Avrille looked at the card long and hard. The face beneath the dark diadem was hauntingly familiar. The features were full of longing and loss. She felt no malice, only emptiness and despair like a mother grieving for her children."

"Why does the Black Queen call to us?" said Avrille turning over the next card.

"The Star!" exclaimed Avrille and Maralinne together. "Lizzie?"

"There is a lot going on here," said Maralinne. "Why don't we just draw and lay all five of them out. Then we can try to see if there is a pattern?"

"Alright, you ask and turn the third card."

"Where is Jareth?" said Maralinne to the card in her hand. Four trees linked by a circle, one in blossom, one green, one russet and one bare, surrounded an hour glass. "Time? How does the Time card answer my question?"

"I don't know," said Avrille handing the deck to Darilla. "Draw and ask," she told the girl. "What will become of the man who is our king and father of our children?" She drew a card and handed it to Avrille without looking at it.

It was not the Black King as Avrille had expected. Her eyes were drawn into the miniature scene of the card. A cluster of people stood in the courtyard of a shining fortress. Overhead a large black-winged dragon hovered ominously then disappeared.

"What is it?" asked Darilla in a small frightened voice.

"The Black Dragon," said Avrille without comment.

"Whatcha doing?" asked Jasenth from the doorway. "Can I play too?"

Maralinne started to object then reconsidered. "Come on in, Jayjay. You can help us. Turn over the top card and hand it to Auntie Avrille." To Avrille she said, "This will tell us what we have to do."

Jasenth carefully took the card. He cocked his head and studied it. "What's the bear doing, Aunt Mari?" he said handing her the card of Strength.

The huge golden bear was standing on his hind legs in front of a cave. In the foreground two women hugged each other. Was it in fear or in awe of the creature? "Let's lay them all out," said Avrille. She lined them up on the table, the Black Queen, the Star, Time, the Black Dragon, and Strength. She studied the plain, painted faces of the cards for a clue but the magic was gone.

Elanille gagged. A sweet liquid was being forced down her throat. It ran down her neck and into her hair. She gagged again trying to sit up but her body would not respond.

"Pretty. Pretty. Feed a pretty."

The liquid trickled down her throat. She tried to swallow.

"Pretty like a sweet?" the voice sing-songed in her ear. She tried to turn her head away from the sound. The liquid splashed on her cheek. Angrily she cried out.

"Pretty wake! Pretty talk! Pretty talk a Spida. Pretty like a Spida?"

"You're choking me. Let me sit up," she cried.

She cringed from the furry claw as it broke the sticky threads over her hands and arms.

"Loose a hands, just a hands, not a feet. Donna want it runaway. Keep it, yes a keep a pretty. Keep it. Keep it."

She tried to sit up but her strength failed. She fell back, her head crashed to the floor and everything went black for a moment.

"Poor, poor, pretty," the voice whispered.

She felt a long furry arm beneath her shoulders.

"Pretty weak. Mussa eat."

The hot sweet breath was close to her cheek. Again the container of liquid was placed to her lips. It was cloyingly sweet but good, like honey mixed with wine. Her empty stomach rebelled at first, then settled down, satisfied. Again she heard the clang of metal and the clomp of heavy boots approaching.

"Come out insect. We know you're in there."

Her captor's breaths quickened beside her ear.

"Come out or I'll throw in this torch."

"No, no! No light! Nassy light hurt poor Spida's eyes."

"Help!" Elanille cried deciding to trust her lot with Delven, who at least looked human.

A furry claw clamped across her mouth. "Shhh, shhh, pretty, shhh."

She jerked her head away. "Help!" she cried again.

Blinding light flooded her prison.

She must have passed out again. When she awoke she was lying on a quilt-covered cot. The sticky webbing that had bound her was gone. She opened her eyes. The room was small and dimly lit. Beside her on a low table was a water pitcher and basin draped with a clean towel. She sat up. Her limbs felt weak and shaky. The room tipped drunkenly from side to side. She reached for the table to steady herself. Grateful for the small luxury, she wet the towel and washed her face.

Yellow torchlight streamed in from an adjoining room. Elanille sat uneasily on the cot and peered out into the light. She could see no one. Dare she try to stand? Slowly she slid her feet to the floor. She took a deep breath and stood up. She was wobbly but she managed to make her way hand over hand along the wall toward the light.

"You awake in there?" called a voice.

Elanille clutched the wall.

"Do you need help?"

The sound of a chair sliding back grated loud in her ears. Heavy footsteps approached. Her legs gave way. Large hands caught her and carried her into the light. When she saw him she screamed.

"Take it easy, lady. I won't hurt you."

Elanille struggled.

"I'm Borat, captain of the Dark Lady's guard. I won't hurt you."

She let her body go limp. What did it matter what became of her? She was free of the whispering menace. What could be worse?

She let him carry her to the chair. His dark mailed shirt pressed hard against her side.

"I see you found the water basin," he said. "I'm sorry I can't offer you a change of clothes, but a soldier's garments would hardly be appropriate. Perhaps the Dark Lady...."

"Dark Lady?"

"When you have eaten and feel stronger I'll take you to her. She has already been informed of your presence and is very concerned with your welfare."

Elanille watched the dark-clad warrior set a plate of bread and cheese in front of her. He poured a mug of wine. When he handed it to her she saw that his face was hard and lined but not fearsome.

"Eat slowly lady. Spida must have almost starved you."

"Spida, what is it?" she asked shrinking from the horrible memory.

"He's a simple-minded creature, a nuisance and a thief. He meant you no harm but you are lucky we followed him and found you."

"Where is Jareth, the man that was with me?" she asked between mouthfuls of cheese.

"That one is a mystery. He escaped without a trace from a secured cell."

"And my son Kylie, a seven-year-old?" she asked against all hope.

"The men had a lad in here a few days ago but he's gone now."

"Gone! Where?"

"They took him to the Dark Lady and that's the last I heard of him."

She choked on the bread. Borat offered her the mug of wine. She coughed and choked again. Her head throbbed. He stomach convulsed. Kylie in the clutches of the dark ruler! She almost sank back into unconsciousness.

"Try to eat a little more," Borat's rough voice sounded almost kindly.

"No, take me to this dark lady of yours," she said with her last reserve of strength.

Borat helped her to her feet. Leaning heavily on his arm Elanille walked with him out into a large hall. There massive doors loomed high in front of them. Borat unbolted the heavy latch. Tendrils of blue smoke slithered through the opening.

"Allow me, lady," he said as he steadied her with an arm about her waist. "There will be a momentary sensation, a vertigo you might say, as we enter."

The doors swung open. Elanille was drawn inside by groping electric fingers. Her feet floated forward. Her breathing stopped. Intense cold gripped her. Borat's arm pulled her down until her numbed feet touched the floor. The doors slammed shut behind her.

Her eyes tried to adjust to the smoky torchlight. She was standing at the far end of a long, colonnaded hall. Her escort had disappeared. She was alone and very much afraid. She tried to focus on the light at the opposite end of the hall. A dark wooden throne welcomed, and at the same time, repulsed her. The shadows above the throne moved like the beating of gigantic wings, and the eyes… Elanille took a step forward. Mesmerizing dragon's eyes drew her toward the mirrors surrounding the throne. She took a few more steps. The patterns in the mirrors swirled and shifted. Suddenly the throne came alive. A dark, seated figure held an enticing golden light in its lap. The eyes watched. The mirrors glittered. Elanille advanced unaware of her halting steps. The dark figure's light reached into the very essence of her being. She fought the golden tide. She both feared and longed for its warmth. The light detached from the shadowed chair. Elanille reached out her arms. Her head pounded wildly. Her body moved against her will, until out of the light stepped a golden-haired child in a long white nightgown. An unbearable pain shattered Elanille's mind as she recognized the child's face.

"Lizzie!" she cried and everything went black.

When the summons came it was just three words. "It is time." The ancient Watcher removed the seal from the door of the inner cave and waited. From the dark recess he heard a low growl as the beast woke from its years-long slumber. Heavy padded steps moved toward the opening. Claws scraped on the floor. The Watcher stepped back as a great, golden bear lumbered out into the light. The Watcher said the long remembered words in a clear voice. "Go. Bring the Queen of All Light to heal the broken mirror. The Oaken Circle will be the doorway to the balance and the future."

The bear cocked his head and looked at him.

"Do this and you shall be free," the Watcher concluded as he opened the outer door.

Sunlight momentarily blinded the bear but soon he was able to move out into the crisp mountain morning. With one look back at the Watcher he headed down the eastern slope.

Jareth said the Watcher's message over and over in his mind. "Bring the Queen of All Light", that had to be Avrille, which meant he was back in his own time again but still wearing a bear's body. The Watcher's last words were, "Then you shall be free". How he hoped that meant return to human form. He thought about the events that had taken place since he said goodbye to Maralinne. He and Elanille had braved the Delven depths in search of Kylie. When they were attacked, he fought bravely but he was overwhelmed and Elanille was torn away from him. The time spent in the dungeons was a miserable blur but he had escaped. Afterward there was the strange time turn in which he acquired the bear's body that he still wore. He had escorted his younger self back through the Dark Realm and delivered him to Gil and Marielle's safe-keeping in Allarion. That done the last thing he remembered was the uncontrollable desire to return to the Watcher's cave to sleep. Had he really slept almost thirty years? How much time had elapsed here in this time? Where was Elanille? Was she alright? What was his mission for the Watcher? Jareth knew he needed to return to the cottage and Maralinne before he could do anything else.

He continued down the mountain. Letting the instincts of his bear's body take over, he fed hungrily on herbs and grubs. He also found a few blueberries left on a rocky crag. By nightfall he arrived at the river. This time he crossed easily, letting his bear's strength carry him effortlessly to the opposite shore. Before moving on he turned over a few rocks in a small eddy to feast on crayfish. Then he shook himself dry and climbed up the bank to the road. The last leg of the journey stretched the longest. It was already night when he reached the clearing.

As he neared the cottage he was faced with the dilemma of identifying himself. To Maralinne, or anyone else for that matter, he was a bear. He waited in the edge of the clearing, churning the Watcher's words over in his mind. The queen was to heal the broken mirror. Avrille had healing powers, but the broken mirror, what or who was that? At least he knew where he had to take her. Five Oaks Circle in Arindon wood was a doorway, but to where he did not know.

Unable to wait any longer to see his beloved Maralinne he approached the cottage. He stood on his hind legs and looked in the window. Maralinne was clearing the table. Her brilliant hair lit the small room, competing with the firelight. Darilla held one baby on her hip as she folded the table cloth. Where was Jasenth? Then he saw him climbing down the loft ladder carrying his sack of toys. Jareth watched him empty out the sack on the hearth rug where two small girls were playing. What were the twin princesses doing here? Avrille came out of the kitchen carrying Darilla's other son.

Jareth dropped back onto all fours. He couldn't just go up and knock on the door. He had to think things through. He made his way to the shadow of the barn. The chickens sensed his presence and raised a clatter. The door of the cottage flew open. Maralinne came out with the broom in her hand.

"Is it a fox, Aunt Mari?" Jasenth called.

"Stay inside, Jayjay."

Maralinne walked cautiously toward the barn. When she rounded the corner Jareth stepped out into the moonlight. She did not scream. She did not run. He was proud of her. She slowly raised her broom and backed toward the barn door. He did not pursue. Wagering on Maralinne's common sense and curiosity, he rolled over in submission and whined pitifully. Maralinne held her ground. He approached a few steps and repeated his submission act. Maralinne's hand trembled on the broom. He took another few steps and rolled over a third time, inching forward until he could lay his muzzle on the toe of her shoe. Maralinne lowered the broom. Her eyes were wide with fear but he also noted the spark of curiosity he had hoped for. He rolled over at her feet whining his most pitiful whine. She reached down and patted his head. It was then she saw the leather pouch still on its thong about his neck. Cautiously she touched it. When the bear did not resist, she untied the pouch and looked inside.

"You are from Jareth? Is he alright?' she exclaimed when she saw the red lock it held.

She misunderstood who he was but Jareth was glad to have reached her at all.

"Avrille, come out here. Alone," called Maralinne.

Avrille left the porch where she had been waiting.

"Don't be scared," Maralinne warned.

Avrille saw the bear and froze.

"It's alright. He's from Jareth," Maralinne assured her holding up the pouch.

"The card! It's just like the card!" Avrille exclaimed. "Two women and a bear!"

Jareth moved in Avrille's direction and stopped. Slowly he approached Avrille again and lay down at her feet. He took the hem of her skirt in his teeth and pulled gently. Then he dropped her skirt, walked away a few steps, and returned to pull at her skirt again.

"What does it want?" she said with a shaky voice. "Does it want me to follow?"

Jareth tried to nod his head. He pulled at her skirt again, and again walked away a few steps.

"Why you and not me?" said Maralinne. "If he can lead you to Jareth then I am going too."

How could he tell her? This was not in the Watcher's plan. What should he do? He growled and pushed at Maralinne's legs until she stepped back.

"Why can't I go to him?" she almost sobbed. "Is he alright?"

Jareth pushed her back again then tugged at Avrille's skirt.

"Why?" Maralinne asked in desperation. "Why her and not me? If he's hurt or…he's hurt…that's it. Avrille's healing…"

Jareth nodded his great head.

"Please," Maralinne begged but the bear growled at her.

"What is it, Aunt Mari?" called Jasenth from the porch.

"Go back inside, Jayjay."

"A bear!"

"It's alright, this is a magic bear. He won't hurt us," said Avrille.

Jasenth jumped down from the porch. Jareth left the women to greet his nephew.

"Are you the bear from Auntie Avrille's cards? Here bear. Here bear," he said reaching up to pat the beast's head.

"Jayjay go get my shawl," said Avrille. "The bear wants me to take a walk with him."

"Will he help us find Uncle Jareth?"

"I think so. Now go get my shawl like a good boy."

Maralinne embraced Avrille. "Bring him home to me," she pleaded. "And I pray your sister is safe with him too."

Avrille took her shawl from Jasenth and followed the bear into the dark woods without saying goodbye.

Moonlight flooded the clearing when they arrived. "I know this place," said Avrille. "This is the place we came to when Uncle Hawke first brought us here."

Jareth walked the perimeter of the circle. Then he led Avrille to the flat stone in the center. A cloud slid across the moon. Darkness fell around them. The earth shook. A distant rumble raced toward them. Cold gripped them, intense and paralyzing, thrusting them into emptiness. Avrille clutched her stomach. The child inside her flailed his tiny limbs as they hurled through time and space. Helplessly she tossed and tumbled through torrents of electric fire. With one final jolt the child curled up and sank again into contentment. Where was she? The smoky air made it hard to breathe. It stung her eyes but she managed to force them open.

A figure in long dark robes was walking toward them. The Black Queen of the cards! She tried to take a step but her feet refused to move. The bear nudged her from behind. An intense longing and sadness enveloped her. The dark figure drew her taking on features not unlike her own. Time stretched toward the future dragging her with it. She cried out in protest. Then she felt herself being snapped back to the present. A gamut of emotions welled out from the figure. Despair shifted to surprise, then to unbridled joy. The dark woman ran to her. Her black hood fell back to reveal her face.

"Mother! Mother!" Avrille rushed into her arms.

"Who is it, Grandma?" called a child's voice behind her.

"Lizzie too!" Avrille whirled around, grabbed her niece and smothered her with kisses.

Lizelle began to laugh. "Uncle Jareth, you look so funny in a bear fur. Poof! I take it off." She snapped her fingers and Jareth's human form was restored.

Chapter 12

Janille ordered tea for her unexpected but very welcome guests. "Where shall we begin," she said. "How did you come here?'

"The real question is how you came here, Mother," said Avrille.

Janille idly smoothed the shiny, dark satin of her gown as she composed her tale. So much had happened in the two years since Avrille and Will's wedding and coronation. She had lost everything she knew and loved in one tragic moment. Now there were so many secrets she was forced to keep or the delicate balance between Light and Dark would forever tilt toward darkness. How much could she tell without jeopardizing Kyrdthin's plans or betraying his loving trust? She drew in a deep breath. "You know the events in the throne room on your wedding day better than I do," she began. "Tell me what you and Willy saw."

"Analinne and Tobar were on the star sign in the center of the floor," Avrille began. "There was this horrid black thing and a fire and they just disappeared." Avrille shuddered as she remembered the tragic event. "There was music and columns of rainbow light. Then the chandelier fell. Uncle Hawke fought the black thing. Then he fell down a big, dark hole. Everyone yelled and screamed. What a mess!" Avrille let her hands drop to her lap. "What a way to start our marriage!"

"Things are not so good between you and Willy?" her mother asked with concern.

Avrille shook her head. "That's another long story, but I need to hear yours first. Where is Uncle Hawke? Is he alright?"

Janille began thoughtfully, "Hawke called to me. I pulled him through to the world where I was waiting but there was nothing I could do. He was dying. There was nothing, nothing I…" her voice cracked as she fought back the tears.

"He's dead!" Avrille jumped up to embrace her mother. "Uncle Hawke can't be dead!"

"Hawke the man is no longer with us…but…well just let me tell my tale and maybe you can understand."

Avrille sat down. She would not accept what she had just been told. She saw her mother's grief. She felt her mother's shoulders shake with unvoiced emotion, but still she did not believe it was true.

Janille continued to tell what had happened. Her words came freer now. "I had no means to live in that alternate world alone, so at dawn I set the greatest funeral blaze I could for him. I chanted the home spell. I wanted to bring him back to give him the honor due to him. I wanted to come home to you and Willy and the babies. Yes, I knew you were pregnant even before you did."

Avrille looked a little disconcerted. "Go on, Mother."

"It was a strange passage, longer, colder than any I had made before. When I arrived I was in a place I did not know."

"Here?" asked Jareth pulling up a chair to join them.

"No…" she answered with much hesitation. "There is so much I want to tell you, so much I am not allowed to tell. Hawke was dead, and I followed him home instead of going home to the kingdoms. I saw things and learned things that no mortal is allowed to know. The gods will not allow me to come back because I could upset their plans. They put me here to wait and watch in silence until the time comes when secrets are no longer needed."

"But why? What is this place?" said Avrille.

"This is Bellarion, the realm once occupied by Belar the Dark Lord. He is no longer a prisoner here because Hawke overcame him and sent him home. But now I am here in this penalty box where the gods put offending players in their great game."

"But Why?"

"I can't say more, daughter. I could change the future, your future if I did. Please don't ask me more."

"When will they let you come home? They will let you come home won't they?"

"Soon I think. Their allowing you to come here may be my testing. I know I will be needed again in the kingdoms before the game is done."

"I need you now!" Avrille wailed giving her mother a desperate hug.

At that moment Borat arrived with tea. Lizelle skipped merrily beside him. "Can I take some tea to Mommy?"

"Elani is here!" Avrille and Jareth chorused.

"Mommy is sick," said Lizelle carefully holding a cup as Borat poured.

"Go see if she is still sleeping," said Janille. "I gave her chamomile with a drop of Freebane a little while ago. Your sister has been through too much to endure. She has broken. Her mind and will are shattered beyond my skills to repair."

"The Watcher said 'Bring the Queen of All Light to heal the broken mirror'," said Jareth. "I knew to bring Avrille but never guessed that Elanille…"

"The Watcher?" said Janille. "What dealings have you had with the Watcher?"

Jareth told his tale beginning with the search for Kylie. Avrille filled in with events of the boy's return to Frevaria.

"My men found the little rascal. He was camped at High Bridge as smart as you please," said Janille with a touch of pride. "They brought him down here just so I could have a glimpse of him. They only kept him overnight…"

"But he was gone two weeks!"

"Time runs slower here in Bellarion. Remember Hawke told us that the worlds coincide only at certain points and each turns at its own speed in time?"

Avrille shook her head. "I remember, but time twists never did make sense."

"They don't to me either," said Jareth half to himself.

"Well my men fed him supper and played soldiers with him until he fell asleep. In the morning I sent a party of five to escort him home."

"Five! There were thousands!" Avrille exclaimed.

"Illusions," said Janille with a sheepish grin. "I confess to wanting to strike fear in the breast of my ex-lord husband for all the pain he caused us. It seems I overdid it."

Jareth threw back his head and laughed.

"Father is dead," said Avrille disregarding Jareth's outburst.

"I did not intend that to happen," said Janille. "I called the storm but that is all. Lightening strikes where it wills once it has been freed. It was the will of the gods, not mine that took his life. Now that my grandson is king I know it was meant to happen and I have no regrets."

"With Cellina as regent," added Jareth.

"An unexpected but wise choice," said Janille. "I am proud of Will."

"I'm not," said Avrille.

Janille looked sadly at her daughter. "I wish I could have sent you more than just a dream of love."

Avrille jerked away. "That day at the Star Spring, you had a hand in that?"

"The gods willed the future but I wove the dreams you both remembered."

"Then my only moment of joy with Will was just a dream?" Avrille wept.

"No, no my darling." Janille placed a hand on her daughter's belly. "It all happened, your dream of love, Will's dream of glory and two sleeping children by the pool, three separate realities, all of them true."

"But I don't want another baby!"

"I have given you a hope and joy to keep you through the lonely years ahead," said Janille trying to comfort her.

Avrille folded her arms on top of her belly. "Lonely! I'd welcome some time alone. I need time to think. This is all so confusing. Three realities! And the one I end up with gets me pregnant!"

"We women are but granaries," Janille mused. "We are keepers of the seed until spring."

"If that's all we are, why do we have powers? Peasant wenches can satisfy kings as well as royal wives. There has to be more to life than this."

"Not for me," said Janille with unfathomable sadness.

Lizelle returned with an empty teacup.

"She is awake?" asked Jareth.

"She talks, but not to me," answered the child.

"The broken mirror," said Jareth half aloud.

"Yes," said Janille. "There is no hurry. Let us continue our conversations here a while. Elanille needs rest." She poured tea for all of them.

Lizelle held her cup with both hands. "Two sugars please, Uncle Jareth."

"There you are, little princess," he said giving her two heaping spoonfuls. "Tell me, how did you come here to live with Grandma?"

"I came when the lamp fell down," she answered matter-of-factly.

"Let me tell it, Lizzie," said Janille. "Here in this room are my mirrors." She swept her arm in a circle around her. When the worlds are aligned I can see into your lives."

"And be seen," said Avrille telling her about Jasenth's scrying.

"Yes, with any of the balances or extremes, the risings or settings of the houses of the gods, the mirrors become windows to what is or what may be. It is then that I have glimpses of those I hold dear. Only Lizzie knew me and responded."

"She used to insist that Grandma talked to her," said Avrille.

"And nobody believed me," said Lizelle setting her teacup down with a delicate clink.

"I foolishly thought that with her powers maybe she could help me escape." Janille lowered her voice. "I know differently now."

"Mommy made me scrub off all the pretty stars," Lizelle interjected.

"When the moon was full one night," Janille continued. "My spell was almost ready when…"

"The lamp fell down," said Lizelle.

"The passage was already open, but you know about the fire and all the rest. Lizzie was drawn here instead."

"Grandma saved me."

Janille patted her granddaughter's bright curls. "I'm so glad for the company. She is a good girl and is learning to use and control her powers. Yet the grief I caused dearest Elanille…" She stopped. Her face knit tight with pain as she thought of her elder daughter lying in the next room.

"We tried to tell her in the sunlight,' said Lizelle.

"The tournament!" Avrille exclaimed. "Elani saw you! Trebil did too!"

"I almost cost you Rogarth and young Anton did die. Whenever I try to reach into your world to guide events I cause some terrible tragedy…" Janille's voice failed her. She dabbed at her eyes and cleared her throat. "Even when what I do brings us closer to the balance, the price is pain to the ones I love." Her eyes fell to Avrille's hand resting on her abdomen. "The prophecy is true. None can change what we are…"

"None can change what we must be," Avrille finished for her.

"What must we do now?" asked Jareth.

"Take me to my sister," said Avrille as she stood up.

Lizelle led her to a small candlelit room. Elanille lay on a divan propped up with pillows. She was deathly pale and thin. "I'd like to be alone with her," said Avrille. When the door closed, she gently stroked her sister's brow, letting her fingertips send out warmth and calm. Elanille cried out in a weak, parched voice.

"No, sissy, no,"

Avrille brushed her sister's hair and tried to rearrange the quilts only to have Elanille cry out again.

"Sissy, no. Go away."

Avrille took a deep strengthening breath and let it out in a slow deliberate hiss. She pressed her hands to Elanille's forehead and let herself slide into the chaos of her sister's illness. A racing jumble of images assaulted her. Faces hovered over her, distorted, babbling, fading in and out of view. Some faces she recognized, Analinne, Sir Keilen, their mother Janille. Others were strangers, towering adults with stern, knit brows and wagging fingers. Their voices were critical and harsh. She felt a wash of fear and indignation as she relived her sister's early memories in Frevaria. She massaged Elanille's temples sending quietude and healing. Sir Keilen's face reappeared, then their father's. The two faces tilted and first one way then the other as their voices rose and fell. Her blood pounded in her ears. Passions rose and swelled, first with the ardor of Keilen's gallant pursuit, and then with anger at her father's stubbornness.

Avrille sorted through the fragments of her sister's memories, trying to fit the pieces back into meaningful patterns. She slid deeper into Elanille's mind until the images swirled inside her own head, assaulting her own perception of reality. She tumbled farther into the chaos, reeling with the faces and the cacophony of their voices. She tried to stop them with her healing spells but they fought back, threatening to engulf her.

A light but insistent flutter inside stopped her accelerating plunge. What was this new presence? She let it call her back into herself. As she withdrew from her sister's illness the fluttering stopped. Avrille placed a hand on the round of her abdomen. Was it her child? She felt a slight movement. Yes, her child had saved her. A welcome feeling of joy and contentment flooded over her as her own healing spells were mirrored back to her.

Elanille tossed in her pillows. "Go away. Go away," she said in a hoarse, childish whisper.

Avrille kissed her sister's cheek and left the room.

Janille ordered a meal for her guests. They sat in awkward silence while they waited for it to arrive. Small talk seemed inappropriate and the larger questions were either too painful to discuss or were forbidden to be discussed at all. The torchlight of the hall threw eerie shadows on the floor and the gargantuan sculptures on the capitals of the colonnade watched with glittering jeweled eyes. The five towering mirrors encircling the dark, carved wood of the dragon throne stood mocking gray and visionless. Borat's arrival was welcome. Their sadness was momentarily distracted by the food, but however well the preparation may have been, they found it tasteless. Jareth was restless, anxious to return home to Maralinne. Avrille was torn between the joy of being reunited with her mother and the fear of leaving her again. On one thing they did agreed, Elanille should return home to Frevaria if ever she were to be made whole again.

When they were finished eating, Borat carried Elanille's limp, sleeping body to the great doors. Tenderly he handed her to Jareth. "The Freebane should last a few hours, beyond that there is nothing I can do," said the dark-mailed servant, smoothing a stray curl back from Elanille's face.

Lizelle stood beside her grandmother. Her tiny mouth was pinched tight. Her eyes brimmed with tears as she looked at what was left of her mother.

"Are you sure we can't take Lizzie?" said Jareth.

"To Frevaria! No sorceress is welcome in Frevaria, not even a tiny one," said Janille giving the child a squeeze. "No, Lizzie and I will stay here together. Right?"

"Right, Grandma."

"Until when?" Avrille asked with pleading eyes. "Mother I need you."

Behind them the great, gray mirrors came to life. "April I need you," Will's voice rang through the hall. The torches on the walls guttered, threatening to go out. "April!"

Avrille ran to stand before the mirrors. "Where are you Will?" she cried.

The images in the left-hand mirror shifted. The iron superstructure of a bridge loomed overhead. The high-pitch sing of speeding tires on the steel grating of the bridge deck surrounded her. She screamed and screamed until the mirrors grew dark again and she felt her mother's arms wrapped around her. "I told him not to go back there. I told him," she sobbed.

"We don't know that he did, dear daughter. Sometimes the mirrors replay the past. They have shown this scene before, and also your gentle nursing his of hurts when he came home."

Avrille looked angrily at the mirrors. "Show me the truth," she demanded. "Show me why Will is calling me."

The central mirror lit up in answer. It was dawn. Pale orange fingers of light spread across the face of the glass and on to the adjoining mirrors. She viewed the Star Castle construction site from a high vantage point. She was freezing cold. The black wings that enfolded her offered no warmth. She tore herself away from the scene. "Will's at his stupid castle, I might have known. Well if he's that cold he should come home."

"April where are you?" his voice filled the hall with loneliness and despair. "Why won't you believe in me?" The mirrored scene receded as if she were flying high away from the castle, then suddenly she was falling. "Willy!" she cried. "Willy where are you?"

Once again the mirrors were gray and lifeless and the torches burned with bright tall flames.

"Let's go, Jareth," said Avrille. "Whatever Will has become, he needs me."

The great iron-hinged doors opened. As the blue tendrils of mist groped toward their feet and drew them into the void her mother's voice called after them. "It will not be long, my precious daughter. I will come to you when you need me most. I will come when the dragon flies."

"April, you can't just sit in a stuffy room all day," said Will. "Soon you will be as crazy as she is."

"She's my sister."

"She doesn't even know you're here. Why don't you come with me?" he said flashing her the grin Avrille had thought was long lost. "Let me show you the dream castle I'm building for us."

She was glad she let him persuade her. As the carriage jolted along the road she felt almost buoyant. Will chattered beside her. She was not interested in masonry and tile setting but it was good to be near Will again and to have him talk to her with such enthusiasm. Inside of her their child gave a little flutter. She reached for Will's hand.

"Feel him kick?'

Will could not feel the tiny stirrings, though the child somersaulted to match his mother's response to the touch. "Is he still doing it?"

"No he stopped now," she said. "He'll be much stronger later. Remember the twins?"

Will laughed. "Yeah and they're still pushing and shoving each other."

"You should have seen them when they met Darilla's twins," she said watching him closely. "They each grabbed a boy and tumbled him into a squalling heap."

Will looked away. "How are the star twins?" he asked with forced casualness.

"Haven't you seen them lately?'

"No."

She resisted the temptation to pursue the subject further. Part of her question had been answered. That was enough.

The scaffold-encased walls of Will's dream castle loomed above the trees. "See how the color of the sandstone walls contrasts with the white gypsum where it joins the towers? I wish those clouds would go away," he said shielding his eyes to look up at the sky. "When the sun is out the effect is unbelievable. Frevarian gold supporting Arindian silver, balanced, interdependent..."

The workers hailed the royal pair as they approached. Will guided the horses past the piles of cut stones and surveyor's lines to the almost completed north tower.

"We got the stairs done yesterday," he said with pride. "Are you game for a climb?" He lifted her out of the carriage. "Sweep the stairs," he shouted to a youth unloading some heavy sacks nearby. "The queen wishes to see the view from the top."

"Is that cement in those bags?" asked Avrille.

"You are observant," Will said with his quirky grin.

"Where in the kingdoms did you…?"

"Only a small appropriation from a place we both know," Will answered. "I'd use more things if these suspicious morons…"

"The Dark Lord did the same thing."

"It's not the same. It's…"

"It is so, Willy."

"Belar built an abomination to the Light at East Pass. We were right to destroy it. But this.…" He made a sweeping gesture across the courtyard. "This will be a glory to the Light. Just imagine it, with silver Arindon on one side and golden Frevaria on the other, this dazzling star will be the center of our universe." Will's face was radiant. "April, when this is done and the glass windows in the towers reflect the sun by day and glitter with torches by night…"

The youth reappeared in the tower doorway. "It's as clean as I can make it with just a broom, sire."

"It will be fine," said Avrille dismissing him with a smile.

Hand in hand the young king and queen ascended the tower stairs. Though Avrille was gasping for breath by the time she reached the top, she found the climb exhilarating. Will led her to the window facing the inner court. The making of his dream spread out before them. The ancient spring lay like a glassy eye in the center. The brush had been cleared but the trees remained. The vines were pruned and the wild flowers coaxed into walled beds. The surrounding area was being tiled in a rainbow-hued mosaic of stones. The walls rose star-shaped, already connecting three of the five towers.

"Are you pleased?" he asked with enthusiasm.

"Where will we live?" she said, not seeing evidence of any quarters beyond the towers.

"Later, later," Will brushed her question aside. "Have you ever seen anything like it?"

"Yes I have."

He gave her a puzzled look.

"I saw it in the cards, not just once but twice. The Fountain card and the Black Dragon card both had this exact same scene."

"So that proves it is our destiny!" he said grabbing her shoulders.

She pulled away from him, knowing she had made the right decision not to tell him about her recent venture into the Dark

Realm. She and Jareth had agreed to say that they found Elanille in the caves as Spida's prisoner. Of the Black Queen and her little companion they would say nothing.

"April I thought you would be pleased," Will said, his disappointment obvious in his tone.

"With a movie set? This is not a home. This is no place to rule a kingdom and raise a family."

"But you said the cards…"

"The Fountain I drew the night before our picnic here. The Black Dragon, Darilla drew for you."

Will laughed. He grabbed the ends of his black cape and flapped his arms up and down. "Beware! The Black Dragon is gonna get you, April," he teased as he danced wildly around the tower room.

"Stop it, Will. People will see you."

"Gotcha!" He lunged, enveloping her in the wings of his cape.

Struck with sudden terror, Avrille wriggled free and fled down the stairs.

Late that evening the second floor of the Frevarian household was quiet. Downstairs in the great hall dinner was over. A song floated up from Dell's harp, filling the time between dinner and sleep. The bard's music hovered in the real space between warmth of family and the cold shattered plane where Elanille drifted. Moonlight slid through the grillwork that barred her bedroom window. Broken patterns of white crept across the carpet and up the draperied bed until a full round face of light peered in on the sleeper lying there. Elanille tossed and cried out, then she snuggled back into her pillows again. This is how she had been since Jareth and Avrille brought her home four weeks ago. She had not recognized any of them. In her waking moments she stared wide-eyed from face to face. Then often as not she burst into tears. The Frevarian physician, fearful of magical maladies, refused to attend her. Queen Avrille had done what she could for her sister but she could not begin to put together the broken pieces of Elanille's mind and heart. At times Avrille did sense a fleeting recognition as her healing fingers probed to ease a troubled thought. Elanille would cry out, "Stop it sissy. Mommy, the baby's bothering again. Take her away." Then she would sob for her mother as if she were a child of three or four and not a mother herself. Confusing though this behavior was at first, in time Avrille realized that she was the baby sister in Elanille's babble.

When Kylie was brought to his mother's bedside, Elanille looked beyond him as if she could not see the child. Kylie had stood there a moment tightly clutching Lady Cellina's hand. "That's not my mommy," he announced, turning his back on the tormented figure in the bed. Lady Cellina followed him out of the room hoping to comfort him, but he was content in his denial and had no need of her.

Now in the moonlight Elanille cried out in her lonely room. She threw back the quilts and slid her thin legs out of the bed. Music played down the beam of light. Elanille responded to the fresh tinkling melody. She threw off her robe with a carefree gesture. The music was inside her, coursing through her blood, filling her, lifting her. Her bare feet padded across the cold stone floor to the door. She lifted the latch.

Through the dark hall and down the stairs she wandered. The household lounged drowsily by the fire, sated with dinner and Dell's song. No one saw the wraith-like figure pause on the landing. No one saw it glide through the door left open to the garden, or saw it slip past the nodding guard at the gate.

The music danced on the moonbeam. The road was dusty, yielding to pressure from her soft bare feet with a dry puff. Elanille seemed to float, drawn by the voices in the music. The moon climbed the sky above her, then sank slowly toward the west. The countryside was still in autumnal slumber. Not even a farm dog barked at her passing. Just as the stars were beginning to fade behind her, the voices enticed her from the road. The empty scaffolds and half-built walls of King Will's castle were but passing shadows as the music drove her on. The trees swayed with the melody. The scent of flowers hung heavy on the breeze. She drifted on singing, gaily unaware of the chill or her now bleeding feet.

"Star flower, moon blossom," she sang.
"Sweet scent of rue.
Fair flowers, fair fairies calling to you."

She entered the glade drawn by the scent of cool moss and ferns encircling the spring. Flowers floated on its still, mirror-like face. The setting moon drew a path across the quiet water. Elanille sang with the voices as she gathered the unearthly blooms. She draped her wasted form with garlands and wove them in her tousled hair.

"Sing of the flowers that circle the spring," her frail voice echoed.
"Bye low, bye bye low, the lone to home bring."

The moon path beckoned. She stepped out onto the cool, white surface of the water and fell. Her gown spread wide, buoying her up for a moment. The blossoms floated away in slow, widening circles then sank with her into the welcoming depths.

Chapter 13

The family was still at breakfast when the workman burst in with the news. In numbed silence they filed out to the gate to await the wagon which bore Princess Elanille home. The workmen who found her drowned in the spring that morning formed a makeshift honor guard beside the wagon. The princess's body was respectfully draped with their coats. Kylie stood at attention as the procession halted at the gate.

"What does your majesty wish to be done?" they asked him.

"Just like for Grandpa," he said. "But let's not wear black. My mommy likes blue. I decree everybody's got to wear blue until Solstice." He looked to Lady Regent Cellina for approval but her face was buried in grief against Mabry's strong shoulder.

Blue banners fluttered above the garden wall making dancing shadows on the lawn where Kylie and Nancie were playing. "I won!" Kylie pounced on Nancie's game piece and removed it with a flourish.

"No, you didn't," Nancie countered. "See I can take two of yours here."

"No, no you can't," Kylie wailed.

"It's just a game Kylie,"

"I am king and I can win if I want to."

"You are king and kings must learn to be just and fair."

"No, they don't."

"Let's play something else," said Nancie.

Dell watched Nancie gather up the game and take Kylie back to the shade of the tower before he tried to redirect his thoughts to the task at hand. Composing an elegy for the Princess Elanille was not easy. He toyed with the phrases but the words seemed ineffective. Golden child or moon wraith, which was she? Too frustrated to continue, he strapped his harp on his back and lowered himself over the wall. The jar of the long drop shook up his stomach but not his thoughts. He let out a deep sigh and set out over the fields toward Arindon.

He avoided the road, following the fence rows instead. When he reached a low knoll he stopped to rest, he looked back toward Frevaria and the elusive lines finally came to him.

"A flutter of blue
In the golden light..."

Yes that was good.

"The flower bloomed,
To hold back the night."

He resumed his walk humming the tune. A farm dog howled. Dell's gaze stretched out across the checkered fields to the village clustered against the blackened husk that had been Arindon castle. The dog howled again.

"Called by the Dark,
The flower fell.
All men and beast,
Sing her mourning knell."

"That's it," he said to himself quickening his stride.
"Ho Dell!" A workman spotted him from the wall of the Star Castle. Dell waved back. He was glad to join the workers now that his grim task was done.

King Will was angry. Mabry had ridden to Arindon village early that morning for an overdue visit with his family and to check on the mill. The workers at the construction site were slowing down and today without Mabry, nothing was going according to schedule. They did not see his dream. They did not feel the driving force that coursed in his blood. It was bad enough that they were only soldiers and farmers. Only a few were real artisans. Today their lack of enthusiasm bordered on insubordination. Once they had loved and blindly trusted their king, but now after weeks of relentless hard labor, they whispered treasons among themselves. Will knew he was losing control. His angry shouts masked his own fears and insecurities. How could he instill fear and obedience into grown men? If they were children he could say like nannies do, "Be good or the Dark Delven will get you." Will threw back his head and laughed out loud. That was it! Why not? He laughed again, this time with malicious anticipation.

The workmen shared their lunch with Dell. They sat in the shade of the wall they had built. Their shovels stood upright in a pile of sand. Dell took another swig from the water jug and cleared his throat. "That was good," he said and reached for his harp. "Here's a new line I'm working on." He plucked an unharmonious twang as he began his song.

"They are workmen strong,
Building the dreams of kings,
Working the whole day long,
While the lazy harper sings."

Loud guffaws and good-natured back slapping followed.
"But I'm immortalizing you," Dell pleaded with feigned offense.
"Sing us something to forget the king's dreams," said a young worker in farmer's overalls.
"Yes, sing us something we all know," added a veteran soldier.
Dell caught the tension. He had heard the whispers. With a glance up at King Will's dark silhouette on the wall he began "The Ballad of Keilen's Stand". The song had become quite popular since Kylie's coronation. The workmen joined in with the chorus.

"...and the fight lives on in Keilen's son.
The fight lives on in Keilen's son."

Will recognized the tune. That was all the push he needed to put his plan into action. He turned his back to the scene outside the wall. In front of him lay the half-finished courtyard and the spring. He reached out, concentrating on the spring, drawing its primal power into himself. From the dark interior of the west tower he began to weave an illusion. Slowly the darkness began to take shape. It grew and divided and grew again until five shadowy figures emerged. He let them feed through him on the raw power of the spring. The figures marched toward him. "Oh have I been clever or what?" Will congratulated himself. "Those uneducated bastards will work their tails off this afternoon or I'm not High King." He leaned over the wall with five Dark Delven warriors flanking him and called. "Ho, Dell. Put that harp away or I'll find a shovel with your name on it."

All eyes looked up.

"From now on," Will continued after he had their attention. "Each section will have a foreman." He gestured to his creations. He paused to measure the effect. "Back to work!" he shouted.

The stunned workmen picked up their tools without even exchanging a glance. Will positioned himself on the west tower wall, gleefully pulling the puppet strings.

"We need a diversion," Lady Cellina declared. "With Will's ridiculous project in the center of the kingdoms there is no time left for anything else." She maneuvered her bulk out of the creaking wicker chair. "I wish it would rain. Then we could have some men around court again."

"It has been dull lately," Lady Liella agreed.

"When is King Will's castle supposed to be finished?' asked Nancie.

"Not soon enough," Cellina commented with emphasis.

Lady Liella helped herself to another apple muffin. "I dearly love these, but they make them ever so much better in Arindon."

"A lot of things were better in Arindon." Cellina settled down in her chair again to console herself with the last muffin. "Will should be rebuilding Arindon instead of wasting time and manpower on that useless monstrosity of his."

"Especially the manpower," Liella giggled behind her napkin.

Nancie tried to hide her amusement by dabbing her mouth with her napkin.

"What we need is a ball, a grand ball," said Cellina. "I'm so tired of wearing this," she said plucking the front of her dark blue day dress.

"But we are in mourning," said her sister.

"Only until Solstice, and what better time to have a ball than Solstice."

"King Frebar, may he rest in peace, promised us parties and balls," pouted Liella. "But Kylie is too little to...."

"The royal dear will give us a ball if we tell him to," plotted Cellina. "His mother loved balls. Remember the one when we helped her win Sir Keilen?'

"And Maralinne and Rogarth's betrothal," said Liella with a sigh.

"Now that was glorious!"

"So much has changed," said Liella. "There are so few of us left."

"But we are left and still unwed," said Cellina bitterly.

Nancie pushed back her chair. "I will go tell His Majesty that his regent wishes to confer with him."

Lady Cellina startled her young maid with a kiss on the cheek. "Nancie, you are indispensable!"

"Just like her father," Liella giggled when the girl was out of earshot.

Queen Avrille was glad to be home again. She set about getting her house in Arindon village back in order from her long absence. She would send for Linelle tomorrow when the twins came back from the cottage. Today she wanted to enjoy the delicious solitude. When she finished unpacking her clothes, she looked through the pantry. "Fresh fruit," she said to herself. "I'm so hungry for fresh fruit and some good bread." She grabbed a basket. Going to Arindon market would be just what she needed. Yes, that was it, the freedom and the company of genuine, simple people. She paused by the mantel mirror to brush back her hair. The image shifted slightly. "Love you, Mother," she said blowing the reflection a kiss and headed out into the sunny street.

"Welcome back, Lady Queen," called Nelsie the tailor's wife. "See you're comin' along fine."

Avrille glanced down at the bulge beneath her dress. "He is starting to make his wants known now," she said patting her front.

"And they never stop. But of course you already know, double," the woman smiled and dropped a belated curtsy.

Avrille bought apples and pears. She bought a loaf of coarse, dark bread and some tiny honey cakes for the twins' return tomorrow. She wandered through the stalls, absorbing all the colors and smells. She chatted with the villagers and they brought her flowers and gifts and wished her well.

By late afternoon she was more than a little tired and hungry. She told the last knot of adoring children to, "Go back and help your mothers", and headed home. As she passed Beck's tavern she noticed a familiar figure cutting through the back yards and alleyways. Dell waved and made a sweeping bow.

"My Lady Queen is playing peasant today?" he called.

"And enjoying myself," she called back.

Dell did not enter the tavern as he had planned. He fell in step with Avrille instead.

"Will I have music to cheer my lonely supper?" she asked.

"You honor an humble bard," he said. "I am yours to command."

"You have news for me?" she said lowering her voice.

"News? Yes, I have news," said Dell. "And black is the color of it."

Three weeks before Solstice the rains came. Will was almost glad. Maintaining the illusion of Delven foremen from dawn to dusk had left him weak and sick. The work was progressing rapidly. The walls were up. The towers were completed all but the glass windows. The courtyard was paved and the gardens were laid out and ready for spring planting. He stood in the west tower doorway watching the rain pelt the stone stairs below. His face was drawn and thin. His eyes were dark-ringed and sunken. He coughed a deep chest-rending cough, and clutched his damp cloak tighter. The small, smoky fire in the tower room gave only a little warmth. He leaned heavily on the doorframe. He could not remember when he had eaten last. Purity of the fast added strength to any magic but that was not the only reason. He had stopped eating lunch with the workmen weeks ago. When the construction first began their elaborate noontime picnics were more like celebrations than work breaks. Then they had shared his dream and had returned to work singing. Now he had to keep a Delven foreman on the wall to ensure their return.

Night brought exhaustion. He longed for the lost evenings he had spent with Mabry, eating and drinking and talking at Beck's tavern. Now in the village he saw fear and distrust rather than welcome and respect. With nowhere else to go, the stark west tower had become his refuge. He ordered nearby farmers to send him supper but lately he was too tired to climb down to where the farm maids left their baskets on the stairs. More than once lately his illusions had begun to fade in the bright sunlight. Seeing this ironically made the men work harder. They feared magic more than what they had thought were flesh and blood Delven.

Will did not dare show his increasing weakness. He spent more and more time at the doorway of his tower. He clustered his illusions, making them easier to maintain and control. Today when the dark clouds rolled in behind him engulfing the castle he gave up. He sent the workmen home knowing that this time they would not return. A shiver ran through him. He coughed again and again. He was sick. He was alone. His stomach was empty beyond hunger. His head pounded, burning with fever. He shivered again. Sweat trickled down his temples. He had to have something to drink. He stumbled around the sparse room looking for the water jug. When he found it, it was empty. His hand shook. The jug fell and shattered on the stone floor. A drink, he had to find a drink. He staggered down the winding stairs. The rough wall scraped his hands as he groped for balance.

When he stepped out into the courtyard the downpour chilled him through and through, but it did not quench the burning inside of him. The spring, he had to get to the spring. He stumbled again and again. At last he dragged himself to the rim of the pool and plunged his whole head into the water. He drank and drank until his stomach rebelled with a nauseous roll. He tried to stand up but his legs gave way. He slumped over the stone wall and huddled beneath his sodden cloak. He did not see the lightening sizzle across the sky or feel the rumble that chased it to the east. Willarinth, High King of All Light, cried like a child for the only comfort he knew. "April, April, please help me," he sobbed.

The twins were playing with scraps of colored cloth as Avrille sewed. Linelle had asked to spend the evening with her family and Avrille had let her go. It was good to have the twins alone with her for a short time at least. She examined the red velvet gown draped over her lap. A ball at Frevaria had sounded like such a grand idea when the invitation arrived. Now she was not so sure. Altering the gown she wore for her last appearance at court had turned out to be more difficult than she anticipated. The line was loose and flowing but now she was not only six months pregnant, she had also put on some extra weight. She would need every inch she could borrow from the pleats and seams. She threaded her needle again, squinting in the lamplight.

"Mummy, Mummy," Arinda cried. "Mummy, mine!"

"The red ones are yours, Rindy. The blue ones are Rella's," Avrille said returning the scrap of blue silk to Arielle. Arinda kicked and screamed in protest, as her twin stuffed all the blue scraps into her mouth.

Avrille rocked her chair faster and faster. Outside the rain dashed against the windowpanes. She wished Linelle would return soon, but she had told the girl to stay the night if she wished. Finally she knotted her thread and snipped the ends. "Look girls," she said holding up the finished gown. "Look at Mommy's pretty dress. It's all fixed."

They stopped crying momentarily. It was then she felt the calling. The child inside her turned over. She gazed into the fire and thought of Will. Outside the lightening shot blue behind the shutters. Thunder rattled the door.

"April, April," a faint voice called through the storm.

"But Daddy," Nancie begged.

"I can't dance. I have enough trouble just walking, so I can't go to any ball," Mabry argued.

"But my lady is planning specifically on your being there," said Nancie putting on her most seductive smile.

"Lady Cellina cannot fix a leg that refuses to walk like a man much less dance."

"But Daddy, you know the steps. You used to…"

"Used to, it seems there is more than one problem with 'used to'," he said knitting his brows in mock ferocity. "I used to have a respectful and sympathetic daughter…"

"You still do, Daddy dearest," Nancie cooed sweetly. "That is precisely why I felt it my duty to inform you of my lady's plans so that you may…"

"Respectfully decline to attend," said Mabry with as much finality as he could.

"I don't think Lady Cellina would like that answer."

"I don't think so either," he admitted.

"Then what will you wear?" said Nancie grabbing him in a wild hug then dancing away. "My lady is wearing pink, bright pink."

"There are times I wish you were not too big a girl to turn over my knee," he said grabbing for her.

"And there are times you love me for being so clever," she said dodging him.

Mabry dropped his arms to his side in defeat and Nancie ran laughing from the room.

Frevaria castle was bustling with preparations. Though the plain blue mourning banners still hung for Princess Elanille, bright colors and ribbons and jewels were the topic of conversation as Solstice approached. Lady Cellina spent long hours with Cook and the steward, planning the feast. Though the guest list was long, she deliberated meticulously with each detail of protocol. To everyone's pleasant surprise Princess Maralinne and Jareth agreed to attend. They were bringing Jasenth of course, and Mabry's Darilla. It was going to be a magnificent event. Afternoon and early evening would be for the children. Kylie had ordered a puppeteer and races and games and such an assortment of sweets to be served that Lady Liella seriously questioned whether it was necessary for the children to attend dinner at all. Every royal and landholder's child under the age of fifteen was invited. Kylie was ecstatic. He shouted decrees until the staff was in an uproar and Lady Cellina had to gently take him in hand insisting he go to his room and play quietly for a while.

After dinner there would be music and a grand promenade and after that dancing. Lady Liella's plans featured many lady's choice dances and progressions to be sure that she would be well partnered. Cellina argued that kind of program was not at all appropriate for mature ladies. She favored couple dances in slower, more romantic tempos. Dell let them argue as he rehearsed his musicians. Later he tactfully helped them arrange a varied program with enough dances to keep all of them diverted until dawn.

* * * * *

"Shut up and drink it, Willy," Avrille ordered.

Will opened his mouth to object and she poured in the tea. He gulped and choked.

"Don't you dare spit it out, not even a drop."

"What the hell are you giving me?" Will's hoarse voice cracked but the emphasis of the question was not lost.

"Yarrow, lemon balm, elderberry and willow,"

"Why don't you just use your magic touch?"

"Not for pneumonia, Will."

"Gods, what stinks?" Will wrinkled up his nose.

Avrille handed him a second cup of tea.

"I'm not drinking something that stinks like that," said Will. "What are you trying to do poison me?"

"It's just chamomile…and a little valerian."

"Valerian, so that's what stinks. You are trying to poison me."

She tried to ignore his remark but he persisted.

"Like to see me suffer? Want to watch me die?"

The cup shook in her hand. Why did he have to be so obnoxious? She swallowed hard then smiled at him sweetly. "Sit up a little more, Willy," she said pushing another pillow behind him.

"I can sleep without your stinking tea," He slid down again.

She set the tea cup down with a forceful clunk. She grabbed Will by the shoulders and yanked him up again. He started to yell. She pinched his nose and when he gasped for breath she grabbed the cup and dumped the contents down his throat. "Swallow!" she ordered and left the room.

Her head pounded. She tried not to think but her anger would not let her thoughts rest. She had taken him in. It was her duty. He was her little brother as well as her husband and king, but she didn't have to be glad about it. In spite of her patient administrations he was not getting better. She cooled his fever with wet compresses. She brewed teas for him. Though he begged for "decent food" everything she gave him except for the blandest porridge came back up. He grew thinner and weaker. Often he raved in his deliriums of wielding dark powers and wreaking vengeance on imagined foes. The twins were afraid of him.

Linelle willingly took them to her mother's house rather than stay under the same roof with her once-loved king.

Avrille tended him alone with all her skill of herbs but she did not use magic. Her one attempt to soothe his troubled spirit on the night he first came to her met with such a blast of resistance that her unborn child leaped violently inside. She had doubled over with so much pain she feared she would miscarry.

She pushed the thoughts away from her and went to the kitchen to fix Will some broth. She was relieved to have finally gotten some medicine into him. As she ladled the thin soup into a bowl over bits of toast, she looked out the window. It was dismal outside. The whole world was gray and wet. She took a deep breath and returned to Will.

"Eat this and I'll cut you a slice of the apple pie Maralinne brought," she said setting the bowl down on the bedside table so she could light the lamp.

"Gimme the pie first."

"You'll just throw it up."

"Then there'll be room for your disgusting broth."

"Willy, be good. I'm really trying to help you." She held out a spoonful hoping this would not become as difficult as giving him the tea. She was too tired to fight him.

He grabbed the hand that held the spoon.

"Watch out or you'll spill!" She fought for balance. He pulled her down. His face felt hot against hers. His lips were dry as they rasped her cheek. His body shook beneath her. She let him hold her, not knowing whether to feel pity or anger or fear. Who was this strange, tormented man in her little brother's body? She held him, trying not to feel his anguish, trying not to care. His chest heaved against her as he started to cough. "It's OK, Willy," she said trying to disengage his embrace.

He clutched her tighter. "Don't let me die, April. Please don't let me die," he pleaded. His eyes were wild with terror.

She pushed back the wet, dark curls clinging to his forehead. "It's OK, Willy. It's OK," she said rocking him like a child.

"Then give me that piece of pie," he whimpered, wiping his tears on her sleeve.

Avrille ran from the room.

Chapter 14

At last Will's fever broke. He woke up one morning shouting, "Hey April, when's breakfast?'

Slowly Avrille roused from her long vigil.

"How come you're sleeping in the chair?" he asked.

"Feeling better, Willy?" she said sleepily.

"I'm hungry."

"OK I'll fix you something."

She padded across the cold floor with numbed feet. Her ankles were swollen. "I should have propped them up last night. I should have gone to bed," she mumbled to herself as she entered the kitchen. She uncovered Trebil's cage. "Morning, birdy love," she cooed. She stirred up the fire. Water still simmered in the pot. Good, she could have a cup of tea before she began Will's porridge.

"April?"

"I can only move so fast."

"It's Ok. I just wondered where you went."

"I'm in the kitchen making your breakfast like you ordered."

"Aren't you sour this morning!"

Avrille stirred the porridge slowly so the boiling did not stop. She readied the tray, tea in the little lidded cup, bowl, spoon, napkin, honey, cream and dried fruit. She spooned the porridge into the bowl then picked up the heavy tray. She walked back to Will's room praying her clumsy feet would get her there without dropping it. Will was sitting up, wobbling on the edge of the bed.

"You look a sight, April. Don't you ever brush your hair?"

She did not drop the tray. She stood there immobile, shutting out everything. She did not see Will rise on unsteady feet. She did not feel him remove the tray from her frozen hands.

"Come on, April, sit down. I'd carry you but with the shape I'm in we'd both end up on the floor."

She sat down on the bed.

"Where's your hairbrush? I'll get it for you."

"On the mantel."

Will started across what seemed to be a vast uneven expanse of living room. How he wished his stomach would stay still. He reached up to the little box by the mirror where Avrille kept her hair things and stopped. The bright surface of the glass caught his eye. He swayed, groping for the rocker to steady himself. The image in the mirror held him fixed. Overwhelming sadness poured out of the vision. A voice from his deepest memories sang the words of the prophecy. "None can change what we are. None can change what we must be."

"Are you OK?" called Avrille.

"Why didn't you tell me this room is five miles long?" Will tried to laugh. He made it back to the bed and sat down with a plop. Avrille reached for the hair brush.

"No let me," said Will.

With loving playfulness he loosened her straggled braids. Her thick, dark hair tumbled its full length down her back and across Will's lap. He brushed with steady strokes until it shone with dark brilliance. She sat unmoving, glad that her back was turned. She did not want him to see the turmoil of emotions that played across her face. This was everything she wanted. This was everything she dare not feel for fear of losing it again.

Will laid the brush aside and pulled her back into the bed with him. He reached around her waist until his hands could feel the rippling movements of their child inside. He buried his face in the silken softness of her hair. Avrille let go of her fears and sank into the deliciousness of the moment. Soon they were both asleep.

Will awoke with the noon sun bright in his eyes. What was that noise? Knocking? The door? Somebody was at the door. He slid his legs over the edge of the bed. "Steady," he told himself as the room did a sudden shift. The knocking persisted. He felt along the wall, making his way to the door. When he opened it the two young boys standing outside took one look at him and ran. Disoriented for a moment, Will did not recognize Mabry's ten-year-old twins, but when he did he called after them, "Tad! Tam! Ho boys!"

They stopped and turned but made no move to come back.

"Queen Avrille is resting," Will shouted to them. "Can I do something for you?"

The boys elbowed each other until Tad took a step forward. "Sire, we had a message to say for her."

"And we're to get the market list," added Tam.

Will beckoned to them. The boy's looked at each other.

"Come on fellas," he called. "I guess I look a sight. I've been sick. You heard, no doubt?"

They nodded. After another moment of hesitation they returned to the porch.

"Who is it, Will?" called Avrille from inside the house.

"Mabry's boys."

"Send them in," she said as she drew on her robe. "Tad and Tam have been my lifeline lately."

The boys bowed with courtly style as their queen approached.

"Aunt Cellina has been working on you two I see," said Will with a mischievous grin at Avrille.

"Sit down, Will," she ordered handing him a small blanket from the rocker. "You aren't better yet."

Will sank deep into the rocker. Avrille arranged the blanket over his knees. "Now we can receive our courtiers," she said. "Master Tad, Master Tam, you have a message?"

"Yes, Lady Queen," Tad began his recitation. "His Royal Highness King Keilen sends his greetings and inquires after his uncle's health..."

"Wishing him well," added Tam.

"I know my part," said Tad with a poke at his brother.

"Lady Regent Cellina inquires after the health of the queen and her children," recited Tam. "And wishes to confer..."

"That's my line," said Tad stepping in front to Tam. "Wishes to confer with her concerning the Solstice Celebration."

Will rolled his eyes. "Our dear aunt is overdoing it, don't you think, April? These boys used to be proper ruffians and now look at them. How are these silver-tongued gentlemen ever going to learn to run my mill?"

"We help Don in the mornings," said Tad.

"In the afternoons we attend his majesty," said Tam

"His majesty?"

"King Keilen, sire."

"We get to go riding, and hawking, and to the practice yard," said Tad with boyish enthusiasm.

"And we can read and cipher, or at least I can," said his twin.

Avrille handed the boys a slip of paper and a small purse. "I added some 'real' food to the list, Will, now that you are better." She turned to the boys and said, "Be sure to stop by the baker and pick out something for yourselves."

The twins bowed correctly but with less formality this time, then they scampered off to the market.

"Speaking of food," said Will. "What happened to my breakfast, you lazy woman?"

Avrille waddled back to the kitchen smiling.

The next weeks were filled with a deep sense of joy and well being. Will's recovery was slow but steady. Days were spent in pleasant banter with Avrille as she sewed baby clothes and puttered around the house. The weather outside was wet and winter dreary but by the fire they were warm and secure.

One afternoon Linelle arrived with a bundle held beneath her cloak to keep it dry. Inside were dresses her mother and sisters had sewn for the royal twins to wear for Solstice.

"Oh Linelle, they're darling!" squealed Avrille holding up the tiny velvet dresses. Arinda's was red and Arielle's was blue. "Now let me show you what Aunt Cellina sent for them," she said reaching for a small box on the mantel. She lifted out two pairs of hair bows. One pair was red satin and silver lace, the other blue and gold. "They are too little to wear tiaras so she made them these."

"They are pretty but Arinda won't keep one in long enough for you to tie the other," said Linelle. "Her hair is always a mess."

"All we need is a few moments for her to walk the promenade. Then she can run naked for all I care,' said Avrille.

"She probably won't wait that long, My Lady."

"I really miss my babies. Why don't you bring them over if this horrid rain ever stops? Will is much better now."

"As you wish, My Lady," said Linelle. "The sky was lighter in the west when I came. Perhaps by teatime…"

"Tea, yes," said Avrille already planning what cakes to serve. "Dress them up pretty. Will hasn't seen them for weeks."

The carriage jostled along the muddy road to Frevaria. It had snowed, then melted, then snowed again. King Will, Queen Avrille and the twin princesses rode in style, bundled up in blankets and furs. Tad and Tam shared the driver's seat on top, sitting tall and proud in their new coats and boots. When they neared the halfway point, Will pulled Arielle onto his lap. "See the castle," he said pointing out the window. "That will be yours when you grow up."

"Mine!" said Arinda climbing up to see too.

"For both my girls," said Will.

"No, mine!" Arinda insisted.

"We could lock each princess in their own tower," suggested Will only half in jest.

"All three of them," said Avrille as she felt the baby kick inside, countering the rhythm of the carriage.

"When shall the three be five?" said Will suddenly. "There are five towers."

"One pregnancy at a time Will, please."

"There are always my two boys. That makes five."

Avrille shot him a look with multiple meanings. Relief that Will thought this could be her last pregnancy was clouded by jealousy that he considered Darilla's twins on an equal level with her own. She chose to make no reply. The remaining five miles of the trip were busy with small talk and keeping the girls occupied.

King Kylie was wild with enthusiasm. The day of the Solstice celebration was sunny and crisp as if made to order. He had been awake and running since before dawn. Lady Cellina was beside herself with keeping tabs on him in addition to supervising the last minute preparations for the grand extravaganza she had planned. By noon she was puffing down the corridor toward the main hall, dabbing the perspiration beading on her forehead with her lace handkerchief when Mabry saw her and took pity.

"Need I carry you off to your room and order you a bite of lunch?" he said taking her elbow and slowing her down to a reluctant stroll.

"Oh you dear man," Cellina panted and blushed even redder than she had been before. "Whatever am I to do with Kylie? He is just impossible today."

"Let him just have fun with the other children. He is a boy first, then a king," said Mabry steering her toward her apartments.

Cellina leaned on him heavily. "You are so right. What ever would I do without your experience with children?"

Mabry smiled to himself as he escorted her to the quiet of her private sitting room and rang for refreshments.

By afternoon the celebration was in full swing. King Kylie and the boys raced their ponies through the snowy slush, around and around the practice yard, swinging their wooden swords in a raucous melee. Rosy-cheeked children were everywhere, oblivious to the cold snowflakes flying in the air. The swing that was set up for the girls in the courtyard was unoccupied but the croquet balls and quoits splashed from puddle to puddle. A sack race was in progress on the flagstone path between the herb garden and the kitchen gate. A juggler entertained in the hall before the roaring fireplace where nurses herded their charges periodically to dry off and warm up. There was a puppeteer and indoor games of blind man's bluff and charades. Most of the little lady guests remained indoors but they were just as wild as the boys outside. Mugs of steaming cider were served and more sweets than their eyes ever wished for or their stomachs could hold. Frevaria castle had never known such noise.

The royalty of the twin kingdoms were gathered in the atrium before the gilded doors of the great hall. The herald was poised waiting for the signal. Avrille retied Arinda's hair bow for the third time. Kylie strutted around the room brandishing his small sword, trying to get a reaction from Jasenth. The smaller boy was held in check by his aunt's steeled grasp. In the corner Lady Liella tugged discretely at her sister's bodice lacings.

"I know this is right, but is it really?" Cellina said behind her hand.

"We have talked this all through, sister," Liella whispered.

"How do I look? Tell me honestly," asked Cellina with almost girlish indecision.

"You look spectacular!" said Liella stepping back.

"Oh Liella, this is such a big moment." Cellina's voice trembled just a little, then she drew a deep breath. She faced the center of the room with her head held high. She cleared her throat. "Herald, begin," she commanded.

The doors swung open. The trumpet blared. "Their Majesties, King Willarinth and Queen Avrille."

The room was suddenly quiet. The royal couple stepped out into the tense silence. All eyes turned to behold those whom they both loved and feared. Will drew his thin frame tall and straight. His ceremonial armor was buckled as tight as possible but it was still too big. He stared ahead. Avrille walked beside him sharing his unease. She set a smile and fixed her eyes on the thrones at the end of the long, long hall.

The trumpet blared again. "The Princesses Arinda and Arielle escorted by King Keilen and Prince Jasenth."

Avrille held her breath. Could they, would they do it? The four royal children walked forward. Kylie, proud in his miniature golden armor held Arielle's hand, supporting her toddling steps in her new blue velvet slippers. A murmur of admiring 'ohs' and 'ahs' rippled through the hall. Jasenth had the more arduous task. Looking grand in copper silk and green leather, he held the hand of his fretting charge in a vice-like grip. Arinda marched beside him. Her wee brows were knit in a defiant scowl. Her hair bows were untied again.

"Behold the red velvet terror," Will leaned over and whispered to Avrille.

"One more minute, please gods, one more minute," she answered between clenched teeth.

Halfway down the hall Arinda screamed, "No hold! No hold!" She wrenched her hand free and broke into a run. "Mummy, Mummy, Jayjay hurt Rindy!"

"Come back here. Come back here, Rindy. I decree!" shouted Kylie running after her.

The hall exploded with laughter then quickly stopped when King Will rose from his chair.

"You bad girl, Rindy," said Kylie catching up with her. "You spoiled my procession."

Arinda burst into tears. Will picked her up and turned to Kylie. "Disciplining the royal princesses is the duty of their parents. It is not the duty of their cousin irregardless of his status." To the assembly he said with an embarrassed grin, "Shall we proceed?"

As the heralds trumpeted Kylie sat down in his little golden chair to nurse his indignities. Meanwhile Jasenth had taken the abandoned Arielle by the hand. He quietly delivered her to her mother and took his assigned seat.

"Princess Maralinne and her consort Jareth," the herald announced.

The tongues that had wagged at her peasant frock at her last court appearance were stopped dead in awe this time. In copper silk embroidered with red and silver leaves, Maralinne presented herself with all the radiance and glamour she had flaunted in her youth, tempered now with confidence and maturity. Her fiery hair fell in braided loops behind her ruby and silver crown. Jareth walked modestly beside her. He wore the colors of the forest in green silk and unadorned gray leather. After the king and queen received them they took their places beside Jasenth's little silver chair.

Once more the herald's trumpet sounded. "Lady Regent Cellina and Lady Liella."

Cellina waited until all heads had turned before she stepped through the doors. In fuchsia satin she exploded into the hall. The rustle of her gown swelled like a symphony, keeping time to the rhythm of her steps and the bounce of her bejeweled bosom. In her wake tripped Liella in a pink lace gown embroidered with wildflowers, a mere shadow to the vibrant full-blown rose that was her sister.

When they had taken their places, Cellina nodded to Kylie. Still sour from his public reprimand he stood up and shouted, "Let our feast begin!"

The hall burst into a flurry of activity. Servants carried in the long tables. Plate was laid in alternating settings of Arindian silver and Frevarian gold. Allarian crystal goblets were set for the high table. Candles and evergreens entwined with ribbons and candied fruit adorned the long white tablecloths. There was roast venison, decreed by Kylie of course, grilled fish and small fowl. There were herbed salads and egg dishes, long loaves of bread, wheels of cheese both fresh and aged, bowls of fruit and pitchers of steaming spiced wine and ale. Cook had out done himself.

Dell's stomach did a roll of anticipation. The musicians would dine well after the feast tonight but now they had to entertain. He nodded the signal and the music began. A gay little melody wove in and out of the festive chatter of voices, filling the hall with joyous song.

When the dining tables had been removed, Lady Cellina nodded to Kylie. "Now," she whispered.

King Keilen stood up to survey his subjects. "My Aunt Queen Avrille has told us about a Solstice custom she and Uncle King Will did in the land where they was fostered. It's called Crismisgifts. And we thought it sounded like fun, so we're gonna do it here, I decree, every year."

Cellina handed him two wrapped and ribbon-tied packages.

"These are for my cousins Rindy, I mean Arinda and Arielle," said Kylie.

"Princesses," corrected his regent.

"Princess cousins," said Kylie.

"Now give them to their mother."

Avrille received the gifts with a smile and with Linelle's help the baby princesses unwrapped the little rag dolls Lady Liella had made for them.

Next Kylie handed a package to Jasenth containing an embroidered shirt also lovingly sewn by Lady Liella. "And I'm supposed to say too that when you're big enough like me you can come to foster in Frevaria."

Maralinne's face registered momentary panic, but she regained her composure to reply, "We are indebted to Frevaria to show concern for the education of my sister's child. When he reaches the proper age we will discuss this generous offer and make decisions based on the circumstances of the time. For now, please accept our deepest appreciation." She paused for a breath. "And now, Your Majesty, Prince Jasenth has a gift for you.

Kylie jumped up and practically grabbed the small bow and quiver of arrows that Jareth had made for him. Cellina nodded her thanks and quickly confiscated the toy saying, "Perhaps Jareth will give you a lesson in the morning."

After Queen Avrille had presented Kylie with a cap, gloves and scarf which she had knit in bright blue wool, King Will stood up with a long flat box in his hand.

"Kylie, this is an educational toy modeled after a weapon in the land where I was fostered," he said opening the box. Inside were three tubes, two blue and one gold, along with several attachments. He removed the gold-painted one. "What you do is take out the stopper in the top like so, and pour in a bit of water." He drained his wine goblet and reached for the water pitcher.

"Not here!" Avrille exclaimed.

Will just grinned at her as he poured water into his goblet. Next he demonstrated the use of the funnel-shaped attachment and poured a thin stream from the goblet into the tube. "Then you stopper it up again and hold it like so." He wrapped Kylie's hand around the curved handle of the tube. "The finger goes on the little trigger piece here. Inside there's this little spring connected, see? Now raise your hand." He showed Kylie how to sight along his arm. "Ready?"

Kylie nodded.

"Squeeze the trigger and shoot."

"Will!" Avrille screamed as a jet of water spurted across the room.

Kylie jumped and shouted with delight. Lady Cellina stood with her mouth agape in horror.

Will laughed. "And my dear Aunt Cellina, so that you don't think I would render Frevaria defenseless, please note that I have demonstrated only one of the three gifts in this box." He lifted out the two blue tubes, identical in function to the gold. "I am told that Master Tad and Master Tam now attend King Kylie."

"Yes sir, Uncle Will. They are my bestest friends."

"You and your friends can learn together the lesson these water pistols were designed to teach."

"Which is?" challenged Cellina.

"Let me see if I can quote the proverb exactly," said Will trying hard to conceal a grin. "For every action there is an equal and opposite reaction." With that he snapped the box shut and handed it to Kylie. "Learn your lesson well, nephew."

"I will! I will!" Kylie shouted as he hugged the box and ran back to his chair.

Lady Cellina rose to speak. "Your young king has been so caught up in the enthusiasm of this new gift giving custom that he asked what to give to myself and my sister. Not wishing to discourage his generosity, a noble trait in a ruler, we agreed to indulge him."

Kylie jumped to his feet. "For my Auntie Lady Liella. Ready? Attention! Company forward! March!"

The palace guard from both kingdoms paraded in side by side, thirty men strong. Lady Liella blushed behind her pink lace handkerchief. The young Frevarian captain bowed and kissed her hand.

"Will My Lady honor us with a dance?"

Choking back a nervous giggle she stood up and took his arm. Dell signaled the musicians and the lilting music began. Each guardsman waltzed with Lady Liella. She blushed and beamed as she daintily turned with light practiced steps. Round the gallant circle she danced. The guardsmen solemnly performed their duty with military precision. Last to partner her was Rogarth. As the music swelled then floated away he twirled her in a grand finale and escorted her back to her seat. Exhausted she sank back into her chair like a wilted bouquet.

The guardsmen filed out and Lady Cellina rose to speak again. Her face was red. Her fingers nervously twisted her handkerchief. "Your Majesty." She dipped a quick curtsy to Kylie. "For myself I wish nothing more than to reward those that have been so very kind and generous to us through all the harsh events this last year." She paused.

Glances were exchanged and questioning eyebrows rose as a murmur rippled along through the hall.

"There is a man," Cellina continued. "A man and his family who have contributed enormously to the well being of the kingdoms and to us personally." She paused again, this time to clear her throat. "Mabry, Master Miller of Arindon, will you please step forward?" she said a bit louder than necessary to be heard.

Mabry sat there, overcome with embarrassment. First his face was white with shock, and then a brilliant red flush started to spread up from his collar.

"Go on, Daddy," Nancie prompted.

Mabry rose slowly to his feet. With irregular steps he limped to the space before the dais. He gave one pleading look at Will then he dropped his eyes to study his boots.

"This man's talents," Lady Cellina was saying, "They were first recognized and put to use by King Willarinth himself. All of you have seen his mill and other accomplishments. His sons, Masters Tad and Tam, now attend His Young Majesty. His elder daughter, Mistress Darilla, serves Princess Maralinne and his younger daughter, Mistress Nancie, serves myself." Again she paused, obviously agitated.

"What's she up to?" whispered Will.

"I'm afraid to guess," Avrille replied.

Mabry shifted his weight, not daring to move even to wipe the perspiration now beading on his forehead.

Cellina continued to speak. "My role as regent is no easy task. To properly nurture your young, orphaned king, I have had to assume the multiple roles of parent, and schoolmistress as well as household manager and stateswoman. This selfless man..." She reached out her hand to the quaking figure before her. "He has generously offered to us the wealth of his experience. Therefore..." She paused longer this time, twisting her handkerchief through her be-ringed fingers.

"Oh no!" Avrille gasped behind her hand.

"Therefore...to this man, Mabry the Master Miller, if King Keilen wills it, I give my hand in marriage."

Silence, complete silence followed her proposal. Not a breath, not a whisper, not a shuffle nor a stir, there was only silence. Then King Will threw back his head and laughed. He laughed heartily like men do leaning over their ale at Beck's tavern. He laughed at the masterful joke played on his best friend. Mabry stood alone in the center of the room, reddened down to his very boots. But as the grave reality of the situation suddenly struck Will, his laughter changed. Everything had started out so grand. He and Mabry had changed the face of the kingdoms together. He laughed on, this time harsh with growing anger. His best friend had betrayed him. His voice cracked and still he laughed, sobbing in self-pity. Hoarse but still unceasing his laughter rang through the shocked, silent hall. It floated up and out of the castle, out across the fields where it mingled with the howls of farm dogs baying at the Solstice moon.

Dell's fingers reached for his harp. He began to pluck a merry tune. Couples spilled out onto the dance floor, eager to escape the tension of the moment. Nurses scurried the children off to their beds so their elders could revel the rest of the night without interruption. A few adolescent maids hid on the landing of the stairs. Queen Avrille smiled when she saw them, remembering her first view of a royal ball from just such a place. How much had changed since then! She looked at Will and surreptitiously reached for his hand.

Rogarth approached the thrones and knelt. "It is customary for the queen to favor her champion with a dance," he said.

Avrille felt Will's cold fingers tighten. "My friend," she said smiling to Rogarth. "Dancing with you is always a pleasure, but tonight, my fair knight champion, my place is here with my lord." She looked at Will's pale agonized face, then turned back to Rogarth. "Honor me by dancing with another lady of my choice."

Rogarth studied her face as he asked, "Whom does My Lady choose?"

"See the maid in yellow on the landing?" she said pointing discretely.

"Cellina's Nancie?"

"Yes, now be a true queen's champion and thrill the little lady with your charms."

He dutifully kissed her hand and walked to the foot of the stairs. "Mistress Nancie," he called.

The startled girl backed away fearing she was to be disciplined for spying on her elders.

"Be a good girl and come down," said Rogarth with a smile. "Your queen wishes you to have a dance with me.'

He reached out his hand. Nancie floated down the stairs. As he offered her his arm, Nancie tossed back her tight brown curls and drew herself up tall and proud. Rogarth swept her into the dance. In her flowered dress and yellow-starched pinafore, she bobbed and twinkled like a butterfly in a sunny field. He led her skillfully through the figures and turns and promenades. When the music ended he escorted her back, not to the stairs but to the corner where her sister Darilla sat quietly with Don the miller's journeyman.

The evening wore on. Dell orchestrated the events with care. The musicians under his direction kept the tunes light and fast, but he felt the pull and sway of powerful forces as the characters of his next epic verse struggled in the room. He sensed their fears masked in gaiety as they tampered with the eternal balance here at the apex of the year. Lady Cellina had been very clever but what else had her meddling done beyond achieving her own ends? She had obviously pitted young King Keilen against Prince Jasenth with King Will and Queen Avrille trapped in the center. The arrangement of chairs on the dais, the meticulous protocol, even the subtleties of speech and gesture thrust and parried the forces at play in the hall.

At last midnight arrived. Dell gave the signal. The torches were extinguished. The music changed to a dull heartbeat on the drum. White streams of moonlight flowed through the upstairs windows flooding the hall. Dancers groped for their candles and put on their masks for the Solstice ritual. Servants carried an unlit brazier to the center of the hall. Dell laid his harp aside. He circled the brazier once, twice, three, four, five times as he chanted.

"One for Dark and one for Light,
One for Day and one for Night…"

The voices in the room picked up the chant.

"One for Silver and one for Gold,
One for Youth and one for Old…"

Hands grasped hands in a long line walking behind the bard.

"Round and round the Seasons turn,
Winters freeze and summers burn…"

Last to join the line, King Will and Queen Avrille closed the circle. Holding their candles in their hands the masked dancers converged on the dark brazier.

"Round and round the circle turns,"
"One for Beauty," soloed the ladies.
"One for Love," soloed the men.
"One for Wisdom," sang the ladies again.
"One for Strength," sang the men.

Dell reached for the flint and steel he had hidden up his sleeve.

"One to chase the dark away,
Before we die and fade away."

"…fade away," the room echoed the refrain.

The masked figures giggled as they clutched their candles and shuffled in the dark. Dell raised his hand to strike a spark but Will caught his wrist and held him back. Will faced the center of the room. He thrust out his arms. Blue flames leaped from his fingertips and ignited the brazier. Several of the ladies screamed and swooned, but before a general panic could set in the fire died down to a friendly orange glow. Queen Avrille lit her candle from the golden brazier and removed her mask. One by one the others followed her example.

It was almost dawn. The dessert tables had been cleared and the revelers had all gone to bed. Dell sat alone by a window trying to capture the night's events in verse but without much success. At first he did not notice a cloaked figure gliding silently toward him.

"Up late or is it early, Dell?" said Will.

"There was much afoot tonight. Eyes that see too much have trouble sleeping," answered Dell.

Will raised his eyebrows and gave Dell a hint of a grin.

"Shall I sing for you, Sire?"

"Not yet, friend, but soon there will be much more to sing about."

"How so?"

"You saw Cellina's well-intentioned bungling. Two kingdom's treasures, both crowns, both thrones, both swords all neatly collected and paraded out for everyone to see. Then Kylie and Jayjay neatly balanced while the scale rocks precariously in Frevaria's favor. Tell me Dell, what holds up the arms of a scale?"

The bard thought for a moment. "The pedestal in the center, sire."

"And where is the pedestal in the center of the kingdoms, my gifted friend?"

Dell nodded as he recognized the clever analogy. "Your new castle lies in the center…"

Will slapped Dell's shoulder. "Yes, there the balance will be achieved. There my children, all five of them, will shine like stars."

"Five, Sire?" Dell was puzzled. "Do you mean your daughters with young Keilen and Jasenth and your child to be?"

Will smiled a secret smile. "You underestimate me, Dell. Kylie and Jayjay have nothing to do with my plan. Stick with me, Dell and come equinox you will no longer be singing idle ballads. You will be chronicling history!

Chapter 15

The wet rainy days of late winter were difficult for the royal household. Will's health took a turn for the worse after Solstice, but now except for a lingering cough he was well again and very restless. The little house in Arindon seemed much too small with the twins' whining and fussing. They all waited anxiously for a clear day, especially Avrille. The dampness made her ache all over. Sitting by the fire did not help. No chair was comfortable any more. Walking and standing made her feet swell and doing any kind of housework or helping Linelle with the twins hurt her back. Being eight and a half months pregnant was awful.

Finally late one afternoon the sky cleared. Will took the girls out to the porch to play. Avrille stretched out on the bed to nap in the welcome quiet. When she awoke it was almost dark. Linelle was feeding the girls their supper but Will was nowhere to be found.

"Did he say anything when he left?' Avrille asked Linelle.

"No, My lady."

"If he's drinking at Armon Beck's again he's in trouble," said Avrille reaching for her shawl.

"Do you want me to go for you?"

"No, Linelle. What I am going to say to him if I catch him there would be considered treason coming from you."

Avrille jumped puddles across the muddy street. The fresh air felt so good she almost lost her anger. The lights from Beck's tavern spilled out into the street with laughter and the clink of glassware. She did not want to go in. Queens did not go into taverns looking for wayward husbands, but what else could she do? She pushed open the door. Mugs clunked down on the long wooden tables. All eyes turned. The innkeeper wiped his huge hands on his apron and executed a court-worthy bow.

"Has anyone seen the king?" said Avrille.

"No Lady Queen." "Not Me." "No, My Lady."

Avrille looked around the roomful of shaking heads. Armon Beck waddled out from behind the bar. He dusted off the best seat by the fire and said, "My humble hospitality is at your command, Your Majesty."

Avrille hesitated. These rough men were her friends as well as her subjects but the queen should not sit in a tavern unaccompanied. She looked down at her swollen feet and that decided the matter. She had to ask their help. She took the chair and before the innkeeper could ask, she ordered, "A glass of plain water if you please."

Armon Beck poured a dipperful of water from the cistern into one of his best goblets. Avrille sipped it slowly, enjoying the attentions of her rustic court until a man in tan shirt and hose approached her.

"Mebbe I got a clue, Lady, on the king's whereabouts."

"Tell me," she said smiling at his awkward bow.

"Mabry's in town. He come flying through here a while back in a new yellar paint cart. He dint stop to jaw with none of us. Gone straight ways to the mill he did."

"Thank you," said Avrille trying to rise up from her chair.

The man glanced quickly to his companions for approval then offered the queen his arm.

"Would some one please escort me to Mabry's mill," she said when she was on her feet again.

"Take my cart," Armon Beck quickly volunteered. "You, Jude, and you, Ross, sweep it out and lay a clean blanket on the seat for Her Majesty."

Avrille waited patiently while they scurried to serve her. They were good simple men. She was proud to be their queen.

Soon she was bouncing along the pot-holed road to the mill at the edge of town. When they drew near she could see figures silhouetted in the yellow-lit window.

Inside the mill King Will was in an uproar. He shouted at Mabry over the new power loom whirring between them. Don reached up and released the belts to silence the machine. Then he returned to where Darilla and her twins were seated in the corner.

"What do you mean build a mill in Frevaria!" shouted Will.

"King Keilen does not share his grandsire's conservative views," Mabry tried to explain.

"You mean Aunt Cellina's views. Kyle is too little to have views on anything, conservative or otherwise."

"I am sure the Lady Regent may have offered advice but it was His Majesty…"

"I am His Majesty!" Will raved. "And I decree that if Frevaria wants use of a mill they will come to Arindon and pay me for the privilege."

"Then it is no longer my mill?" said Mabry with a new boldness.

"It's my mill. Everything in Arindon is mine. Everything in Frevaria is mine. I am High King in case you have forgotten, Mabry. Aunt Cellina may rule you now but that is the extent of her powers."

Avrille chose that moment to open the door.

"Will Arinth, you had me worried sick!"

"What do you want?" Will growled.

Avrille glared at him. She thrust her hands on her hips and walked straight toward him. "I want you to tell me when you are going somewhere. You are still sick, not to mention that your wife is about to give birth at any moment."

Will shot a glance at Mabry. The man was trying hard to be respectful. He was trying not to laugh. Will turned his back on him. "Now that you're here, April," he said. "Have a look at the face of the future. Journeyman," he called to Don. "Demonstrate this power loom for your queen."

Don handed Veren back to Darilla. He slipped the leather belts back over the whirring wheels and the loom came alive. The shuttle cock flew back and forth unaided and the warp frame rose and fell rhythmically. The cloth inched forward as the beater bar pounded the rows and the rollers squeaked winding up the finished product. Avrille watched with interest. It was an amazing accomplishment. But soon she was tired and started to cough from the mill dust.

Finally Will was persuaded to go home. Mabry offered his own horse and cart for the king and queen's convenience. As Will flicked the reins Avrille looked back. Don and Darilla stood in the doorway each holding a twin. It was almost dark but she was sure Don's free arm was around Darilla's waist.

Maralinne was determined. Jareth was not going anywhere without her. Neither of them were going anywhere without Jasenth. There were some times in their rustic, idyllic life that

Jareth forgot his wife was a princess. This was not one of those times.

"Don't give me the king and loyal subject argument either," said Maralinne. "This time Will has gone too far. This idea is not only unnecessary and absurd, it's immoral! The twins are half brothers and sisters!"

"Betrothing Will's two sets of twins to each other would secure the kingdoms and breed a strong Allarion power that neither Arindon nor Frevaria could ever match."

"Breeding! Power! These are children, Jareth, not livestock!"

"Admit it, Maralinne, you still are holding out to put your sister's son on the throne in Arindon, or better yet as high king," Jareth countered.

"I'd rather Jasenth were the gamekeeper's son," she answered, her anger suddenly gone. She loved her nephew. She and Jareth had nurtured him as their own since Analinne and Tobar's deaths. But he was not their child and that was the pain that pushed her to tears. "I want what's best for all the children," she said wiping her eyes. "I just don't understand how Avrille could go along with all this."

Jasenth came in from his play. "When's supper, Aunt Mari?'

Their conversation stopped abruptly but she knew it would be taken up again.

"Go wash up, Jaybird."

The subject still churned in her mind as she headed for the kitchen. Ever since Will came to them with his plan two days ago she and Jareth had been arguing about it. Will was losing power, that was obvious. He was no longer Arindon's beloved and trusted king. Maralinne pitied her half brother. But even more her heart reached out to Avrille, her long-time friend. Power was rising in Frevaria. Will was becoming desperate. By betrothing Avrille's daughters to Darilla's sons Will claimed the balance would be achieved. He wanted to perform the betrothal ritual at his Star Castle next Equinox. That was only three days away. Why did Avrille just stand by and let it happen? Why did she stay with Will for that matter? Did she really love him, or was it just a pregnant woman's basic need for security that bound her to him? And why did Will have to involve Jareth? She kept asking herself question after question as she set out the plates for supper. Couldn't someone else witness the ceremony? What dread magic would Will unleash if this all took place? What dangers would again threaten the man she loved? She had argued about the politics and morality of the issue, yet all the royalty of the Twin Kingdoms were related by one bloodline or another. That the twins were closer tied did not really matter. Only Jareth mattered.

She stood there poised in the middle of the kitchen with the spoons in one hand and the forks in the other. Jasenth returned to the kitchen. He looked up at her with a puzzled face.

She rapidly started laying the silverware at each place. "Those hands are not clean, Jayjay." She grabbed his shoulders and headed him back to the washbasin again. "Use the little brush this time."

Jareth joined her in the kitchen. He set out the glassware and the napkins. When the table was ready he untied her apron strings as an excuse to be close to her. "You still love me?" he said slipping his arms around her.

"You know I do," she said turning toward him. "I'm just afraid to lose you again with all this madness. Please promise me you won't let anything take you away from me again."

"Never willingly," he answered. "But we must go along with this game. Somehow I know it is right, even if we do not understand why."

"I won't let you do it, not alone."

"Then we will all go, all three of us."

Dell arrived early. The sky over the Star Castle was gray, threatening rain. He climbed the east tower stairs and stepped out onto the wall. The wide courtyard spread out beneath him. The paving was a multicolored mosaic of geometric designs and symbols. A gigantic star sign was set in the stonework in front of the walled spring. The flowerbeds were bare, waiting to be planted at the end of the rainy season. The white towers with their new glass windows looked down on the empty castle shell. There were no quarters for family or servants, no kitchens, no stables, no guardhouse, no armory, no great hall. Only the austere towers offered any human shelter. For what strange purpose had King Will labored to build this place, balanced halfway between Arindon and Frevaria? What was his king's dream, here at the fulcrum of the Twin Kingdoms? Dell did not know. He turned his back on the inner courtyard to look down over the outside wall. A moving speck raced over the fields toward him. That would be Will. Another, larger speck emerged from the trees on the Arindon road. He watched it grow until he was sure it was the queen's carriage. With a resigned shrug of his shoulders he climbed back down the winding tower stairs to wait for them.

"I don't know why I'm doing this," Avrille declared after turning the first three cards. "The Sun, the Moon, and the Star, how obvious can it be?"

The carriage sped along the bumpy road. Avrille and Maralinne were both tense. Luckily Varan and Veren were asleep with their bottles and for the moment at least Arinda and Arielle were content with their baskets of sweets.

"Can I pick a card?" asked little Jasenth.

"You must ask it a question first," said Avrille handing him the deck.

"Where are we going today?" said Jasenth drawing the top card. "It's a pretty place," he said handing her the Fountain Card.

"This is ridiculous!" Avrille exclaimed. "Of course it's the Fountain. Will designed the place from the card."

"I thought it was from a dream," said Maralinne.

"Both, first the card and then a dream," said Avrille dropping the cards on the seat beside her. The carriage bounced over an especially large bump. She grabbed for the cards but the top one went sailing to the floor.

"Rella get it," said Arielle sliding off the seat.

"No, mine," said Arinda attacking her sister.

"Stop it!" Avrille shouted. "Give the card to mommy."

"Mine!" Arinda wailed.

"Give it to me or mommy spanks."

Arinda held out the bent, sticky card.

Avrille gasped. "When the dragon flies..." she said handing the Black Dragon card to Maralinne.

"Lemme see," begged Jasenth. "Wow! We gonna see this?"

"I don't know, Jayjay," said Maralinne with a shudder.

King Will arrived on horseback at the Star Castle ahead of the royal carriage. Dell helped him carry the ritual artifacts from the west tower where they had been secured since Solstice. The heavy thrones were placed side by side in the courtyard facing the star sign mosaic in the paving. Will pushed them together until the half rainbow arches carved on their backs touched. A rainbow of light shot up from the thrones. Will laughed when Dell jumped back. "That's just one note of the song you will hear today, my loyal bard."

The worn leather box that held the crowns was set in front of the thrones. Will buckled on his father's silver sword and muttered through clenched teeth, "I shouldn't have given Frebar's sword to Kylie. But what's done is done."

Dell took his assigned position on a stone bench to the right of the star sign and tuned his harp. Will paced, anxiously waiting for the royal carriage to arrive. He stopped to look up at the lead-gray sky then resumed his pacing until Jareth drove through the gate.

"It's just like my card," Jasenth exclaimed as they came to a halt.

"You must be very quiet and very good from now on," warned Maralinne. "All of you," she added with a look specifically aimed at Arinda.

"The boys are asleep," Avrille said to Will when he opened the carriage door for them.

"Good. We'll position the girls first."

"Scowling Arinda was lifted, honey-smeared hands, rumpled dress and all onto the red velvet cushioned throne of Arindon. Arielle sniffled but let Jareth place her on Frevaria's blue seat of state next to her sister.

"April, you stand across the circle facing the thrones," Will ordered. "Jareth you're on the left and Maralinne on the right."

"What about Jasenth?" asked Maralinne clutching the child's hand.

"I don't care. Just keep him out of the way."

Dell leaned back on the bench and fingered a dreamy little tune. Avrille looked at him then closed her eyes in concentration. Now if never before her twins needed a calming spell. Will returned to the carriage and came back with his sons, one cradled in each arm.

Dell sang the first words of the prophecy.

"When the Sun and Moon
Shine double in the sky."

Will laid the sleeping infants on the cushioned thrones beside the girls.

"Then shall the cask be opened," sang Dell.

Jareth unlatched the box and lifted out the crowns. He laid the silver one in Arinda's lap.
"Mine!" she squealed pulling it away from baby Varan. He whimpered but did not wake. Arielle sat still like a porcelain doll as Jareth laid the golden crown on her knees.
From the vantage point of his bench Dell studied the scene arranged around the star sign. Queen Avrille looked tired and worn. Her cloak did not meet across her front. No woman in her condition should have been allowed to leave her home much less be subjected to this. She barely responded as Will strutted forward to perform the ritual. Maralinne held Jasenth as if she expected the child to be wrenched from her at any moment. Her eyes pleaded with Jareth but he did not notice. His attention centered on the task before him. Dell watched Jareth hand Will the thin white betrothal ribbons.

"One for Silver, One for Gold," sang Dell.

Will tied each pair of tiny hands. Dell's harp sang a lullaby. His fingers caressed the strings as his beloved instrument sang. Jareth's eyes were glazed as the song unlocked his memories. Tears ran unnoticed down his cheeks. He was a child again. The song the harp sang was his mother's voice and the tragedy of his loss wrenched his heart anew.
"Dell!" King Will commanded.
Dell snapped back to the business at hand. He sang the next line of the prophecy.

"When shall the Three be Five?"

Will whirled to face the thrones with sword drawn. Above him the clouds burst open. The noonday sun struck his upraised blade. The blaze shot like a fiery arrow to the glass windows of the west tower. It leaped to the east, then crossed and crossed again and again above them. The five towers awoke anchoring the dancing image of a star before the vision faded.

Dell's harp vibrated with life. King Will stood frozen facing his queen, stance wide, sword thrust high. His shadow cut a dark path behind him severing the twin thrones with its long dark arm. The air grew heavy and still. The rhythm of Dell's harp intensified. His hands flew over the strings as the harp spoke. The diamonds in the crowns pulsed. A rainbow of stars swirled about the thrones. The base strings of the harp throbbed louder and louder. Dell's voice rose. Jareth's voice joined him, swelling to a perfect fifth below the bard's clear tenor. Dell plucked one last note and the string broke with an almost human cry. The babies screamed. The earth beneath the thrones convulsed and split open. The sides of the gaping rift tilted in toward each other. Silver throne slid into gold. Arindon's crown and Frevaria's crown eclipsed each other. Twin slid toward and merged with twin.

Dell's broken harp wailed, like a mother torn from her child. A cloud of iridescent mist swirled between them, separating them from each other. They all cried out, child for parent, husband for wife, friend for friend, but no one could hear any voice but their own. As suddenly as it had appeared the mist vanished. A single rainbow-colored throne stood before the star sign. It was empty! The twins had vanished! A double diadem of silver and gold entwined around two huge diamonds, cut as the sun cradled in the cusp of the moon, lay on the seat of the throne.

"Where are my babies?" Avrille screamed. "Will, what have you done?"

As if in answer, the crown began to move. It fell from the seat of the throne and rolled across the stone-paved star sign in a lazy arc past Will to Avrille's feet. In suspended time she reached down and picked it up. No one else moved. No one else breathed. When her hand touched the enchanted crown the muscles of her abdomen tightened like steel bands. She doubled over with a scream of pain. Maralinne and Jareth rushed to her side.

The earth began to shake beneath their feet. Black smoke seethed through the cracks of the star sign mosaic. It swirled around King Will, engulfing him. His arms flailed. His black cape billowed up behind him. The earth rumbled with a deep and terrible voice. A silver shot of light leaped from the blackness and

Will was gone. A dark cloud rose above them. It expanded across the sky until it hovered over the Star Castle like gigantic dragon wings.

Another wave of pain gripped Avrille. "Mother! Mother! I need you now!" she cried.

"Look, look, Aunt Mari," Jasenth's voice rose above the storm. He was pointing to the spring.

They all turned to face the pool. The water bubbled. Colors swirled, weaving with pure light. Gradually something solidified in its center. They stood in awe as the colors took shape. Three figures emerged, one an old woman, one young, and one but a maid. Around them the water merrily splashed and played. Avrille moved toward the figures. Peace, comfort and calm reached out to her. The light shifted and the smaller figure separated from the other two. The child stepped daintily between the fountain sprays holding the hem of her white gown with one hand. In the other she clutched a tightly rolled paper.

"And the Star arches alive." Dell sang the last line of the prophecy.

"Lizzie!" gasped Avrille. "Where are Rindy and Rella?"

"Grandma says to tell you, 'Princess Arinda Arielle is being fostered in a safe place'."

"And the star babies?"

"Varen? He's back with his mother," said Lizelle with nonchalance. "I made a present for my new baby cousin. Want to see, Auntie Avrille?" She unrolled her paper to display a neatly crayoned star. "He says his name is Allarinth, the Star King."

As Avrille reached to take Lizelle's gift a third contraction gripped her. "Take me home. Please take me home, Jareth. It's time," she groaned and sank into his arms.

"Bye, Jayjay, my betrothed," called Lizelle. She blew a kiss then vanished with a giggle into the sparkling pool.

"Finders keepers, right Aunt Mari?" said Jasenth holding the silver sword of Arindon. "I got a real sword now just like Kylie.

Late that night Dell the Bard sat on the porch of Beck's tavern mending his beloved harp. The day's events raced through his mind. Try as he would the words of the song he was trying to write would not come. The song of prophecy had already been written, not once but many times. What could he add to it? "There, my love," he said. "Good as new I hope." He gave the instrument an affectionate pat and plucked the new string. The note rang true. Again he tried to sing. This time the words as well as the melody came from the soul of the harp.

"When the Sun and Moon
Shine double in the sky...
Two babes for silver and two for gold,
Twice two babes but one year old.
Two he got on the queen he wed.
And two he got in the miller girl's bed."

Dell chuckled. "You are a naughty girl," he whispered to his harp.

"Then shall the cask be opened...
The Star King's crown lay darkened, forlorn,
Locked in a box of old leather worn,
One half of silver, the other of gold,
Two halves of the diamond star
Severed and cold."

He drew his cloak tighter against the chill as he gazed off into the sleeping village. One house was still bright with light. "Another ballad in the making," he said looking toward Queen Avrille's house. "Or the ending of this one, who knows."

He had just decided to wait up for news of the royal birth when something caught his eye far down the road. A hooded figure walked briskly toward town. In its hand bobbed a little yellow light. He watched them approach. Soon he could discern a middle-aged woman with a covered basket on her arm. A golden-haired child skipped beside her.

"Hurry, Grandma, hurry," the child was saying.

Dell slung his harp on his back and followed them. "And so we play the same scene over and over?" he said to himself. "Over and over until we get it right."

Appendix I

The Characters

Kyrdthin (Kurd thin), Hawke
    Magician

Janille (Jan eel), Janie, Aunt Jane
    Former wife and queen of Frebar. Mother of April and Elanille. Foster mother of Will.

Avrille (Av reel), April
    High Queen of Twin Kingdoms. Daughter of Janille.

Willarinth (Will ar inth), Will, Willy
    High King of Twin Kingdoms. Son of Arinth and Marielle.

Analinne (An a lin), Ann, Annie, deceased
    Princess of Arindon. Wife of Tobar. Twin sister of Maralinne. Daughter of Arinth and the late queen Veralinne

Maralinne (Mar a lin), Mari
    Princess of Arindon. Beloved of Jareth. Twin sister of Analinne. Daughter of Arinth and Veralinne.

Elanille (El an eel), Elani
    Princess of Frevaria. Daughter of Janille and Frebar. Sister to Avrille. Mother to Kylie and Lizelle

Marielle (Mar ee el)
    Queen of Arindon and Allarion. Mother of Will.

Arinth (Ar inth), deceased
    King of Arindon. Father of Analinne, Maralinne and Will.

Gil (Gil)

Consort of Marielle in Allarion. Advisor to Arinth and later to Will

Lady Cellina (Sel in ah), Celli
    Spinster sister of the late queen Veralinne of Arindon. Twin to Liella.

Lady Liella (Lee el ah)
    Spinster sister of the late queen Veralinne of Arindon. Twin to Cellina.

Belar (Bay lar)
    Dark Lord of Bellarion.

Borat (Bor at)
    Servant to Belar, later to the Dark Queen

Frebar (Fray bar)
    King of Frevaria. Former husband of Janille. Twin brother of Tobar.

Tobar (Toe bar), deceased
    Prince of Frevaria. Husband of Analinne. Twin brother of Frebar.

Jareth (Jar eth)
    Gamekeeper of Arindon wood. Consort of Maralinne. Advisor to Arinth and later to Will.

Rogarth (Roe garth)
    Captain of the king's guard in Arindon, later Master of War. Queen Avrille's tournament champion.

Keilen (Ki len), deceased
    Chief bowman of Arindon. Husband of Elanille.

Kylie (Ki lee), Young Keilen
    Son of Keilen and Elanille.

Lizelle (Liz el), Lizzie

Daughter of Keilen and Elanille.

Jasenth (Jay senth), Jayjay
    Son of Tobar and Analinne. Nephew of Maralinne

Mabry (Mab ree)
    Miller of Arindon. Friend and mentor to Will

Darilla (Dar il ah)
    Daughter of Mabry. Mistress to Will. Mother of Varan and Veren

Armon Beck (Ar mon)
    Innkeeper of Arindon

Dell (Del)
    Bard

The Watcher
    Guardian of the caves

Spida (Spy dah)
    Man-beast inhabitant of the caves

Arinda (Ar in dah) Rindy
    Princess of twin Kingdoms. Daughter of Avrille and Will. Twin to Arielle

Arielle (Ar ee el) Rella
    Princess of twin Kingdoms. Daughter of Avrille and Will. Twin to Arinda

Varan (Var an)
    Bastard son of Will and Darilla. Twin to Veren

Veren (Ver en)
    Bastard son of Will and Darilla. Twin to Varan

Cook
    Master Cook of Frevaria castle. Mentor to Kylie

Nancie (Nan see)
    Mabry's daughter. Maidservant to Lady Cellina

Tad
    Mabry's son. Twin to Tam

Tam
    Mabry's son. Twin to Tad

Linelle (Lin el)
    Nursemaid to Arinda and Arielle. Daughter of Armon Beck

Sir Anton (An ton)
    Knight of Frevaria

Appendix II

The Cards

The House of Light
    White King, White Queen, White Dragon, White Knight, White Fortress

The House of Darkness
    Black King, Black Queen, Black Dragon, Black Knight, Black Fortress

The Gifts of the Gods
    Beauty, Wisdom, Strength, Honor, Compassion

The Abodes of the Gods
    Sun, Moon, Star, Rainbow, Fountain

The Elements of Creation
    Fire, Water, Air, Earth, Time

Appendix III

The Prophecy

When the Sun and moon
Shine double in the sky,
Then shall the cask be opened.
Then shall the Three be Five.

Twice two shall weep
When the eclipse is done.
Magic will die
When the Darkness is chained.
And the Star arches live.

NORMANDALE COMMUNITY COLLEGE
LIBRARY
9700 FRANCE AVENUE SOUTH
BLOOMINGTON, MN 55431-4399